I0788569

STOLEN MATES BOOK ONE

THE FERAL'S CAPTIVE

SARAH SPADE

CHAPTER 1
FATE

Fate sucks.

Rearing back my foot, I kick the baseball-sized rock in front of me. The toe of my worn leather boot connects with it, shooting it sky-high. The rock flies a good thirty feet before it pelts the thick trunk of a hickory tree in the distance. I hear the thud, my inner wolf yipping at me when the bark splits and the ancient hickory groans.

I wince. Fate still sucks, but the tree didn't deserve that.

I know better than to treat the forest with disrespect. A member of the Sylvan Pack since birth, I've lived along the edge of these woods for the last twenty-six years. They're almost as responsible for me as our Alpha is.

Probably more since I'm nothing but a delta.

We have at least fifty-six packmates at last count—fifty-eight if Kara had her twins—and there's definitely a hierarchy. Alpha is at the top. Beta is next. Our Omega doesn't have the dominance that the higher-ranked wolves do, but her role as peacemaker for the pack is essential so she's up there; of course, being the younger sister to our Alpha doesn't hurt, either. Gammas are the older wolves who have earned a peaceful retirement after protecting the pack. Then there are deltas. Regular rank-and-file packmates, deltas make up both the bulk and the base of the hierarchy.

Of course, among deltas, there's a hierarchy of our own. Some deltas are members of Bishop's pack council. Others are patrollers; protectors who are responsible for keeping the borders of Hickory secure. We have deltas who are cooks. Who teach. Who sew. A couple of deltas are tasked with leaving pack land and mingling with humans, buying the supplies we need as a community.

And then there's me. Quinn Malone. I... I'm just a delta.

I used to have a job. I fulfilled a purpose for the Sylvan Pack. Jokingly referring to my duty as stylist/groomer, I was the one my packmates came to when they needed a haircut or—after one memorable tumble through the blackberry bushes with his mate—they had canes and tangled thorns all up in their fur. I'd needed my clippers that day, and Frankie's wolf had a bald ass for a week after that.

But that was before.

Something similar happened to Sofia. I should've anticipated my fate after seeing hers, but I hadn't. That was my fault.

Sofia is the female half of our Alpha couple. Bishop's mate, she came from the River Run Pack on the East Coast where she taught the local pups math and science.

When the Luna whispered her name to Bishop during his Alpha ceremony five years ago, he sent for her, and she accepted his mate bond. They performed the Luna Ceremony during the full moon that followed, and, once they were fully bonded, she was no longer a plain, boring, nobody delta like me.

Her dominance level didn't change by mating Bishop, but her rank sure did. From the bottom to the top, she couldn't be a math teacher anymore. Being the Alpha's forever mate was a full-time job of its own.

So is being the Beta's mate, I've discovered.

That's supposed to be me, but it isn't, and I'm still shit out of luck when it comes to my place in our pack after all this time—and all because of the Luna and her twisted idea of Fate.

Six months ago, I smiled at Weston Reed, the Beta of the Sylvan Pack. I'd done it a hundred times before. We were friends, growing up in the same age group, even though being a born beta wolf meant he was a much higher rank than us deltas. I knew that, one day, West would succeed our old Beta, Harris, and it didn't hurt to be buddy-buddy with him while he still rubbed elbows with the rest of us.

Truth be told, I'd always been drawn to him, but friendship was all he could offer so I took it gladly. For as long as I could remember, he had been together with Helene, our pack's Omega. And while their official relationship ended about three years back when Helene was promised to the future Alpha of a neighboring pack, West... he didn't get the memo.

He's been trying to convince her to choose him over Rafael ever since. Still is even now.

I was on his side when the pronouncement first came. As much as I had a crush on West, he loved Helene. I knew that. Anyone with eyes could see that. I thought she loved him, too. She didn't have to leave Hickory when Rafael eventually became Alpha if she didn't want to. She could reject him and choose West instead.

She refused. Pack gossip said that she was content to wait until Rafael could claim her by shifter tradition. That she had decided to accept her fated mate. It also said that Helene gently suggested that West do the same.

But *he* refused to do that—and, six months ago, when I smiled at him and, suddenly, something snapped into place, our goddess whispering to me that West was *mine*... he still refused the idea of taking any mate other than Helene.

Worse, he *rejected* me.

He rejected the idea that *I* could ever be the female meant for him.

Oh, not with words, though. That's not West's style. He's never been cruel. He just pretended that he didn't feel it when a bond sprang up between us, and because he's the Beta, the rest of the pack did the same.

One problem: ignoring the bond doesn't mean it isn't there.

Following his lead, I stayed away, too. I didn't push him. I gave him the space he needed to work out his feelings for Helene before he did what nearly every other shifter did and claimed his fated mate as his own.

But Fate sucks, remember? And West is the rare wolf who seems to be able to fight her pull.

I just wish *I* could.

Even worse, the pack still considers me his mate. Does it matter that West doesn't? Nope. The Luna says I'm the Beta's mate, so I am.

You know what that means?

No one comes to me for a haircut anymore. They don't want to bother the Beta's mate for something so trivial, and now Gregory is the new pack stylist.

I've gone from a flirtatious she-wolf needing to fight off interested males to basically being the shifter version of a freaking nun, only without a wimple. None of the males treat me like a prospective mate anymore. Why would they when they already believe I'm taken?

Worst of all is how when other packmates need West, they come to me as if I hold any sway over him. Then they apologize when I point out that they'd have better luck going to Helene.

I was understanding in the beginning. As much as I was over the moon to discover I was meant for West, I knew he loved Helene. I just thought... maybe he could love me, too.

But, once again, I was wrong.

Ugh!

I don't kick another rock, but that's only because I still feel guilty for striking the tree before. This is my safe place. The clearing on the edge of pack territory where I can go to bitch and rage and get out all of my frustrations before I go back to Hickory where all I have to look forward to are pitying looks.

They all know I'm the rejected mate. The one cast aside. West never had to say it, but it's obvious.

And that makes it so much harder to take.

ONE OF THE DOWNSIDES TO BEING THE BETA'S FORGOTTEN mate? If I'm gone too long, West won't even notice—but someone else in the pack will.

I lose track of how long I was sitting on the grass, absently weaving flowers into my hair. I used to keep it short, usually shoulder-length, but in the last six months, I let it grow. I guess I lost the taste for cutting even my own hair, and now the deep black strands go nearly past my boobs when I'm standing up.

Hiding out in this clearing isn't new to me. I've been coming here since I was a randy teen and I needed a place to meet up with shifter males who wanted nothing more than a good time. I've never been the type of virginal, holier-than-thou she-wolf who wanted to wait until I took a mate. Shifters are earthy creatures. Sex is a biological urge. And, fuck it, it just feels amazing when done right.

I haven't been laid in six months. That's my longest dry spell since I started crooking my finger at horny males, inviting them to join me out beneath the hickories. Maybe that's why I'm feeling kind of twitchy all of a sudden.

My skin feels like it's stretched over my bones. Letting go of the wildflower I plucked, I rub my neck. A bird sings in the distance. My shifter's ears tune in. I hear... I hear...

Rustling?

The twitchy feeling turns into something else. Unless I'm imagining it, it's like I feel eyes on me. Like someone's watching me.

But who? There aren't many who come this far. Most of my packmates prefer to stay close to the cluster of cabins where we each have our homes. The pack circle is there—the cleared area with picnic tables where we can meet and talk and eat together—and it's within reach of the Alpha cabin where Bishop lives with Sofia.

I've brought plenty of males here over the years, but none recently. And those who know that I consider this part of the woods mine would never approach without permission. This is my territory, and a male encroaching on a possessive she-wolf learns very quickly how far she'll go to protect what's hers.

Especially because I never would've found it if it wasn't for West.

Before he was the Beta, he was another shifter who enjoyed exploring the woods. He showed me this spot years ago and I immediately proclaimed it as mine. He didn't mind; he already had his own. While I came out here for the peace and, later, the privacy, West always visited a grove on the far borders of Hickory where countless types of wildflowers grew; similar to the ones that are growing by me, but more plentiful. It was a thing he had with Helene. Whenever they were separated during the time they were a couple, he'd bring a flower back for her.

They're not a couple anymore, but he still does it. I

used to think it was cute. These days, though, I get a funny feeling deep in the pit of my stomach whenever I see him from a distance, stalking toward the Omega cabin, a stem clutched between his fingers.

I did a few weeks ago. Just like now, I'd sensed someone near a few seconds before my wolf started to whine once she recognized West's. He was in the woods, and he found me on my own, even stopping to say hello for the first time in ages... but all I could focus on was the flower in his hand.

Is that who is out there now? Should I go look?

Will my battered heart handle it when I see him holding another flower for Helene?

This isn't the first time I've longed to get up and run to West. Once again I'm sitting here, wondering if I should work up the nerve to head upwind and confront him in his own private sanctuary out in the woods.

It's getting harder to resist. I have to remind myself that he's chosen Helene, and I'm better off by myself— even if I'm not.

So, yeah. That's my big secret. My dark shame. I pretend like it doesn't faze me one bit that my fated mate follows another female around like a besotted puppy dog. On the rare occasion one of my old friends tries to see how I'm doing, I shrug and say that it happens. If the Luna got it right every time, there would be no rejected mates. No broken bonds.

Heck, one of the biggest cautionary tales in the shifter world is Jack "Wicked Wolf" Walker, a cruel Alpha who —at one time—ruled almost the entire West Coast of shifters. He turned his pack into a haven known as the

Wolf District, and he lorded over it with an ever-changing retinue of Betas—and no mate. His fated mate rejected him before he bonded her to him, choosing to mate the Alpha of a nearby pack instead.

It's an open secret. While the Wicked Wolf was still the biggest threat on the West Coast, every shifter knew why he went through she-wolves the way I used to go through males. After losing his fated mate, he didn't want to choose another. He was happy by himself, and he was one of the most powerful—and feared—Alphas in the whole Luna damned United States until a challenger finally caught up to him and he lost everything except for his head.

I try to tell myself that I could be like the Wicked Wolf. Not the sadistic bastard part, but a shifter who doesn't let the pain of a jagged bond stop them from living life to the fullest.

Unlike me...

Another rustle and, so soft I'm not sure it's real, an animalistic snuffling sound that has my wolf cocking her head.

I take a deep breath, trying to see if I catch a familiar scent. I'm out here so often that I can recognize the wild wolves that visit, the prey animals that skirt around our territory, even the other shifters who take a break from pack living by passing through.

Is there a whiff of sandalwood?

I exhale. Nope.

Nothing. I get nothing. Everything is the same as usual.

And that makes the weight of the stare on me even weirder...

Brushing my hands against my jeans, I rise up from the ground. The sensation that someone is close by is only growing stronger. I can't shake the feeling that I'm being watched.

Maybe it's a packmate. Maybe it is West. Maybe it's someone—or some*thing*—else entirely.

Whatever it is, I don't like it.

I'm not scared, though. Please. I'm a wolf shifter. There's nothing out there I can't take.

Well, maybe not a vampire, but you have to be much more dominant than me to take on a vampire. Good thing you can scent one of those undead corpses from a mile away. Between their icy auras and the scent of blood and rotten meat that clings to their supernaturally beautiful forms, they'd never get close enough to Hickory before the whole pack would work together to take them down.

Still, scared or not, I've been out here too long. The last thing I need is Bishop sending West after me again. It's always super awkward when I have to talk to him. We have an unspoken agreement to pretend we're strangers most of the time, and whenever we don't, it's fucking terrible.

Just like it was a couple of weeks ago when I hated the azalea he held almost as much as I wish I could hate *him*.

But I don't. I *want* him.

He doesn't want me.

And there's not a damn thing I can do about it.

Purposely giving my back to whoever—*whatever*—

might be out there watching me, I start to stalk back toward Hickory. It isn't long before I leave that strange sensation behind me. By the time I cross back into the inner border of pack land, I've forgotten all about it.

I want to go straight to my cabin. Despite having a decent enough afternoon by myself in the woods, I'm not in the mood to deal with any of my packmates today.

Who knows? Maybe I'll feel like being social tomorrow. Not likely, but you never know.

Of course, that's when I hear someone call my name from off to my side—

"Quinn!"

I freeze.

The voice... it's familiar and, for a split second, hope fills my chest. And, sure, his aura marks him as a delta, and he doesn't smell like sandalwood like West does, but I'm so far gone over my fated mate that I'm willing to be delusional until I turn toward him and see—

"Tucker." *Crap.* "How've you been?"

His smile is blinding. Something about Tucker Madden always reminds me of toothpaste commercials I see on television. He has bright white teeth, gleaming golden eyes, and dark blond hair styled in soft waves. Like all protectors, he has a lean body that I know intimately.

From the heat in his eyes as he looks me up and down, he's thinking the same thing about me.

"Missing you, but other than that I'm alright. I've been thinking about how much fun we used to have. Good times, huh?"

"Yeah. Sure."

"I was also thinking... it's been a while. You know. You and me. Maybe we could have some fun again? Go visit that spot in the woods you like? I know it's not too far. And it's real nice and private."

Ah, Luna. As if I need another reminder that I'm single as fuck. With West making his rejection obvious, the males I used to fool around with still see me as a sure thing—but they're the only ones.

Funnily enough, even they left me alone for the first few months. West is our Beta, and he has the respect of the entire pack. I'm his fated mate, and they figured he'd come to his senses eventually and accept that.

But he didn't. In so many different ways, he continues to reject me. To reject our bond. Tucker coming up and reminding me about old times isn't an insult to West so long as the Beta acts like I'm nothing to him. Tucker is just a horny male shifter who wants to get his rocks off, that's all.

And he probably guesses I'm the hard-up she-wolf who might say yes to his offer because he doesn't try to be coy or sly at all when he says, "I'm going on patrol after dinner, but that gives me a good hour. I was heading out to take a walk in the woods now anyway. You want to join me?"

A walk in the woods... every adventurous shifter in Hickory knows what that's a euphemism for.

I should. The longer I stew over a male I can't have, the more bitter I'm becoming. Maybe a quick romp with another packmate is just what I need to get my mind off of West.

But I can't. As insane as it sounds to want to be loyal

to a male who doesn't want you, if I sneak off with Tucker, it's almost like I'm cheating on my fated mate.

Speaking of—

My wolf yips when she senses him. The little hairs on my human arm stand up, almost like I've been shocked by a tiny jolt of electricity. I instinctively know where he is and, shifting my stance a few degrees to the right, I look over Tucker's lean shoulder.

And there he is.

Weston Reed, the Beta of the Sylvan Pack.

My heart stutters in my chest. I'd always thought he was good-looking before. Since the bond appeared, he's more than that.

He's *breathtaking* to me.

West isn't as conventionally handsome a male as Tucker is. He wears his dark brown hair cut short, and his eyes are unusual for a shifter. Normally dark grey, they only turn gold when he's lost control of his emotions. Since that's almost never for a disciplined beta wolf like West, I've only ever seen it happen twice: the day we recognized each other as fated mates, and when he discovered that Helene was fated to belong to Rafael Cruces once he took over his pack.

West isn't alone. Though it takes a second for me to stop staring at his profile, I force myself to look away from him. Even before my gaze lands on the beautiful, blonde Helene Dupuis, I knew exactly who he was talking to.

The look of pure adoration on his masculine features made it obvious.

My heart aches. There's no other way to describe it.

My fated mate is right there, barely twenty feet away, and I've never felt farther apart from him.

And wouldn't you know, I'm also not alone.

My heart still aches while my stomach sinks.

I shake my head. "Maybe some other time, Tucker."

Tucker follows the direction of my stare, making a soft sound of understanding when he sees West and Helene together.

"Yeah. Well, you know where to find me." He reaches his hand out to pat me on the shoulder. I try not to wince when he pauses, only an inch separating us, careful not to actually make contact. "Until next time, Quinn."

He couldn't touch me. West is over there making goo-goo eyes at Helene, Tucker wanted in my pants two minutes ago, and once he noticed the Beta nearby, he couldn't even touch me.

Until next time?

Yeah. I don't think there's going to be one.

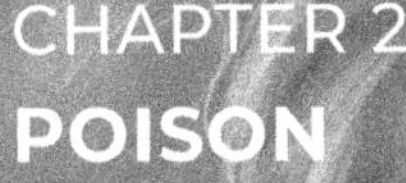

CHAPTER 2
POISON

Sometimes I wish that West would just reject me completely.

It's easy enough. Up until the moment we perform the Luna Ceremony and get her blessing, all it takes is one half of a promised pair saying the words with meaning: "I reject you." *Boom*. The bond snaps, and though I'll have lost any chance of ever having my fated mate, at least I wouldn't be existing in this state of constant ache.

I know he doesn't mean to give me hope. He never has. In his own way, the Beta is being a decent wolf. He knows how much it'll hurt me to hear the truth so he just doesn't say it.

He doesn't have to.

As Beta, he's the second highest-ranked wolf in our pack. Bishop is first, and though we have two other budding alphas living in Hickory, West ranks higher than them because of his title. He's Bishop's right-hand wolf, the only one—besides Sofia—who can look Bishop in the eye without immediately baring his throat in submission. All of our fellow packmates follow his lead. As soon as he pointedly ignored the fact that the Luna paired us up, so did everyone else.

As far as the Sylvan Pack is concerned, West rejected me in every way that mattered—except actually setting me free.

I must be a fucking glutton for punishment. I walk around like a pariah, the topic of whispers and rumors that they know me and my wolf can hear. They feel pity for me, but they also wonder why I don't just leave.

Sometimes I wonder the same exact thing.

Hickory is my home. I was born on this land, and until the Luna upended my life, I planned on dying on it. My dad did—a victim of a challenge against another delta that he didn't win—and my mom, unable to live without her lifemate, who followed soon after.

I was twelve when all that happened. The rest of the Sylvan Pack rallied around me, giving me time to mourn, but also making sure I didn't want for anything. If I walk away because I can't have the one male meant for me, it's like I failed or something. I've never given up when things got hard. I'm stubborn to a fault.

Petty, too, I admit. If I have to live with the urge to go to West every single day, I'm not gonna make it easy for him to get out of doing the same. He's gonna see me. I know what an unfulfilled bond feels like. No matter how much he loves Helene, it's hard to beat Fate.

Am I hoping that he might wake up one day and realize what he's been missing out on? Not really. Maybe at first I did. If so, it was short-lived.

Am I waiting for Helene to leave Hickory for her promised mate?

I... I might be.

I'm not sure what that says about me. I never wanted to be another she-wolf's sloppy seconds or a male's second choice. During my wild early years, when I was exploring my sexuality without the pesky complications of settling down with a mate, I had half the males in my age group sniffing around my tail. All I had to do was run into the woods, content in the knowledge that an interested male would chase.

Not West. Never West. He's always been hovering over Helene.

No one knows when she'll be leaving the pack. As our Omega—and the Alpha's beloved younger sister—Helene will stay in Hickory until her promised mate performs the Alpha Ceremony, taking over the Gravetail Pack. Only then will they perform the Luna Ceremony that will bond them together, and West will finally have to accept that he can't have the mate he wants.

Will he come crawling back to me?

I don't know.

Will I be waiting for him if he does?

I... I don't know that, either.

Another reason why I wish I could just get rid of this pull I feel for him. After the last six months of pity and need and loneliness, there's a good chance I would jump him the first time he acted like he wanted to be with me.

A she-wolf's gotta have some pride, right? When it comes to West Reed, I'm pretty sure I don't.

Ugh.

He won't do it. He won't snap our bond. Why? I have no clue. But six months after we both recognized that we were fated, all he's done is grow colder, more distant, while focusing all of his intention on a female he can never have.

And me? I spend all of my time on the edge of Hickory. Still near enough to the pack that I don't accidentally become a lone wolf, but with enough space that I can shake off the mantle of being the Beta's rejected mate.

There are other options. If Helene *did* forsake her own fated mate and choose West, our bond would break. Even less likely, I could choose another male. Since my packmates would never dare try to steal their Beta's mate —though, as Tucker proved the other day, fucking me is okay, but mating me is definitely a no-no—and I have no intention of leaving Hickory, I'm gonna have to just suck it up and get used to being the pack outcast.

It's like I've got a scarlet letter on my damn chest. Only, instead of Hester Prynne's A, I've got an R.

R for rejected. Yippee!

You know, I've heard rumors about a Luna-touched female with the gift—or curse, depending on your point of view—of breaking bonds with her little finger. One touch and, so long as one of the mates was willing, it was as though it never existed.

As much as it must suck to be her, if she's real, maybe I should see if I could track her down. With West content to go on as if our bond doesn't exist, she might be the best chance I have.

I'm just thinking about which of my packmates might know more about the mysterious Luna-touched female when, suddenly, a very familiar aura wraps around me. Just like the other day when I was talking to Tucker, I sense him before I pick up his scent, and by the time I turn to find West walking toward me, all I can think is: Mate. *Mate. Maaaaate.*

As handsome as ever, his face is an expressionless mask. I can't tell if his thoughts are running along the same lines as mine or if he was even expecting to run into me like this in the first place.

I peer closer. There's a look in his eye I recognize. Shortly after Bishop proclaimed him as his Beta—and long before I realized he was my fated mate—I used to tease him that it was his "business" look.

Wonderful.

"Quinn. There you are."

As if he's surprised to find me. Whether he wants to admit it or not, with our bond open, he's as viscerally aware of me as I am of him. It wouldn't have taken much to know that I was sitting on the front porch of my cabin.

Unless... unless he keeps our bond closed on his side. It takes a lot of effort to cut off a mate, and it would probably be more uncomfortable than leaving it unfulfilled, but it *is* possible. I don't do it because, really, what's the point?

Is that what he's doing to me?

I don't ask. I can't. Honestly, I'd rather not know the answer.

Instead, I shrug. "Yup. What's going on? You need me for something?"

Please need me...

He nods. "I know you spend a lot of time out among

the hickories and the oaks on the edge of our territory." Gee... I wonder why. "Some of our patrols have picked up a few unfamiliar tracks recently. No scent, and that's what's weird about them. You should probably stick closer to the heart of pack land until we figure out what's going on."

My heart stutters against my ribcage. I don't want to read too much into West coming to warn me personally, but...

"Are you telling this me because you're the Beta and I'm a packmate, or because—"

West's perfectly chiseled jaw goes tight. "Because I'm the Beta and I have a duty to every wolf in Hickory."

Right. Message received.

So we both know where we stand. As if I wasn't already aware.

I offer him a mock salute. "Will do. Thanks."

West nods. His dark grey eyes travel over the fake smile I pulled on my face. For a second, I think he wants to say something else. I'm almost begging him to.

He doesn't.

With another nod and a short wave, he turns on his heel and starts to walk away. Probably going to see Helene again.

I wait a moment. When he doesn't turn to glance over his shoulder at me, I think about West's warning—and then I completely blow it off.

I'm not worried about there being a threat in the woods. True, I could've sworn I felt someone watching me the other day, but nothing happened. If it was really that big of an issue, Bishop would forbid any of us from heading out there instead of just giving us a warning. He'd amp up pack patrols on the edge of our territory, too.

Besides, I'm scarier than anything else that could be out there. I'll be fine.

And if this is my own way of saying, "Fuck you," to West without it being a challenge, then that makes my decision to retreat to the woods again that much sweeter.

THE BEST THING ABOUT BEING A DELTA? I'M NOT IMPORTANT enough that I can't slip away without one of the higher-ranked packmates noticing.

If I'm gone too long, they will. Our pack is strongest when we're whole. Bishop takes his role as Alpha seriously. If he can't account for all of us at any given moment, it sets off his wolf—and that usually sets off West.

It's bad enough I ran into West a couple of weeks ago, carrying another Luna-damned flower for his precious Helene. No doubt in my mind that it was an accident, and that he only stopped to talk to me because his wolf spurred him to. With all of Hickory between us, he can usually avoid me. When we're that close? Even he isn't strong enough to resist the pull. Part of the reason I call bullshit on his warning me about the woods earlier today. Sure, he's the Beta, but any other protector could've done the same thing. It didn't have to be West.

Of course, then I remember how, after I ran into Tucker a few days back, I saw West watching Helene with such open adoration—the Omega the only one worthy of him showing any hint of emotion toward—and I realize I'm still fooling myself.

Come on, Quinn. He's just one male. One dick. If he can beat Fate, so can I.

Right?

Well, not in the last six months I haven't…

Our tie has another downside besides the fact that it rules me: if I'm missing for too long, Bishop will definitely send West in particular to find me. Neither of us wants that. He'd be able to, too, and not only because he's the Beta. Mates can find each other by following their bond to the other end; unless it's closed off, of course. It's how I know that, whenever he's not busy with his pack duties, West spends all of his free time outside of Helene's cabin, waiting for her to give him a moment of her attention.

Me? I spend mine in the woods.

That afternoon, as I move soundlessly through the trees, I rub my chest with the heel of my hand.

It's getting worse. Can't deny it anymore. The jagged edge of our neglected mate bond… it *hurts*. At this point, if I could use my claws to gut myself open and rip it out, I would. Anything has to be better than walking around with the sting of rejection as my constant companion.

Usually just being close enough to take in West's scent soothes it for a little while. Talking to him, hearing his voice… it helps.

Not today, though.

When I get to the small clearing I consider mine, I plop down on the ground. My legs are stretched out in front of me, I'm leaning back on my hands, my eyes cast toward the sky. The caps of leaves on the crowded hickory trees block out most of the sunlight, leaving a few stray beams filtering through.

I exhale roughly. It's not much, but at least I find some peace here.

Later, I'll look back and accept that everything that happened next wouldn't have if I'd only swallowed my pride and listened to West's warning. But I didn't, and by the time I discovered there was some merit in it, it's too late.

A big, black wolf has stalked out of the woods about twenty feet away from me.

I only noticed because his eyes are a vibrant gold, and as shadows fell around me, their shine caught my attention. I never scented him. Never heard him. I don't know where he came from or how he snuck up on me, but it doesn't matter. He's here.

Lips parted, I breathe in deep, sampling scents. Big mistake. Something burns the back of my throat.

I choke.

Wolfsbane.

No wonder I didn't catch his scent before his eyes flickered in the distance. No wonder the pack patrol found prints and no other trace. Wolfsbane can cover up anything except muddy prints.

He's not a real wolf. I hadn't thought he was, but the wolfsbane gives him away. That's a shifter out there. The wolfsbane makes it worse. He's not only a stranger, but he has to be an enemy. No supe with good intentions carries wolfsbane on them.

And that's when his aura rushes at me. It took a few seconds, thanks to the wolfsbane messing with my senses, but I can't miss it now.

He's a shifter—and he's an alpha. Explains why he's so huge.

The way his gaze is locked on me also explains why he's here.

I have no clue what the hell he wants with me, but there's no denying the predatory gleam in his gaze as he pads closer.

He's moving slowly on purpose. He doesn't want to spook me. He's treating me like prey and, Luna, does that rankle.

I hop to my feet. He pauses, then continues to stalk forward.

My first instinct is to shift. I run faster as a wolf. His every move screams he's ready to take off if I do, and I'm not sure I can waste the precious seconds it would cost me to explode out of my clothes and change shapes.

I'm still a wolf whether I'm in my skin or not. I know these woods like the back of my hand. I know every member of the Sylvan Pack. The black wolf is undeniably a stranger. So he tiptoed up to the edge of our territory. I can lose him, then make it further into Hickory where the rest of the pack can help me.

That's what we do. When push comes to shove, we help each other.

I bolt. Just like I figured, he comes racing after me.

I can make it. Weaving around the trees, taking the quickest path back toward Hickory, I can lose him—

Nope.

With all of his brute strength, the wolf barrels into my legs. It's a cheap shot. I'm lucky he didn't snap a bone with his impact, and when I go flying before landing on my belly in the dirt, all of the air is knocked out of me.

A second later, his wolfish body is covering my human one.

Shit. I knew he was big, but pressed against me, I realize he's *massive.*

What *is* he?

He looks like a wolf, but he sure doesn't act like one. Wolves rarely give pursuit when they're hunting. They prefer to ambush their prey.

Then again, isn't that what he's done to me?

Once I'm down, I figure it's worth the split second of vulnerability. The force of my shift will tear my clothes off of my back, but the supernatural magic inherent to our kind will also push him away from me if only for a second.

That might be all I need to get away from him. My wolf is much squirmier than my human form. Faster, too. Shifting now should give me the best chance of escaping him.

I'm quick. He's quicker. As if he expected me to change shapes once he got a hold of me, he grabs my scruff between his fangs. Though, as a shifter, I only have sex when I'm in my skin, never my fur, there are some primal memories I can't deny. A wolf on top of me, his fangs pinning me by the scruff?

He's mounting my wolf.

No fucking way.

He's an alpha. Not as strong as Bishop—as if anyone

could be—he's still twice my size and probably triple my power. He must've thought I was an easy target.

If so, he was wrong.

I jerk my head. His fangs rip through my skin. Ignoring the pain, I whirl on him, snapping my fangs back, trying to bite any part of him I can reach. I'm especially partial to any dangly bits. An unknown wolf attacking me on pack land? I have every right to defend myself, and if he ends up castrated, he'll learn that even a low-ranking delta she-wolf has claws and fangs.

I lock onto his foreleg. Blood gushes into my mouth. Swallowing it greedily, I tear.

Feel that, asshole!

The wolf growls. Instead of trying to get me off of him, he pushes against my fangs, feeding me more of his fur, his muscle, his blood.

I choke on it. Breathing through my snout, I refuse to let go.

He shifts. I'm ripping human flesh now, but I don't care. In fact, without the fur in my way, I'm sure I'm doing more damage.

Why isn't he fighting to be free? Or fighting back? From his aura, I can tell he's an alpha. Just because I'm defending myself, it doesn't mean that he won't take this as me answering his challenge. By shifter law, he can put me down without any consequence. He's certainly strong enough to. Failing that, bastard could force me to submit. He's too dominant for me to ignore.

I'd never win.

Only... he isn't. He's willingly allowing me to gnaw on

him as the heat of his naked body pushes me to the ground.

I stay in my fur. I need my fangs to be at their sharpest, I need my jaw to be strong, and I need to keep my naked human body away from the monster erection digging into my back.

That's not the only thing I feel poking me.

Still clamping down on him—now that he's human, his foreleg is now his upper arm—I jerk in time to see he has something in his other hand. I don't know where he got it from. Clothes never survive the shift so it's not like he pulled it out of a pocket. Jewelry that's been charmed might, but he's not holding a necklace or a bracelet.

That's a shot. The vial is filled with a viscous, silvery grey liquid that shimmers against the glass casing—and he's buried the needle part of the injector past my fur.

I know what that is, too.

Mercury.

Quicksilver.

Poison.

Before I can react, he uses his thumb to press down on the plunger at the top of the injector.

Fucker.

It's not enough to kill me—he'd need pure silver to do that—but quicksilver isn't just a poison. It's also a sedative. Pour a couple of drops in a drink and it'll do something funny to a shifter's beast. Shoot one with an injection of the stuff and I'm gonna be on my ass before I know it.

He runs his fingers through the fur on the top of my head, obviously pleased with himself. His mouth reaches one of my ears. I flick it angrily, but that doesn't stop him from leaning closer.

"Remember," he whispers in a gruff voice, "it didn't have to be this way."

As the quicksilver worms its way through me and I start to go under, I suddenly remember something I should never have forgotten.

Real wolves will rarely pursue prey. But give a wolf shifter the chance?

He'll *always* chase.

I also realize something else.

There's no escaping him, either.

CHAPTER 3
CHAINS

My eyes flutter open.

I already know something is wrong before I'm completely awake. As a shifter, my senses are usually firing on all cylinders. My nose can tell me almost as much about my surroundings as my sight does. My ears, too.

None of them are working right.

My nose is stuffed up. Supes don't get sick like humans do, but this is what I think it must be like. It's as if someone shoved a wad of cotton up each of my nostrils because I can't smell a damn thing.

Same with my ears. Everything is dull. I move a little, and I hear something heavy sliding across the floor, but it sounds like it's coming from far, far away.

The room is dark and, except for me, it's empty. There's one window, high above my head on the wall at my back, and it's closed. Shades are drawn, letting in a sliver of light, so I know it's still daylight out there. Normally the meager light would be enough for me to make out every detail—but it isn't. The most I can see is that the room is made up of four solid grey cinder block walls with a single dark brown door breaking them up. If I didn't know any better, I'd think it looks like some kind of cell.

And that's when I remember.

The quicksilver. The black wolf.

The chase.

My senses are trash. Now that I remember that I was dosed with quicksilver, it makes sense. Quicksilver is a sedative, but it also cuts a shifter off from their wolf. It wears off in time. Based on how... how *human* I feel right now, I can tell it hasn't yet. My wolf is eerily missing.

And that's not all that isn't quite right.

Wherever I am, I'm laying down on a blanket that's protecting me from the hard cement floor beneath it. I jerk up, and that same sound from before follows my movement. I feel heavy, too, like whatever I'm dragging is attached to me.

Uh-oh.

I look down.

The first thing I notice is that I'm human again. Last I recall, I was in my wolf form, but the human arms and legs I'm looking at are undeniable. Of course. With the quicksilver coming between me and my wolf, I would've reverted back to my human form in order to contain my beast.

The second thing?

I'm not naked.

Not that I would prefer to wake up without any clothes on in an unfamiliar room. Considering I had shifted during the attack, I *should* have. My clothes are a mess of tattered remains in the forest while I'm here, wearing a slinky, dark red dress that covers me all the way down to the middle of my thighs. No bra, no panties, but at least my tits aren't hanging out. Small victories.

Then there's the tiny matter of the third undeniable thing...

I've been chained to the bare wall behind me.

Each of my ankles has a shackle on it. A length of chain—from the faint crackle I sense coming from them, I know they're made from silver, just like the shackles—is attached to each one, threaded through a sturdy-looking ring screwed into the cinder block over my head.

I don't scream. He's already proven that he sees me as his prey, and no matter what his intentions are, I'm still as much a predator as he is. My heart might be racing, my stomach tight and queasy as the reality of my situation sinks in, but losing my head won't help me get out of it.

Think, Quinn. Focus.

Okay. First things first. I can't reach my wolf. I can't rely on my shifter's senses. I still have a brain.

What happened after I was out? That's something to worry about.

Rubbing my thighs together, I'm relieved to find that I don't feel any tenderness or pain. On the plus side, my mysterious captor might've dressed my naked body before chaining me to a wall, but he didn't force himself on me.

Yet.

Once I pay closer attention to the shackles on my ankles, I no longer expect him to.

I already knew he was a shifter. He appeared on the edge of Hickory as a black wolf before turning human. The chains only reinforce my belief.

A human in the know might still be stupid enough to go for steel or iron chains if they wanted to trap a she-wolf. At my full strength, I could snap those easily; they'd never hold me. Only silver could, but even if they were tipped off to one of a shifter's few weaknesses, I'd expect them to wrap me up in them, not caring if they burned the crap out of me or not.

I'm just a captive, right? Depending on what they want with me, so long as they keep the chains away from my goods, what does it matter if I suffer in other places?

But the person who locked me up in these chains? They were careful to keep the silver from my bare skin. The chains are stretched out and positioned far from me so I wouldn't accidentally brush against them while I was unconscious, and there's fabric padding between me and the silver shackles.

I might be trapped. The silver might weaken me further.

At least I'm not being burned by it.

Just in case, I give an experimental kick. The chains swing, then go taut, but they don't break. Even when I can tap into my wolf again, I don't think I'll be able to snap them. The silver is too powerful.

Crap.

Now, I'm not pissed about the chains. Not really. Maybe a human chick would be, but us supernaturals see things a little differently. While I don't know exactly why he took me captive, I can't deny it wasn't smart of him to lock me up. He doesn't know me. He doesn't know how I'll react. She-wolves of my rank are still vicious and strong when we're backed in a corner, and that's exactly where I am right now.

I've also heard stories about shifters on the edge of going feral who chose the chains for themselves. Usually they're alphas, but most dominant shifters have a close call or two. I did. When I first understood—really understood—that West was rejecting our mate bond, I wanted to lash out. It didn't get so bad that I needed to be restrained from taking out my pain on him, but it was rough.

So the chains? The chains I can understand. But the quicksilver burning through me, keeping me from getting in touch with my wolf?

He never should've done that.

I'm a shifter. You hurt my wolf, you hurt my soul. And you'll pay for it.

Unfortunately, attacking the black wolf who ambushed me is out. Even before the quicksilver, he was too strong for me. I either need to outsmart him, or get the heck out of Dodge before he realizes I'm awake.

I look down at the chains holding me back again and wince.

This is gonna hurt, isn't it?

Supes, as an advanced species, are powerful. We're long-lived, have amazing regenerative properties, enhanced strength and speed, and the ability to form mate bonds; a vampire has their beloved while a shifter can find their fated mate or choose one to bond with forever. When humans know we exist, we're respected and revered.

All that power comes with a price. As strong as we are, we're not invulnerable. While each type of supe has a few weaknesses specific to their race, we all share one: *silver*. It's deadly to supernaturals. In small amounts, it's like acid against our skin, and a drain on our abilities. In larger amounts, it doesn't need to be a weapon to kill us, though a silver stake, blade, or bullet will certainly do the job.

I'm hoping that the quicksilver he shot me with is enough to temper my wolf's reaction to the real stuff. I'm still a shifter, but with my wolf out of my reach, maybe I can try to break the silver chain without too much damage.

It's worth a shot.

Reaching down by my leg, I grab the nearest length of chain and yank.

As soon as the silver touches my skin, it begins to sizzle. I bite back a scream, gritting my teeth as I tug. I won't give him the satisfaction of hearing me yell. I'd much rather he come back to this room only to find a set of snapped chains and me already gone.

Serves him right from trying to steal me, I think, and seething past the agony, I tug again.

IT WAS A GOOD PLAN. IF ONLY IT WORKED.

I've burned almost all of the skin from my fingers for nothing. The silver chains are as unbreakable as they were when I first came to, only now I'm pissed off, my hands feel like acid has bitten through most of the flesh, my throat is raw from the screams I refused to let out, and, to cap off my shitty, shitty day, my aching, empty stomach is starting to grumble.

I'm a little bit worried, too. The reality of the chains has sunk in. The padding beneath the shackles makes it obvious this isn't some kind of sick torture play—my captor doesn't want me to suffer needlessly because of the silver in the chains—so that means he wants me in one piece.

Not only that, but he wants me in one place. He went to a lot of trouble to get me here, so he must have a reason.

And I'm pretty sure I know what it is.

Realistically, there are only a couple of options. We're shifters. We fight. We fuck. We feed. Life is about survival, making sure the pack is safe, and our future pups are provided for. We feel things more strongly than the cold-blooded vampires, or even humans. Our wolves, at their core, are just like their counterparts in the wild. We see things in black and white; there are no shades of grey.

There's no denying the black wolf took me. Whether he targeted me on purpose, or I was just the bonehead who went to the edge of Hickory that day on my own, he brought me here. The quicksilver sedated me before, and is still subduing me now. The chains make it impossible for me to escape.

He wants me here. It doesn't take a genius to know *why*.

He's a male. I'm a she-wolf. His aura reads as alpha,

though it's pretty different than Bishop's level of dominance. I'm a delta with just enough spunk to put up a fight against him, proving that I'd be a good protector to any pups I might have.

How much do you want to bet he wants a mate and I'm the lucky gal he's chosen?

It's a lone wolf thing. All shifters belong in a pack or a clan or a brood. Wolves are the most notorious for needing to be among their own kind. Sometimes, if one of us goes out on our own, we start to forget how to act like a shifter.

Some rely more on their human side. Others go wolf. With our wolves in charge, pesky things like right or wrong—or letting another shifter know you're interested instead of just straight up *taking her*—fall to the wayside. He might not know how much he fucked up.

That's okay. I'll make sure to tell him.

Even with these chains I have the advantage. He wants something from me, and I want to get the hell out of here. If he really wants me to mate him, he'll try to prove himself to me. I can work with that.

Unless he's a feral.

When it comes to the broken shifters, more wolf than man, there's no guessing what they'll do. They are as vicious and cruel as they are territorial and protective. A feral might force a female, then tear out her throat in an attempt to mark her as his.

Worse, he might force a female, then tear out her throat because he'd gotten what he wanted, and she was a casualty that didn't matter once he finished.

I shiver at the thought. I can handle anything but *that*.

Being rejected, catching the attention of a lone wolf on his own, even walking away from the Sylvan Pack if that's what I decide to do. But a feral?

I'd be better off slitting my own throat. At least I would save myself from anything else a twisted feral shifter might come up with.

No. He can't be feral. Ferals are rabid, untamable wolves walking around in their human shape. They're ruled by their urges. If he looked at me and wanted to mate, he would've fucked me in the woods just outside of Hickory.

The black wolf that stalked me was methodical. He knew exactly what to do to take me down, and he capped it off by injecting me with quicksilver. That takes planning. Precision. Human reasoning.

He has to be a lone wolf. One aching for a female of his own.

Shame he chose me.

And once he finally shows his face again, I'll make sure he knows it.

———

HE'S SOMEWHERE NEAR. AS THE HOURS PASS, THE quicksilver is finally beginning to work its way out of my system. I can't reach my wolf just yet, but I'm able to rely on some of my shifter's senses.

My nose recovers first. Breathing in deep, I catch notes of a male scent overlaying everything in this room —including me. The chains carry his scent. The dress I'm wearing is entrenched in it. *I* kind of smell like him, and when I trace the most potent source to my hair, I wonder what that's about.

Did he pet my hair when I was unconscious or something?

His musk lingers everywhere. It seeps in under the door. It hangs in the air. I don't hear him, but his scent keeps renewing. He's near, and, after a while, I get annoyed that he's left me here to rot.

He fucking kidnapped me. The least he could do was make sure that his quicksilver didn't stop my heart and kill me after he dressed me up like his own personal doll.

The longer I'm in here, the easier it is for me to be angry instead of worried. I need someone to take it out on, and he's the perfect choice.

"Hey!" My voice is rusty from not using it. I clear my throat, then try again. "Hey, you! I know you're here! You can't leave me like this!"

He can. Of course he can. But I'm sure as hell not gonna make it easy on him.

"Where are you? Let me out of here!"

No answer. I didn't expect one, but I let out a full-throated shout that irritates the entire length of my poor esophagus. At least it makes me feel a little better to get that out.

I'm a she-wolf. While I admit it was a shock to realize that I've basically been put in a cage, I'm not going to sit here like some damsel in distress. Maybe if he realizes that I'm a complete pain in the ass, he'll think better of keeping me.

Hey. It's a thought, and one I perk up at.

I can do that.

Just as I'm about to start shouting again, a new scent mingles with that of the wolf. Once it hits me, my mouth waters as my stomach grumbles loudly, and it's all I can think about.

Meat. Beef, if my nose is right. I think it's steak.

Why do I smell steak?

I want steak.

If he's cooking himself dinner while I'm chained to a wall, I'm going to lose it. If I didn't already want to break free, the promise of a steak has me just about ready to see if I'm strong enough to snap my chains yet.

I glance at my fingers. Thanks to the quicksilver, my regenerative properties aren't as fast as they usually are. My palms are covered in pale pink blisters—better than the angry red ones from before, but barely—and my fingertips are tender.

Damn it. Better wait.

Frustrated, I kick out my legs, putting the chains as far away from me as possible. The blanket beneath me is soft and luxurious, but I'm still lying on the floor. I need to get up. I need to move.

I also have to pee. Something I'm going to have to deal with sooner or later, though I'm not above pissing in this dress if I have to. He wants to put me in this room? I'll mark it as mine if he doesn't let me use the toilet.

It's a win-win. He either has to deal with me marking my territory, or he has to unchain me so I can go to the bathroom. If he thought he was going to get some docile female out of this, he chose wrong. He needs an omega like Helene.

Damn it, why didn't he go after Helene?

I know the answer to that. Li'l Miss Pack Princess would never be caught out on her own. And if she was? Both the Alpha and Beta would be on the black wolf's ass so fast, he'd be nothing but a pile of fur and guts by the time Bishop and West finished with him.

And then there's me. If I want out, I'll have to free myself.

I will. Bet on it.

Another couple of minutes go by. Without a phone or a watch or a damn clock on the wall, I have no idea how many. Could be five. Could be thirty. With the scent of cooked meat teasing me, it feels like forever before I hear something on the other side of the door.

Suddenly, it eases open.

It wasn't closed all the way. When I noticed it before, I'd thought it was because he just hadn't bothered on his way out. The silver chains make it so that I can't get out of this room unless I gnaw off my ankles and I crawl out, and if I tried, he'd be after me before I got that much further. I'd put money on it.

Maybe that's true. Could be. When the door inches inward, I discover the real reason.

Wolves don't have opposable thumbs.

With his height, he'd be able to reach the knob if he stood up on his back legs, but he'd never be able to turn it with his paws. The black wolf from the woods uses his head first, then the brunt of his shoulder to push the door in.

He's just as big as I remember. I'd thought my panic made him seem huger in my memories. Nope. The black wolf is probably the largest shifter I've ever seen, except for maybe Bishop.

Alpha. Right.

His golden eyes have that same insane gleam as before, too. As he pads into the room, they're almost flashing as he turns his unblinking stare on me. A muffled grunt is probably his idea of a greeting.

Wait... muffled?

He has something in his mouth. It takes me a second before I realize that he has a hunk of meat hanging from between his clamped fangs. A quick sniff reveals that it's the steak I caught cooking before.

The black wolf is walking right toward me. Any bravado I had earlier fades when I see that his eyes don't just look insane. They look *hungry*.

And he's staring at me.

"Who are you?" I ask, scooting back on the blanket. It's fluffy and thick, the only hint of softness in this gloomy, dark room. It shifts when I move, following me. "Where am I?"

He doesn't answer me. Of course not. In his wolf form, the most he can do is communicate with howls, yips, grunts, and snarls, none of which will tell me what's going on.

But the way he crosses the room before he spits the hunk of meat out of his mouth, dropping it in front of me?

That does.

CHAPTER 4
STEAK

h, Luna. He's got to be kidding me.

"I'm not eating that."

The black wolf grunts again.

Too bad. "I mean it. Get that away from me. I'm not touching that."

Acting as though I didn't say a damn thing, he has the nerve to nudge it closer to me with his snout.

Despite how hungry I am, I flip him the bird. Probably not the smartest move when I'm guessing I know exactly what he wants with me, but I don't care. If he thinks I'm going to accept food from him, he's crazier than I already think he is.

He curls his muzzle over his fangs, showing off his canines.

The fact that he's walking around in his fur, baring his fangs at me, just makes me more pissed off. It's a shifter thing. If I'm in my skin, he should be, too.

"What's the matter? Come on, tough guy. Use your

words. Answer me. Who are you, and what do you think you're doing?"

He growls.

"Sorry"—I'm not sorry—"but that shit you pumped into me is cutting me off from my wolf. I have no idea what you're trying to say."

It's a lie and we both know it. I don't need my wolf to translate when it's obvious. He wants me to eat the steak.

I absolutely refuse.

As if the padding around my ankles isn't enough, I can't deny what this strange wolf is after. In shifter culture, food has a very important meaning. Parents provide for their pups until they come of age. Even if you're separated from your folks before then, it's the Alpha's responsibility to make sure that none of us go hungry; that's why Bishop and Sofia make sure there is breakfast, lunch, and dinner ready for any and all pack-mates, no strings attached.

And, of course, there are mates.

As a she-wolf, if a male offers me food, it's a precursor to mating. Simple as that. Not just fucking, either, but it's his way of initiating a relationship that might eventually become permanent.

The first time I saw West pick out the thickest, most perfectly sauced chop during dinner before plating it and offering it to Helene in front of our packmates, I knew that I'd never have him. There were plenty of other clues in the beginning—the most significant one being the way his gaze often passed over me as though I wasn't there—but that was the one I couldn't deny.

It wasn't bad enough that he was basically begging for

a minute of her attention. Even knowing that the Luna picked me for him, he tried to feed Helene.

She's the Omega of the Sylvan Pack. Considered almost like royalty among our kind, she's always been prized, protected, and coddled. The only one allowed to feed her—apart from her promised mate from the Gravetail Pack—is Bishop. As both the Alpha of her pack and her big brother, there's no sexual intent behind it, so Helene can accept food from him.

When West offered her that meal, he was saying: *I will protect you, I will feed you, and you'll want for nothing if I'm around.*

Of course, Helene gently refused him, and instead of eating the chop himself—or throwing it my way in an act of pity—West disappeared into the woods, tossing the food to the wild wolves that sometimes visit our pack.

Did that stop him from trying again? No. At least once a week West still tries to feed Helene, and the more he did it, the more I felt the eyes of my packmates on me as if watching to see how I'd react. That's why I stopped eating with the pack. Over the last six months, I've gotten used to grabbing my plate and heading back to my cabin instead of sitting down to a pity party of one.

I can't believe this shit. The first time a male shifter propositions *me* with food and it's a lone wolf who stole me away from Hickory. If I eat this meat, I'm basically telling him I'm interested—and that I don't mind what he's done.

Yeah, right. Not in this lifetime.

The black wolf is watching me unblinkingly. After a few tense seconds, he taps his front paw against the floor.

The claws clink. I cross my arms over my chest. He chuffs, then scoots the steak closer to me with that same paw.

What is wrong with him? Not only have I already refused his meal, but I'm obviously in my human form. That means my human brain is currently in charge. As a wolf, I have no problem hunting a deer or a rabbit, then eating the bloody meat raw, ripping it right off the bone. As a human? All I keep thinking about is how dirty his paw is, how he had the meat in his mouth, and how he keeps dragging it across the floor.

He finally gets it. When I turn my nose up at his offering again, he pads away from me. He moves slowly, his head hanging as if trying to figure out what to do next, and I only hope he'll leave me the hell alone so I can figure out what *I'm* going to do.

The black wolf doesn't. Instead, he crosses the room, then lowers himself down into the corner opposite of me. He folds his back legs beneath him, stretching out his forelegs. His golden eyes locked on me, he settles his muzzle on his legs, almost like he's settling in for a good, long wait.

Oh. I see. He's gonna lay there until I accept his steak.

I snort softly. Good luck.

Even if I don't know exactly why he thinks his tactics are going to work, I understand *what* he's doing. A lone wolf is still a shifter, and I've spent twenty-six years around my male packmates. I don't think there's a more stubborn creature on the planet—except, perhaps, a she-wolf who's been wronged.

However, there is one thing I don't get. If he really is treating me like a prospective mate, why is he giving his wolf control? While a mating would never work unless both halves of each shifter were in agreement about their future mate, our wolves are easy to convince. If a mate is attractive, a good protector, a good provider, and a good parent to any future pups, our wolves will be on board long before our human halves are sure.

That's why so many shifters wait to find their fated mates. Whether the Luna pushes us together, or we just sense it like how I was always drawn to West even when he was dating Helene, it's hard to deny a fated mate. There's usually a moment when the pair just clicks, and both halves know they're looking at their forever.

Unless, of course, you already chose your mate. Then you can reject Fate, hoping that the mate of your heart would choose you back.

And when she doesn't, all three of you are left heart-broken and alone...

I bite down, pushing thoughts of West out of my head. I've gotta stop thinking about him. As soon as the quicksilver started to fade earlier, I purposely cut West off from my side of our useless bond. If I keep letting him back into my head, it'll only be a matter of time before I slip up and he can sense something's wrong, no matter how closed off his side is.

How long have I been gone? Long enough that my pack has noticed I'm missing from Hickory? I'm not sure, but if it is, they'll turn to West to find me. They'll have to. Between the wolfsbane and the quicksilver, my captor covered his tracks. And that's assuming he carried me out of Hickory. If the lone wolf had a vehicle, it'll be impossible to scent me unless they know where I disappeared off to.

Considering I have no idea where I am myself, the odds of them finding me are pretty much nil—unless West tracks me using our fated mate bond.

I can't let that happen. If West did come, it would only be out of a sense of duty.

And if he didn't come…

I know he doesn't want me. I know he's rejected me in every way except telling me bluntly that he'll always choose Helene over me. I know that, if I want a mate of my own, it'll be one *I* choose.

But I'm still tied to West. If he abandons me to a lone wolf because I'm nothing to him, I don't think I'd be able to survive that last level of rejection. No. It's better to deal with this situation on my own.

After all, I got myself into this mess. I'll get myself out, too.

Talking to the black wolf is like talking to a brick wall. I'm not going to make any progress there. I need him to shift.

But he doesn't, and not because he can't.

I know he's able to shift to a human form. I didn't get a good look at him before, but my wolf latched onto a human arm at one point when he was trying to subdue me. His naked body seared my back right before he jammed that needle past my fur.

He spoke. In a raspy, hoarse voice that followed me into unconsciousness, he spoke to me, trying to make it seem like getting shot up with quicksilver was my fault for resisting him.

For that alone, I snag the slab of meat from the floor. It's just like I guessed. Barely seared, it's mostly raw, and it squelches against my grip. I can see the fang marks from where he carried it in his mouth to me.

I might be hungry, but I'm not *that* hungry.

The wolf lifts his head when he notices I've finally reached for the meat he gave me. If I eat it, it's a clear sign that I'm accepting his attention. At the very least, I'm telling him that he might've ambushed me and chained me away from my pack, but that's okay since he brought me food.

I'd rather starve.

I fling the steak across the room, aiming for the black wolf. It hits the wall about two feet higher than where his head is. The slap echoes, then the steak thumps as it lands between his ears. He flattens them against his skull before he shakes his whole head roughly, tossing the battered steak to the floor.

The black wolf looks at the steak, then at me, then back at the steak. I think me throwing the meat finally got through to him because, instead of trying to force it on me again, he digs in. In a matter of bites, it's gone.

Good for him. At least one of us enjoyed it.

AFTER THE DISASTER WITH THE STEAK, I DON'T THINK HE'LL come back for a while. He leaves the same way he came, in his wolf form, though he doesn't drag the door behind him when he goes.

Almost immediately, I scent more food cooking. I

can't imagine that he's making it for me after I refused the steak, and I figure that the meat he scarfed down hadn't been enough for such a big brute. It must be for him—and I believe that until a looming figure appears in the open doorway not much later.

With a surprised gasp, I finally get my first good look at my captor in his human form.

Luna damn it. It would be so much easier if he was hideous. A beastly male might have to resort to stealing a she-wolf for a mate, but one glimpse of him and I begin to second-guess everything that's going on.

Because this wolf? He's way too good-looking for me.

He's handsome in a rugged way that's so different than West, but still enticing to me and my wolf. Though I can't quite shift yet—probably because of the silver chains—I can sense her rousing deep inside of me, and her head jerks up when he stalks into the room.

His skin is the soft bronze shade of someone who earned the coloring from hours in the sun. Considering he's wearing a pair of low-slung jeans and nothing else, it's easy to see his tan is unbroken. His thick, shaggy hair is the same color as his pelt, his eyes a shade darker than his wolf's.

He has broad shoulders, a sculpted torso, and a patch of dark hair on the height of his chest; it's also the color of his fur. As he moves into the room on soundless, bare feet, the light flickers against something, and that's when I notice that he has a golden necklace around his thick throat. Two charms hang off the chain: a white sliver of who knows what, and a slender golden cylinder about three inches long.

He has a plate in each hand. Learning from before, he brought me a steak, but it looks like it's medium this time instead of super rare. French fries are piled high next to it. On the other plate, there's a mound of bacon higher than the fries, and a few pieces of lettuce mixed with tomatoes that might generously be called a salad. He has a glass of water tucked under his muscular arm and—

I blink, then blink again because I can't believe what I'm seeing.

He has a bite mark on his upper arm, just above his bicep. *My* bite mark. I can see the imprint of every one of my fangs, plus where I tore the skin as I was fighting for my freedom. It's not still bleeding, but it's nowhere near as healed as it should've been. Actually, depending on how long I've been stuck in this room, it should be way gone by now.

But it's not. And that... that's almost as weird as a half-naked shifter bringing me a meal.

Handsome or not, I can't let him get away with this.

I glare up at him. "What do you want with me?" As if I didn't already know. "You have to let me go."

Like he did when he was a wolf, he pretends not to have heard me. Instead, he lowers himself to a crouch, placing both plates down on the ground. The glass tucked under his arm is next.

Once he's done, he cocks his head. Then, for the first time since he tackled me, he speaks.

"Will they come for you?"

His voice is as gruff as I remember it. More than that, it's deep, so deep it does something to my insides.

Or maybe that's because I can't stop glancing at my bite mark staring out at me from his upper arm...

I shake my head. I mean it to clear the unwelcome thoughts inside my mind, but he takes it as my answer.

"Good. You're mine now. It's better that they forget about you. I won't let them take you from me anyway. And if they try? I'll just go after you and take you back with me."

Wait—*what*?

Forget the fact that he misunderstood. Forget the fact that, despite how low I rank in my pack, I know that Bishop would never abandon me.

He thinks he can keep me here just because he wants to?

"You can't do this," I snap at him, kicking out at the nearest plate. Thanks to the weight of the chain and how short it is, I can't really reach it, but my big toe brushes it. The pile of bacon scatters on the plate.

He frowns when it falls before his attention is back on me.

"That's what you say."

I don't like how he put it like that. "Okay. What do *you* say then?"

"That I already have." He points at the steaming plate of food. "Now eat before it gets cold."

No way. I might've been hungry before, but I've totally lost my appetite.

"You can't keep me here," I insist instead. He has to understand how insane he sounds. "You misunderstood me before. They will come. My mate will get me."

He will. Out of a sense of duty if nothing more, if I open up our bond, West will come and get me.

My captor's eyes flash angrily. "Mate?" he says. "What mate? I will be your only mate."

"You can't be. I already have one!"

Yeah... in retrospect, that was probably the worst thing I could've said to him while he was trying so desperately to feed me.

I knew that's why he wanted me. For me to be his mate. I already knew that. The chains, the blanket, the food... in his twisted way, he was providing for me. He brought me here to be the plus one to his lone wolf.

Thing is... wolves mate for life. If I already have one, I can't be his.

So what if me and West will never be? Technically, I have a mate—and it isn't my captor. He had to know that. Every shifter within miles of Hickory knows about me and West.

Too bad me pointing that out sets him off way worse than I ever would've expected.

With a roar, he just... he loses complete control. There's no other way to explain it. He snaps. Shoulders hunched, eyes a blazing gold, he lunges. Not at me, thank the Luna, but across the room.

Swinging wildly, he bashes his fist into the nearest cinder block he can find.

Something cracks. Since the cinder block wall is still standing strong, I think it might be his hand—or paw, really.

Because that's a fucking paw at the end of his wrist.

I don't know what happened to him, but he's shifted into some form of monster I've never seen before. He's still on two feet, his arms covered in fur. So is his chest. Terrifying fangs jut from a twisted mouth, and his cheekbones look sharp enough to cut paper. His tanned skin seems stretched over bulging muscles. His arms are too long, hanging forward, and those are definitely claws attached to his paws.

What the...

Shifters have two forms: the one that mimics *human*, and the one that mimics *wolf*. Two-legged or four-legged, but never anything in between. Our fangs don't elongate like vamps do, and while our nails tend to grow like claws, they're still recognizable fingernails.

Not him.

He's engaged in some kind of terrifying partial shift: half-human, half-wolf, and all something straight out of a horror flick. This? This is what unaware humans think werewolves look like. This mangled creature with patchy fur, a broken body, claw-tipped fingers, and a mouth full of fangs.

Even more amazingly, he didn't lose his clothes. Not that I was looking forward to seeing his jeans explode into tatters as he went from man to wolf, but that's what happens. If you don't strip before you shift, your clothes are toast.

After a few more furious punches, he prowls around the room, his muscular, animalistic form pushing against the seams on his jeans, but he stays covered.

At least now I know why he didn't bother with shoes or a shirt. They never would've made it.

The partial shift lasts for about thirty seconds more,

though it seems like an eternity. He doesn't come at me, instead spinning to the other side of the room where he punches the cinder block wall enough times that his furry knuckles are shredded and the rusty tang of blood perfumes the air.

As I fold myself into a much smaller target, huddling in my corner, I suddenly understand why he hasn't acted at all like I've expected him to.

He's not a regular shifter. He might be a lone wolf, but that's not all.

Feral, I realize. He is a feral.

And I'm in deep, deep shit.

CHAPTER 5

FERAL

This isn't just some shifter who decided they liked the smell of me, or who mistakenly believes that I have any worth to my pack just because the Luna said I was supposed to be with the Beta. Sofia would've been a better target if he was going after Bishop, and if he wanted to bring West to his knees, Helene is the she-wolf he needs, but neither of those two was dumb enough to leave the heart of pack territory.

Up until now, I really figured him for a lone wolf. Not common, but not unheard of. Since shifters are a mix between human and beast, our instinct is to search out a pack and make a community of it. It takes a lot for a shifter to willingly live on their own—and more for them to turn feral.

Packs stabilize a shifter. It keeps our two halves in sync. We *need* the balance. Ferals are what happens when the dark side of both halves takes control. Between the wolf's single-minded focus to survive above all else and a human's capacity for viciousness and evil, a feral shifter is almost as dangerous as a rogue bloodsucker.

The only thing *more* dangerous?

A feral alpha wolf.

Like my captor.

His dominance is undeniable. As a broken wolf, it was easy to ignore it; with the quicksilver running through me, my senses were dull. But almost all of that shit is out of my system now, and in his human shape, it pours off of his hard body.

As the urge to submit to him hums through me, he pulls it back. The aggression. The rage. The dominance. He finds control—and that, more than anything else, is terrifying to me.

He makes no mention of how he lost it in the first place. Following his lead, I clamp my mouth shut. He just flicks his wrist hard enough to re-set it, then points down at the plates again.

"Eat."

I gulp, but I still can't bring myself to accept it. Especially now. "No, thanks."

I lost my nerve. Sue me. It's easy to be brave when I thought he was a lone wolf who's been out of touch. But a feral? One wrong word and I can trigger him. I have to be careful.

But, oh, he doesn't like me being overly careful, does he?

With a scowl, he says, "Eat or I'll pin you down and force you to. Your choice."

One look in his golden eyes and I know he'll do it, too.

What else can I do?

"I will," I tell him, "but only if you accept that it's because I'm starving and not because I'm letting you feed me."

"You'll eat because you have to." Reaching behind him, he pulls a fork out from his pocket and sets it down on the floor. No knife, but even if he gave me one, I'm not sure I'd be strong enough to use it on him. "And I'll make sure you're fed no matter what I have to do."

It's not a 'no'. Deciding that means he agreed with my stipulation, I lift the first plate onto my lap, then grab the fork.

Growing up in a pack, I'm used to having an audience when I eat; to shifters, eating alone in our cabins is weird since we often have communal meals. Even so, I've never had a male watch me do so with such intense interest. His arms crossed over his chest, bare feet planted in front of me, the feral is witness to every single bite I take. When I finish one plate, he shoves the next at me, then plops the glass of water within my reach.

It's delicious, though that has to be because I *was* starving; shifters need to eat constantly to replace the calories we burn when we shift, and I've already missed a few meals. Regardless, I refuse to thank him. Why should I? Bringing me here makes me his responsibility. Feeding me is the least he can do.

Once I'm done, he gathers up the plates, grunting in approval when he sees that they're just about licked clean.

If I wouldn't be spiting myself more than him, I'd stick my fingers down my throat and hurl everything I just ate out onto the floor. Of course, then he'd probably decide that I didn't deserve to have my hands free. My legs are chained. What's stopping him from locking up the rest of me?

Better not chance it.

As if he's thinking the same thing I am, he piles the dishes by the door, then comes back to me. Crouching down so that we're on the same level, he holds out his hand.

"Arm."

My initial instinct is to refuse. Unfortunately, I make a mistake. Feral or not, he's still an alpha. His dominance rolls over me, and I might've been able to withstand it if I hadn't glanced up.

Our eyes meet. With my hold on my wolf tenuous at best right now, I can't resist the power in his golden gaze.

I submit. Thrusting out my right arm, I'm not able to look away from him until he's cradling my arm with his hands.

It's only after I do that I realize just how dangerous that was. Prolonged eye contact with a dominant shifter is usually a sign of a challenge. Even if I didn't mean it, a higher-ranked wolf might take it that way. He must really think of me as his future mate because any other alpha would've at least snapped their fangs at me.

And that's not counting what a feral is capable of.

Take my arm for example. The strength in his grip tells me that he could easily snap my bone. The gentle way his fingers stroke the crook of my elbow is a sign that —for the moment at least—he won't.

I should've realized he had an ulterior motive. While

still stroking me with one hand, he reaches up to his chest. His fingers grope for the cylindrical charm hanging off of his golden chain. Tugging the bottom part, it pulls free, revealing a loaded shot about two inches long.

Well, now I understand how he got me last time. The charm on his neck isn't some kind of decorative pendant like I first guessed. It holds another injection, and if the cylinder was charmed to survive a shift, he'd be able to carry a shot full of quicksilver whether he was in his wolf form or his human form.

Oh, yes. This feral is very, very tricky—and more dangerous than I already believed.

He moves the quicksilver shot toward my elbow, his intentions obvious.

The only reason I don't jerk away is because he could still snap my arm if he wanted to. Doesn't mean that I'm not going to try my best to stop him from shooting me up a second time.

"If you do this," I snarl, letting the edge of my wolf into my tone before she's cut off from me completely again, "I'll only hate you more than I already do for taking me."

Still holding onto my arm tightly with one hand, he uses the other to caress my cheek; the injection is tucked beneath his fingers. When I jerk my head out of his reach, his eyes gleam, but the notable insanity in them dies down almost immediately.

He leans in. The heat of his skin nearly sears mine as the edge of his jaw brushes against me, the stubble on his chin burning my cheek. His grip on my arm tightens further an instant before I feel the prick of the needle.

"Having you here with me is worth your hate," he whispers into my ear as he presses the plunger. "Now sleep, and we'll try again tomorrow."

I'm already dropping. With this new dose mingling with the quicksilver already in my veins, it hits me harder this time around. My eyes flutter closed as he wraps me up in his arms, laying me out on the blanket beneath me.

My last thought—*if I'm lucky, there might actually be a tomorrow*—runs through my muddled brain, and then I'm out again.

Feral dickhead.

A LONE WOLF WOULD NEVER HURT A FELLOW SHIFTER, especially one he was trying to mate. My worth is in my body, and an interested male would try to prove he was smart and strong and a fierce protector so that he could earn access to it.

But a feral...

A feral is unpredictable.

An intelligent feral like my captor is even worse.

He has just enough hold on his broken mind to protect me from the silver chains while also injecting me with quicksilver to keep me under control. That says he doesn't want to hurt me, but he also isn't willing to let me get the upper hand. I'm his captive until he gets what he wants—or until I find a way out of here.

Or he kills me in a fit of rage. Can't forget that.

I think of West again. He is so calm. Contained. He would never lose control like that beast did and—

Shit. I check my bond. The block I threw up yesterday is still there, and I only hope that it held while I was sedated.

Even if it didn't, I'm betting he wouldn't pay any attention to me until he was forced to. Once someone noticed I was missing—and the tattered clothes and destroyed shoes I left behind are a pretty big clue I was forced to shift in a hurry—Bishop would use West to try to track me down. I'm just about sure of it.

I can't let him come after me. I can't let any of my packmates try to find me. Right now, so long as the feral thinks of me as his, I'm as safe as possible. After the way he fucking lost it after I mentioned that I already had a mate, he'll see any other male as a rival. And that's assuming he doesn't know that West is the male I was talking about when I threw it in his face that I already have a mate.

What would he do if my fated mate came to rescue me after all? He already said he'd go after me, but he might challenge West, too. While I know that the Beta of the Sylvan Pack is a strong shifter, he's not an alpha. He's definitely not a feral.

He'd never survive.

If the feral challenged him, West would fight. I'd have to live the rest of my life knowing that he died because a feral decided he wanted me for a mate.

There is no other choice. I have to stay.

Besides, I also have to admit that *I* can't fight my way out of this because if I accept that West could never, then I'm definitely shit out of luck. Sure, he let me get away with biting him in the middle of him abducting me.

Something tells me that that was my one freebie and I shouldn't expect another.

Sitting up slowly, refusing to let my growing frustration pull me under, I realize I don't know how long I was out for after he dosed me with that quicksilver shit again. Longer than last time, I bet, since my shifter senses aren't as muted as before; either that, or I'm recovering from the poison faster. It's light outside once more, but that doesn't mean anything since my cage is still dark and gloomy.

I've got the same wine-red dress on. The same chains on my feet. I'm laying on the same blanket as... yesterday? I'm gonna go with yesterday. Another one, as silky as the dress I'm wearing, is spread out on top of me.

Shifters run hot. A heavy blanket would've made me melt, even if the room carries a chill. The flimsy, silky covering is closer to a sheet than a comforter, and it's perfect.

Of course, the thoughtfulness just pisses me off. I fling the covering from my body, scooting it away from me with the heel of my foot, then glare at it.

I'm pissed, but I'm also starving again; however long it's been, it's enough that my hunger's returned. So has the need to pee. A quick check down below reveals that he still hasn't taken advantage of me being sedated, plus I managed to keep from pissing myself while I was out.

I'm just beginning to think that I'll have to start marking this room after all when, suddenly, my captor walks into the room.

He's in his skin, which is a good sign. He's carrying two more plates and another glass of water. That's even better.

"Breakfast," he growls.

I planned on being cautious. Careful. That lasts as long as it takes for the feral to set down the plates, the glass, and slowly rise up from his crouch. As he does, his hand reaches to his crotch. The way he adjusts himself, whistling in a breath as he pushes against his junk, draws my attention to that spot.

Oh. Wow. Either he's bigger in the dick department than any male I've ever seen, or he's already sporting a woody in there that's equally as impressive. That bulge is huge, and his sensitive hiss is a sure sign he's aroused.

Uh-uh. Nope.

I haven't forgotten the way he pinned me down in his fur before shifting back to his skin.

I point dead at his chest.

"If you try to mount me again, I'll rip off your dick."

He has the nerve to look surprised that I made such a threat.

"I would never do that." He frowns as he dips his head. A hunk of black hair falls forward into his face. "That's not why I brought you here."

Yeah, right. He calls himself my mate, he's hard as a rock as he walks into my new cage, and he expects me to believe that he doesn't have sex on his mind? And, sure, maybe he's not going to force me to mate him or anything like that. He probably has grand ideas of *seduction*, of making me choose him.

Maybe if he hadn't drugged me, I might've.

Now?

Good luck.

"Same goes for my mouth. Put your cock anywhere

near my mouth and I'll bite it off instead." I snap my blunt human teeth in warning. Never underestimate a ticked-off she-wolf. We don't just threaten—we promise. "You might've taken my claws when you cut me off from my wolf, but I still have these."

"The quicksilver is for your protection. You shouldn't have struggled."

Asshole. He's really going to blame me for putting up a fight when an unknown wolf was stalking me?

I kick out a leg, making the silver chain rattle. "What about these?"

A shadow passes across his face. "Those are for mine."

Smart feral.

Since he seems more chatty today, I decide to keep the conversation going. "What's your name?"

No answer.

I'm not surprised. He wouldn't tell me yesterday, and he point-blank ignored me when I tried to find out where I was or what he wanted with me.

Does that stop me from trying another, more brash tactic?

Nope.

"How long do you plan on keeping me here?"

A muscle tics in his cheek. "You already know."

I didn't, but I could guess. Shoving the idea that he plans to keep me here with him forever far, far away, I open my mouth to ask another question when a low rumbling sound fills the quiet.

He's growling at me again.

I close my mouth.

"No more talking." He points at the food. "Eat. Now."

Then, crouching down a few feet away, forearms resting on his thick thighs, he stares at me. It's clear he plans on staying right there and watching to make sure that I obey.

I have no choice. Last night proved that he'll get his way in this. I tell myself that it doesn't mean anything. That I'm only using the food for fuel. It doesn't matter. I have to eat it, and I do.

When I'm done, he moves into me again, staying low so that we're on the same level. This close, I can either look into his golden eyes or stare at the bite mark on his upper bicep that I gave him.

Bicep it is.

It was half-healed yesterday. I wanted to see if it was gone or, like me, he was having a hard time regenerating. I'll admit, it was a deep bite, but even a feral should've been able to shake off the damage I did to him after a few hours.

And that's when I see that the wound from yesterday is still there as a noticeable silvery scar today.

He took my bite and kept the mark.

That... that can't be good.

He's still wearing jeans. I can't tell if he's hiding any other scars or marks beneath them. One thing for sure, the rest of his upper body doesn't have a single blemish on it—except for my bite.

Due to our regenerative properties, a shifter can keep any mark we want, but it has to be a conscious thing otherwise we heal completely. Scars have two meanings: either a memento from a fight that was significant enough to leave a reminder of it behind, or a mating mark.

As I stare at him, he closes the remaining gap between us. Starting at the hollow of my throat, he takes a deep breath. He's sniffing me, and he trails his nose along the column of my neck, the edge of my jaw, the curve of my ear, before burying his face in my hair.

It's a little bit greasy. It's kind of flat from where I slept on it. He groans under his breath anyway, then slowly inches away.

I'm too stunned to come up with any kind of comment—until he pulls a tiny key out of his front pocket and reaches for the nearest shackle.

"What are you doing?"

"Bathroom," he explains. He makes quick work of the lock, popping it open without ever brushing against the silver. He turns to the next. "You must need it by now."

I do, but I'd rather my bladder burst than admit it. "I guess."

Just goes to prove that he isn't intimidated by me at all. He removes both shackles, leaving the fabric padding wrapped around my ankles in place. I can see now that it's been taped together so that it stays there. The fact that he doesn't also take the padding off says he plans on chaining me up again.

Joy.

He hovers over me as I slowly stretch out my legs, then climb to my feet. Between the quicksilver and the chains, I'm not all that sturdy. No wonder he doesn't think I'm a threat. In this state, a pup could take me on and win.

That makes me angry again. Good. Hopefully the fury can burn through the quicksilver faster, letting me rely on my wolf to make me strong again.

After taking a steadying breath, purposely ignoring him, I scoop the mass of my greasy hair over my shoulder, trying to stretch out the crick in my neck.

Behind me, he starts to snarl. The pitch is low, but it grows and grows until I can no longer ignore it.

I mean, a strange feral is making threatening sounds at my back. Of course I'm going to spin around. My instincts have me throwing my hands up in a vain attempt to protect myself.

He scowls. "Don't be afraid. I won't hurt you."

"I'm not afraid," I lie. My heart is pounding. He can probably hear it. "I just don't want a feral snarling behind me."

I wait for him to deny it. Either the snarling part, or the feral.

He doesn't.

Instead, he frowns. "Couldn't help it. You moved your hair and I saw that my bite was gone."

"Bite? What bite?"

He gestures to the back of his neck, then gives me a pointed look so I know he means mine.

I blink. Hang on... does he mean when he had me pinned in the woods? When he sank his fangs in my scruff, holding me down so that he could jab me with the quicksilver shot?

That bite?

CHAPTER 6

CHASE

My fingers fly to the same spot on my neck. I probe it gently, letting out a sigh of relief when I find that the skin is completely healed.

He growls under his breath.

"Stop that," I tell him, though I keep any heat from my voice. Don't want to set the feral off. Gotta keep it cool —though a girl also has to have her limits and I'm already way past mine. "And of course it's gone. I'm as much a shifter as you are. Obviously I heal."

"Yeah? So do I," he grunts before he shifts his shoulder, drawing my attention back to the silverish-white fang marks standing out in sharp relief against his tanned arm.

Don't freak out, Quinn. The unstable shifter is wearing your bite like a badge of honor he's earned, but don't freak out.

I shake my head royally. "You deserved that, you know. If you kept the scar, that's your business, but I'm not going to apologize for biting you. In fact, give me the chance, and I'll do it all over again."

"And I'll keep that one, too. I'll keep any mark my mate wants to give me."

Don't freak out...

"I'm not your mate."

His expression darkens. I'm not sure how I know, but I'd put good money down that he's thinking about the unbroken skin on my neck. "Not yet. But you will be."

Right. I give him my back as I leave the room. Keep dreaming, dickhead.

Aware that he's right on my ass, I pause as I get my first glimpse of the space outside of my cell. It's a narrow corridor with a flight of stairs at the end. No windows, though a few weak overhead lights flicker down on us. I expect to head toward the stairs, but he moves in front of me, guiding me to a door built on the other side of the hall.

He opens the door, gesturing for me to go inside.

The bathroom looks new. A sparkling toilet is gleaming. A porcelain white sink is perched on the wall with a wooden cabinet built beneath it. He even has a perfume-free bottle of soap on top of the sink.

I step inside. He doesn't.

Interesting.

"Do I get privacy?" I ask him.

With another dark look, he says, "For now."

After the way he seemed to think I would've kept his bite as some kind of mate mark on my skin, I'm not too happy to hear his answer. *For now...* at least he's not going to follow me into the bathroom just then.

With a feral captor, I'll take what I can get until I can finally find a way out.

***

FOR THE NEXT TWO DAYS, THAT'S OUR ROUTINE. HE BRINGS me a plate of food for breakfast, lunch, and dinner before he disappears into a different part of the house to sleep. He unchains me after every meal, leading me to the bathroom at the end of the hall so that I can do my business and wash my hands.

I peeked in the cabinet. I found a toothbrush, toothpaste, and extra toilet paper. I helped myself to all three. If he cared, he didn't say, and I feel a lot better with my mouth clean.

After my bathroom trips, he brings me back to my basement prison. I hope that he'll decide that I've been well-behaved enough to go without chains, but I guess I'm not that good of an actress.

I still snap at him. I badger him with questions he won't answer. He feeds me, and at least twice a day I try to refuse the meals before I eventually give in.

One time, I got frustrated at how he'd rather stare at me than take the chance to get to know me. I tossed my fork at him.

I didn't mean to stab him. Honest. Not gonna lie and say that it didn't make me happy that my wolf lent me the strength to fling it like a spear, but I hadn't meant to hit him hard enough that the tines lodged in the muscle of his pec.

Of course it did. He still goes without a shirt. The bite mark on his shoulder mocks me every time I see it.

I flinched when the fork got stuck. But my captor... he just smiled, then pulled it out of his chest with a firm tug. He offered it back to me, his blood still slicking the tines, and it was all I could do not to hurl up my hamburger patty.

Definitely not the reaction I was expecting.

Something's different about him. I can't put my finger on what it is and that makes me suddenly wary. When dealing with a feral, *different* doesn't mean *good*.

He's a little more quiet this evening. At breakfast, he didn't give me my daily dose of quicksilver, though he put the chains back on me before he left my room. I think it was a test, and one I failed because I spent way longer than I probably should've trying to break the chains again. I couldn't shift, but my wolf was prowling around inside of me, yipping her encouragement.

It didn't work. When he came back with lunch and saw that my hands were destroyed, he dropped my food before storming out again. I figured I had pissed him off enough that he'd leave me to eat in peace. Nope. He came back seconds later with a salve that healed me up in no time.

It was my turn to scowl. I would've been healed before long. I didn't need his help.

I didn't know what to do with it when he gave it to me so readily, either...

Now it's dinner, and apart from taking my hand in one of his massive paws, checking it out before he pressed a fork against my palm, he's sat in the far corner, watching me again.

Routine, right? I eat my food, then shove the empty plates away from me. Knowing what comes next, I put my ankles in his reach so that he can unlock the shackles.

I was trying to skip a step. As if he'd ever let me.

He sniffs me like he usually does. I guess I don't pass the test this time because he tells me gruffly, "You need to shower."

"What's the matter? Didn't think that I might start to be a little ripe after three days of being stuck down here?" I snap. "The sink only does so much, and I didn't see a shower stall in the bathroom."

His jaw goes tight. "I have to bring you upstairs."

The last few days, I came up with a plan. It wasn't foolproof, but it was the best I had.

Step one: get out of the room.

Step two: get out of the basement.

Step three: get out of this place.

I jiggle my leg. "Let's go."

***

I'M ALMOST A LITTLE DISAPPOINTED AT WHAT I FIND ON THE other side of the stairs. I expected blood and bones, ripped furniture, claw marks slashing through everything. He's a feral, after all, and if he lost control, I thought his home would reflect that.

It doesn't.

In fact, it looks like one of the cabins we have in Hickory. He has an unlit fireplace in his living space, a couch big enough for him to curl up in his wolf form—and, based on the amount of fur covering it, he *does*—and a television that doesn't even have a single crack in it.

I feel cheated.

The few windows I see are closed. He has his shades drawn, as if the light outside hurts his feral eyes. Every inch of his space smells like him. Apart from mine filtering up from the basement, it's the only scent here.

I'd guessed he lived alone. Now I'm sure of it.

He lets me get a good look around before telling me to go ahead. Smart feral. He must've seen me eyeing the door that would lead to the outside.

There's only the single floor, not counting the base-ment below. Behind one closed door is a kitchen, he explains, and another is a bedroom. The last one is a full bath.

Thank the Luna. A shower.

I walk inside. He follows me in.

That's new. Every time he's led me to the bathroom before, he's left me to do my business in privacy.

Not now.

He closes the door behind me. In the back of my head, I remember the way he said, "for now," like that when I asked about privacy. It implied I wouldn't have it for long.

Yup. Looks like the clock ran out on that one.

Especially when, in a throaty voice, he tells me, "Take off your dress. Get in the shower."

Does he think I won't do it? Is that it?

Please. I'm a shifter. So long as he keeps his paws to himself, I don't care if he sees me.

I raise my eyebrow. It's the right one, with a tiny nick where the hair never grew. It looks like my eyebrow is split in half, and it's something I always had. Males seem to like it, and that's how I got into the habit of raising that one instead of the other.

I like to show off. Always have. Besides, in a pack, nudity doesn't mean anything. How can it when we always come back naked when we shift from fur to skin? The only time it matters is if there's sexual attraction—which is exactly why I'm surprised he's demanding I strip.

Handsome as he is, it's hard to be attracted to your captor. There's no denying that he's got it bad for me, though. I mean, he stole me from my pack to be his mate. Yeah. He wants me.

Call me petty, but I have no problem showing him what he'll never have. Especially since I'm sure he's already gotten more than an eyeful after he dosed me with quicksilver the first time and I shifted back from fur to skin.

Still...

"Don't forget what I said. Look all you want, but if you get too close..." I hold up my hand. My wolf gives me her claws. I slash at him. "Got me?"

"I won't touch you," he grumbles, moving around me at a quick clip, turning the shower on. Water streams down, splashing off the porcelain tub. "Not until you ask me to."

So. Never, then, huh?

Good.

He sidles past me again, moving in front of the door.

He blocks it, so I can't leave, then turns his sculpted back on me.

What's that about?

"Why the back?" I ask. "You already saw everything I have to offer when you took me."

His shoulders hunch. "Didn't."

I know he's not pretending that he didn't straight-up wolfnap me. "What was that?"

"Said I didn't." He keeps his back to me as he adds, "I covered you with a blanket when I put you in my truck. Kept you covered when I pulled the dress on over your head. I never looked."

Oh. That's... actually a bit surprising. I could tell he hadn't touched anything more than my back, my arms, my shoulders, and my hair, but I expected he would've at least gotten a nice, long peek first.

"Why? Don't you like my body?"

His hands turn into fists. He tightens them, then flexes his long, claw-tipped fingers before rubbing the side of his thighs. "Yes," he finally says. "Too much. But I'll earn my first glimpse. I won't steal it."

"Really?" For some reason, his newfound nobility pisses me off. "You mean like you stole *me*?"

"I had to."

Uh-huh. Sure.

I give him two minutes before he's sneaking a peek.

There's no mirror in here—just another toilet, a sink, and the combination shower/tub—so, if he does, I'll notice. He won't be able to catch my reflection in anything. No. He wants to see the goods, he'll have to turn his head.

I pull the slinky red dress up and over mine, dropping it to the bathroom floor. It pools like blood at my feet.

His posture goes stiff, but he refuses to turn.

Taking my time pulling the shower curtain away from the tub, I push my ass out, waiting to see if he's going to look. I'm not so sure if I should be relieved or offended that my feral seems to be a complete gentleman.

Shrugging my shoulders, I step beneath the spray. The second the warm water hits my skin, I forget all about him. I tug the curtain closed, then focus entirely on how good it feels to be clean again.

He has shampoo, conditioner, and a bar of soap waiting for me. I make quick use of the shampoo, gleefully rinsing his scent out of my hair when he clears his throat and says over the echo of the shower spray, "Chase."

I call back, "That another threat to chase me down if I try to leave, tough guy?"

He's silent for a moment. "It's my name."

Oh. Never would've guessed that.

I grab the bar of soap, lathering my belly. If he wants to be friendly, I might as well give it a shot.

Hey. What can I say? This shower has put me in a much better mood.

"I guess it's finally time I tell you mine," I tell him. "I'm Quinn."

"I know."

My fingers bite into the edge of the soap bar. There goes my good mood. "You know?"

"Yeah. I know."

My stomach drops. For just a few moments here, I'd

forgotten that I was his captive. He picked me, he drugged me, he stole me. He decided I was his mate. He locked me up.

Of course he knows my name. And after only three days of treating me like his personal pet, he deigns to give me his.

I grit my teeth, grateful for the thick shower curtain. If he could see me now…

Making quick work of the soap, I lather up, then rinse the rest of my body. I finish with the conditioner. As much as I want to linger because it helps wash away the last of the fog left behind from the remains of the quicksilver, I turn off the shower.

After wringing the water from my long hair, I shove my hand out. "Towel?"

He places one in my grip.

I wrap the towel around me, covering up. I've lost the taste for showing off. Just then, I need to make sure he's not watching me.

And he isn't.

I've never dried off so quickly before. I end up doing a shit job of it because the dress is sticking to my damp skin when I hurriedly pull it on over my head. Doesn't matter. With my newly formed plan running frantically through my mind right now, I can't risk Chase figuring out what I'm thinking.

How strong are his alpha senses? I don't think he can tell when I'm lying, but does he know when I'm plotting?

I'm about to find out.

"Hey, Chase?"

The big feral shudders. He obviously likes it when I say his name. "Yes?"

"I'm covered. You can look now."

He slowly turns on his heel.

I react.

Taking the towel still in my hand, I throw it in his face. It blinds him for a split second, but that's all I need. I hurry forward, plowing him in his junk with the point of my knee. As a howl tears out of his throat, I fold my hands together, then swing up at his jaw.

I don't hold back. Swinging with all of the pent-up aggression I have, I connect. His head shoots over his shoulder. I feel the reverberation of my hit all the way up to mine.

He stumbles, then drops to his knees. It's too much to hope I knocked him out. At least he's seeing stars.

And I have my chance.

Leaping over him, I dash out of the bathroom, running right for the front door. He roars again, and I pour on the speed. To escape the feral I just pissed off, I'm going to need it.

I never make it.

I get to the door, at least. I throw it open and even manage to get a few steps out onto the wraparound porch before he catches up to me.

One arm goes around my neck. The other wraps around my waist. The dress rides up as he pulls me back against him.

His chest is hard—and so is his cock. I can feel his erection through his jeans, prodding me in the ass as he secures me in his hold.

Looks like violence turns him on, doesn't it?

I huff as I sag against his hard chest. *Feral*. I should've known.

I don't fight Chase. I had my chance, and though I got him down, I just wasn't fast enough.

That's partly my fault. I might've been if I hadn't been stopped short by the rusty, tangy scent of blood and rotten meat that permeates the forest outside of his house.

"Phew." He's conveniently left my arms free. I use both hands to cover my nose. "That's awful!"

For the first time, I'm grateful my nose is still a bit stuffy. How much worse would the stink be at full strength?

Chase leans down, his jaw pressed against the side of my head. "Now you see why I keep the windows closed."

"Where *are* we?"

To my surprise, he actually answers. Then again, with that stink, it's undeniable.

"My land is just off of Sacre Coeur."

Sacre Coeur. It's the French name for one of the infamous cities that every local shifter has heard about. It might mean 'Sacred Heart' to those who don't know better. I'm not one of them. I know exactly what Sacre Coeur is—and it's nowhere as nice or pleasant as its name suggests.

I whirl on him. Just like I thought. *Vampires*. "That's a Fang City."

Chase nods, a hint of a satisfied smirk tugging on his lips. He's won this round, and I hadn't even known we were playing. "Even if you find your way out of the woods, you'll never survive the vampires out there. Not without me."

Suddenly, I realize what that white crescent moon-shaped charm hanging off of his golden chain is: a vampire fang. It's a pass that gives its wearer some protection from the vampires that make up the nearby Fang City.

I can't believe it. My captor is a shifter who lives on the border of a notorious vampire settlement. Our sworn enemies, and he's their neighbor.

"You're not just feral," I breathe out. "You really are insane."

His eyes spark, a vivid gold that only highlights just how right I was. "Ah, Quinn… it's about time you figured that out."

Chase doesn't use the chains on me again.

What's the point? He's proven that he's stronger than me, faster than me, and he put me in a small cabin in the middle of the woods where no one would ever look for me.

Because it's surrounded by vampires. You know. A shifter's ancient enemy.

Supernaturals are technically at war. Vampires versus shifters, it's referred to as the Claws and Fangs war, and it dates back to the animosity that's existed between our races since the beginning of time. It's not a constant fight, but every few centuries or so, a skirmish flares up and we battle ruthlessly.

The last real fight was two hundred years ago. It was easier to hide the truth of supes from humans then, and the bloodshed went down in human history as another of their wars; Luna knows they have plenty. Since then, we live in a constant state of wariness.

After the last real battle, the Alpha of the main pack

involved met with some of the surviving vamps. They decided that the only way to prevent future casualties was for wolves and vampires to keep their distance. Wolves formed packs on secluded tracts of lands far from humans, and vampires—who needed humans for their blood—created vamp-run communities called Fang Cities.

Led by an elected leadership known as the Cadre, Fang Cities are havens for vampires. They run the town, protecting their kind and keeping shifters out. Any humans living within their protected borders—whether they know about supes or not—are also under the Cadre's protection. If you defy the leadership, you die. They're kind of like the vampire version of an Alpha in that way.

No one challenges the Alpha and hopes to survive except, perhaps, another alpha wolf.

I thought Chase was insane. I mean, you can't be a feral and have your sanity intact. That was one of the defining characteristics of *being* a feral. But purposely choosing a cabin that butted up against a town full of vampires? It would be crazy even if he didn't have some kind of agreement with the local Cadre.

Which he does.

I was right about his necklace. By wearing it, he can come and go in Sacre Coeur without any vamp going after him because he's a shifter. Once he realizes I'm not going to fight him again, he explains how he got it.

His land borders the edge of their settlement. Because vampires are almost as fanatical when it comes to patrolling their territory as us shifters, the head vampire

—the leader of the Cadre—has some of his bloodsuckers roaming Chase's woods.

That's how he earned his necklace. By keeping to himself and allowing the vampires to come onto his land, he was given the fang.

And look at me. I don't have one. A fact he points out when he mentions that, if I get caught by a vampire, they might drain me first, ask questions later.

It's not even just the vampires that have me reluctantly following him back inside the cabin. Any hope of a quick escape dies an ugly death once I know where I am. Sacre Coeur is near enough to Hickory that I've heard of it. Too bad that *near enough* just means it's not on the other side of the country. In our fur, it's a good couple of hours away. A car might shave off some of that time, but Chase's woods are just as dense as mine. Anyone approaching—or escaping—the cabin would have to go on foot eventually and risk being caught by vamp patrollers.

Good thing I kept myself closed off to West even as I was breaking for the door. It was bad enough when I was trying to protect him from only the feral. Now I have an entire town of vamps loyal to Chase to worry about...

I expected the chains. Actually, considering I just kneed an aroused feral in the nuts, I expected retaliation.

At the very least, I expected to see him turn into that monster again.

He doesn't. Chase just leads me back inside, then guides me down the basement stairs again. I flop myself down onto my blanket, leaving my ankles free for him to reach. I still have the fabric padding wrapped around them. They're pretty much soaked. So used to having them there, I guess I didn't bother removing them for my shower.

Wonderful. Putting silver shackles over wet fabric... that's not gonna be comfortable.

To my surprise, Chase doesn't grab the shackle. He reaches for my ankle instead, using one of his claws to slice the padding in half. He does the same for the other. For a second, I wonder if he's gonna slap the shackle on without it so I can feel the silver, some way to make me pay for attacking him, but he doesn't do that, either.

Rising up, kicking the chains away with the side of his bare foot, he moves them away from me.

"No more chains?" I ask.

He shakes his head. "No need."

He's right.

"But I have to stay in the basement, right? On a blanket, like a dog. You just showed me that I'm more stuck here than I thought. Can't I at least get a bed?"

Chase's expression turns thoughtful. Holy shit. Did that actually work?

I'd meant what I said. Now, that doesn't mean I've given up on getting out of here. I haven't. I belong back in Hickory, and I refuse to stick around this feral just because he got lonely and decided to take me home with him. Since he has, though, I figure I should make the best of a bad situation.

He makes sure I eat. He finally let me shower. Sure, my hair is quickly drying into a tangled mess since I don't have a brush, but maybe I can work on that one later. For now, I really, really don't want to sleep on the floor again.

If I have to, I'll shift into my wolf. It's been days since she's been free, and I can already sense her begging to come out now that the quicksilver is gone and I'm not wearing silver chains that weaken the both of us. I know she wouldn't mind curling up on the floor. Still, I'd prefer a bed.

Chase rocks on his heels. His hands slip into the back pockets of his jeans. "You won't leave me? If I bring you upstairs... you won't go for my cock again? 'Cause that hurt, Quinn. I didn't like it."

Whoa. The grumble in his voice when he says 'cock' like that... it shouldn't be anywhere near as sexy as it is. He's my feral captor! I shouldn't think he's sexy at all! But, come on. I'm only half-human. His mind might be broken, his sense of right and wrong way off, but he's a hunk of a male who hasn't worn a shirt the entire time I've known him, and he seems more upset at the idea I might try to run out on him again than the fact that I tried to break his dick with my knee.

An apology is on the tip of my tongue before I remember: *Hello! Captor!* I swallow that back, then say, "I won't."

"Promise me." His eyes light up. "Vow to the Luna you won't leave me."

I hesitate. I didn't plan on running out before I came up with a foolproof plan to bypass the vampires, but if the opportunity presents itself...

A vow to the Luna isn't unbreakable. However, good chance I'm already on her shit list because me and West haven't bonded yet. Do I really want to risk pissing off our goddess? Maybe she'll erase the tie I have to West and decide that a feral loner might be a better mate for me. What would I do then?

I mean, he might be convinced. I'm not.

"Chase—"

"Tonight," he amends. "Vow to the Luna you won't leave me tonight."

Okay. I can do that.

"I vow it. But only if you vow you won't try to mark me again."

I'll only heal it, and that'll just bring out the feral. None of us wants that.

His expression shadows. I wait to see if he'll refuse, but I should've known better.

I gave him a promise. He wants to prove himself. Of course he'll give me one back.

"With the Luna above as my witness, you have my word."

Good.

THE BLANKET HE PROVIDED FOR ME WAS SOFT ENOUGH while he kept me tucked away in the basement. That's nothing compared to the oversized, overstuffed mattress that I plop onto after Chase leads me to a bedroom.

The whole space smells of him. Besides the bed in the middle of the room, a blanket that looks like the twin to mine in the basement on the floor, and a single dresser, it's pretty empty. No knick-knacks. No photographs. The walls are bare, the windows closed and covered just like the rest of the cabin.

If his scent didn't overlay the room, I'd think it was a spare one no one used. There's no personality in here. No sign that anyone actually sleeps in it unless you count the blanket in the corner.

When I asked him if it was his room he was giving me, he ignored the question. Instead, he gestured for me to sit down on the bed.

I do, and then I watch him warily as he begins to pace. The room's big enough that I don't feel crowded by him, but it pays to stay on guard. If he snaps and lunges, I don't see anything I can use as a weapon, so I decide to crawl under the bed if I have to.

Something's wrong with him. Him being on edge has *me* on edge. I don't get it. He wasn't even this agitated after my escape attempt earlier and that was after I aimed for where it hurt the most.

When I can't take it any longer, I snap at him. "For the Luna's sake, can you either sit the fuck down or get out? Your pacing is driving me crazy!"

Chase freezes on the opposite side of the bed from me, his head shooting my way. His predatory gaze narrows, locked on his prey.

On *me.*

Smooth, Quinn. Because antagonizing a distressed feral is a genius plan. Way to go.

I clear my throat. "I mean, there's no reason for any of that. I promised I'd stay. Lock me in if you feel better. I don't care. I'm tired and I want to go to sleep. You should go to your room"—which is probably this one, but he didn't confirm it, so I'm gonna play dumb—"and leave me to it."

When he starts to stalk around the far side of the bed, I have a hard time believing it was that easy. Turns out that's because I'm right. Chase doesn't leave the room. Instead, he lowers himself to the blanket tossed in the corner.

He stretches his legs out in front of him, looking like he's making himself comfortable.

Oh, come *on*.

"Really? Are we really doing this?"

"What? I just thought I'd sleep here."

"On the floor."

He nods.

"With me sleeping in the bed over here. By myself," I emphasize.

He nods again.

I jerk my chin at his lower half. "In your jeans?"

His gold eyes flare, turning molten. Shifting against the blanket, his hand covers the button. His claw scratches at the metal as he fiddles with it. "I could take them off if you want me to."

I walked right into that, didn't I? "No, thanks. You can keep them on."

He nods, letting his hand fall to the side. He'd expected that answer.

Chase goes quiet. The eerie way he stares has me grasping for some way to break the silence. One of us needs to fill it, and from experience, I know it won't be him. But since he seems a lot more talkative lately, I figure it's about time I get some answers of my own.

"Hey... can I ask you another question?"

"You can ask me anything, Quinn."

Really? He might live to regret being so agreeable.

"Okay, then. Why am I here? And I don't mean in this bed. I mean *here*. With you."

Chase's big body stiffens. His jaw clenches. Typical. "I already told you that."

"Because you want a mate." He's made that clear from the moment I came to in his basement. "Why me, though? Was it because I was by myself in the woods that day? If it had been any other female, would you have grabbed her instead?"

He shakes his head.

I'm just about to call 'bullshit' on that when he says, "It couldn't have been anyone else. You're the only female that visits those trees."

How does he know that? He's right… but how does he know?

I scoff at him. "Big deal. My scent's all over the place." So I might've marked the clearing as my territory a few times. It's a shifter thing. When my wolf is out, she can't help it. "That's how you know."

Chase shakes his head again. "I know because I watched you for almost nine months. You were always alone. Me, too. That's part of the reason I picked you. If we were together, we wouldn't be lonely."

I'm not lonely. I mean, I *wasn't* lonely. I had a pack.

And a mate.

I'm smart enough not to mention West. If Chase can be believed—and I can't think of any reason why he couldn't—then he was watching me *before* the Luna picked me for our Beta. As if I need another reason why the feral is out of his head thinking we could ever be together. If we were meant to be, the Luna would've made him my fated mate instead of West, right?

Nine months... I really don't want to believe that. Nine months he watched me and I had no idea? What kind of patrols did Bishop have checking out our borders? No one knew he was out there? What the hell?

That makes me think of something else, too. He stalked me both before and after I found my fated mate. That was six months ago. What happened between then and now that he only just decided it was time to bring me to his cabin?

And what about him? Ferals aren't born, they're made, and usually after a tragedy so terrible, it breaks their mind. What happened to Chase to make him like this?

I open my mouth. Think better of what I'm going to ask. Close it.

Chase notices.

"Quinn? If you have something to say, say it. Don't hold back. Never hold back with me."

Holy shit. Leaning toward me, one knee folded, a brawny arm curved around it, the big feral is pleading.

Surprised as I am by that, I can't stop myself from blurting out, "Do you have a mate?"

Okay. Say I believe this. Say I fall prey to freaking Stockholm Syndrome or something and I stick around long enough that even a feral starts to look enticing. As a she-wolf who's already been rejected by her fated mate, if there's one thing I absolutely refuse to do, it's get involved with a male who is only settling for me because he can't have who he really wants.

I don't realize how much I'm suddenly invested in his answer until Chase immediately says, "Yes. *You.*"

Ah, Luna. Maybe I should've explained better. I know he's convinced that I should be his, but even if he did choose me for reasons of his own, what about his fated mate? Has he found her? While lower-ranked wolves could go their whole life never being told who their fated mate was, most alphas are blessed by the Luna with a name long before a mate bond snaps into place. It usually takes place during the Alpha Ceremony, but not always.

Now, a lone wolf wouldn't have an Alpha Ceremony. Does that mean Chase doesn't know his fated mate?

Is she out there somewhere?

Would a feral who went to so much trouble to take me captive reject me just like West did?

I huff in frustration, unable to articulate what I'm feeling just then. "That's not what I mean, Chase."

"I know what you meant."

I give him a pointed look. "Then answer my question. You said you would."

"I did. You're the only mate I've ever wanted, Quinn. The only one I've ever had. When you finally agree to stay with me forever, I'll claim you as mine, and there will be no one else for either of us. Forever."

If only I could believe that. He might, but I can't.

"You could walk out that door tomorrow and meet your fated mate. What then?"

"Fuck Fate."

I blink. For someone whose personal motto is "Fate sucks," that's a little harsh, even for me.

"What? What's wrong with what I said?"

"Nothing."

It's his turn not to believe me. "It's true. Fuck Fate. We make our own fate, for good or for bad. Just like we make our own choices. And I choose you."

It's not blasphemy, but it's pretty damn close.

Most shifters revere Fate almost as much as they worship the moon. It's why I was shocked when West refused to acknowledge our mate bond. If it was up to me, I would've locked him down the same night I recognized him as my fated mate. Not because I loved him. I didn't. I still don't. At least, not any more than I did when I thought of him as an old friend. But shifters believe that the Luna can do no wrong, and a fated mate is a wondrous gift to have. I might not love him now. If the Luna paired me with West of all other males, there had to be a reason. I'd learn to love him.

He never gave me the chance.

I admit, as much as I would've hopped into West's bed if he let me, I can't deny that it irks me to have my choice taken away. As a delta, I'm at the bottom of the pack. My whole life, I never got to choose anything. First, my parents were in charge, then the packmates that rallied around me after they were gone.

Bishop, of course, makes decisions for the whole Sylvan Pack daily.

Just when I was on the cusp of maybe making a choice for myself—if I didn't take Tucker as my first lover after West rejected me, it could've been another shifter— I had that taken away by a feral who thought *his* choice was more important.

Fuck Fate, sure. But fuck dominant wolves who think they can control me.

I'm Quinn Malone. I can take care of myself.

And I won't give up until I've proven it.

Unfortunately, tonight's not the night that I get to.

I thought that Chase would get tired of staring at me from his place on the floor. Why, when he's done nothing to give that impression at all, I have no clue, but I was ready to wait him out.

An hour of silence following our last awkward conversation was about as much as I could take.

I point-blank asked if he really planned on watching me sleep all night long. His only answer was a solemn nod as he placed one leg over the other, crossed his arms over his chest, then rested his head against the wall at his back.

I should've guessed.

Well, at least I have the bed.

I expected it to be harder to fall asleep. It annoys me that it isn't. With Chase watching over me, instead of suddenly developing a bout of insomnia, I'm out within minutes—and unless he slipped quicksilver into my dinner hours earlier, it has nothing to do with being sedated.

My sleep isn't unbroken for long, though. At some point in the middle of the night, I hear a noise that has me stirring. I fight to stay asleep as long as I can, and it isn't until I lose the elusive grasp on unconsciousness that I realize what it is.

It's Chase, and he's whimpering.

Leaning over the side of the bed, I see a dark, shadowy shape on the blanket. My shifter's sight is strong enough to see that not only has Chase fallen asleep, but he reverted to his fur either before or after he did.

His destroyed jeans are ripped up and tattered, scattered on the floor. At first, I wondered if he shredded them off while I was sleeping, but no. I've seen ruined clothing like that before. He shifted while he was dressed, and now his jeans are toast.

I've heard of something like this happening before. Sleep-shifting. It isn't something we usually do once we're out of puphood, but it's a sign of a shifter losing his hold on his other half.

In other words, it's something a feral does.

He's not snarling, though. He's completely his big, black wolf, instead of that partially shifted beast I once met. As his wolf, Chase is curled up on his side, one of his back legs jerking, almost like he's running in his sleep.

Or in his nightmares.

A pang hits me right in the chest. Before I know it, I'm sliding across the sheets, moving toward him.

Another whimper escapes him. This one sounds pained.

I can't leave him like this. Pulling my blanket over my head, pretending I don't see him suffering... I can't do it.

That leaves me one other choice—and it might just be the dumbest thing I ever do.

As I remove the silky red dress, folding it up so I don't

ruin the only piece of clothing I own right now, I remind myself that he hasn't flipped out again like he did my first night here. Not when I refused him. Not when I went for his balls. Not when I ran.

In fact, the only time he turned feral like that was when I mentioned having a mate. So long as I don't bring West up, I can almost convince myself he's just another male wolf. Maybe even just another packmate.

Wolves are pack animals. Us shifters have the same mentality. The same instincts. We thrive better when we're part of a community. I've lived alone for years. I was never lonely, though. Our cabins are built close enough that we take comfort in knowing our packmates are near.

With the Fang City surrounding Chase's land, there isn't another shifter around for miles—except for me. Maybe... maybe he wasn't just looking for a female to fuck. Maybe, when the feral inside of him decided it needed a mate, it was just looking for someone who would be there so he wasn't alone anymore.

If we were together, we wouldn't be lonely...

I'm here. For better or for worse, despite how I got here, he's not alone. I'm here.

Before I think better of what I'm doing, I shift from naked skin to sleek brindle fur. Once I'm on four legs instead of two, I curl up next to Chase, joining him on the floor.

With my wolf in charge, I can pretend I haven't laid down next to the insane, broken, possessive bastard who thought stealing me from my pack and making me his captive was a way to win my heart. I'm just doing what I would do for any other packmate.

So long as I give my word to stay with Chase, we're a pack of two. That's all. That's why I'm doing this. Not because it pains me to see him suffering when I might be able to do something to help him.

Here's hoping that I don't get attacked in the process...

The moment I lay my muzzle on his back, his whimpering stops. His choppy breathing slows. His back leg settles down, no longer jerking in spasms.

My wolf curled up with his, Chase calms down almost immediately. After a few seconds, he sighs before he falls into a deep sleep.

And all because I'm near.

Oh, yeah. I don't know what that means, but I'm guessing it can't be good.

CHAPTER 8
KISS

There's no sign of Chase—in his skin or his fur—when I wake up again the next morning.

That's a good thing. Honest. I don't feel a sting when I realize that he slipped out from beneath me, leaving my wolf to sleep on the blanket all alone.

Nope. Not at all.

I don't want to be the support she-wolf for a feral. It's better this way.

And maybe if I tell myself that enough, I'll believe it.

Blowing a frustrated rush of air through my snout, I slowly climb back to my four legs. His fresh scent lingers in the room so I know he hasn't been gone long. Cocking my head, I see if I can sense him nearby.

It's been days since he dosed me with any quicksilver. I had already slowly gotten used to his aura while I was chained in the basement. Without anything affecting my senses, his dominance is like a beacon to me. When he's not with me, I can usually focus and pinpoint where he is in the cabin.

Before, it was vague directions. Now that he's allowed me to see the rest of his home, I have a better guess of where he is.

Kitchen. Why am I not surprised?

If he's prepping another meal for me, he'll be back soon. I might've been willing to strip in front of him yesterday if only to show him what he'll never get from me. That was yesterday, though. Something changed after I curled up next to him. What? I'm not so sure, but I do know that being naked around Chase isn't a good idea.

The silky red dress is still folded on the side of the bed where I left it. For a heartbeat, I almost decide to stay in my fur. That's how much I don't want to put that dress back on. I might've been able to shower. The dress hasn't. It's rank, especially to my wolf's nose, and a reminder of the days I spent chained.

Only one problem. If I don't shift back, I won't be able to communicate with Chase. After last night, my wolf also has a bit of a soft spot for his. I let her stay in control and who knows what'll happen.

Nothing my human half wants, I bet.

Another wolfish sigh before I quickly shift back to my skin. Snagging the dress, I yank it on again. It looks shorter than before, though that could also be me becoming more aware that I still have no bra, no panties, and what amounts to a slip to cover my body up from a wolf who has made it clear he wants me.

After I'm dressed, I think about what I'm supposed to do next. Now that he's sure I'm not going to run again—as far as he knows—Chase told me I had free rein of the house. It's so different from how he's treated me since he first brought me here that I don't know how to feel about that.

Should I go find him? What kind of signal would that send? The fact that I have the urge to track him down in the kitchen has me going a little queasy. I don't chase males. They chase me.

In the case of my feral, I mean that literally.

I sit down on the edge of the bed, gripping the mattress until the desire to find Chase passes. It's easy to get distracted when the scent of eggs cooking floats into the bedroom, followed by the crackle and hiss of bacon sizzling.

I can hear him moving about somewhere down the hall. Well, not Chase. He's pure predator, soundless on his bare feet, but the pans clanging and the dishes clinking let me know where he is and what he's doing.

When the noise stops and he moves closer, I scoot further back on the bed, crossing my legs and shaking out my bedhead a split second before he walks into the room.

Why did I do that? That's something the old Quinn—before the mess with West—would've done. I liked attention. I liked attention from males in particular. And though I already have it from Chase otherwise he wouldn't have bothered to take me, I put myself in a pose that makes me as attractive as possible without even realizing I've done it until it's too late.

Chase has a prowling walk. Sometimes he stalks, sometimes he stomps, but he usually prowls on the balls of his feet. He's doing that now as he steps into the room, a plate in one hand, a glass of orange juice in the other, and a plastic shopping bag hanging off of his wrist. He's back in jeans. Still no shirt, but at least I know it's a new pair since the remains of the ones he fell asleep in are still scattered on the bedroom floor.

He stops short when he sees me. A soft rumble builds from deep in his chest as he falls back, regaining his balance just in time to keep a drop of OJ from spilling to the floor.

I grin. "Morning."

Chase clears his throat, erasing the rumble. He hasn't blinked yet, his fierce eyes locked on the thigh I'm flashing him. "Uh. I brought you breakfast."

I uncross my legs, then cross them so the left one is on top now. His nostrils flare, his expression hungry—and I don't think it's for breakfast. "Thanks."

He holds the plate out to me. I notice he has a white-knuckled grip on the edge of it, but he passes it easily. The juice, too.

I plop the plate down on the bed. I take a sip of the juice.

His gaze tracks my swallow.

I hide a smile behind the glass. And, okay, I know I'm playing with fire. I can't even explain why I'm doing it.

It's fun, though. I deserve a little fun after the last five days.

When he reaches behind him, muscles on his forearm flexing as he grabs the fork he has for me, the shopping bag bobs. Chase gives his head a little shake, staring down at the bag. I think he forgot he was carrying it.

After he hands me the fork, he shimmies his hand, removing the bag. He holds that out to me next.

"What's this?"

"For you," he says gruffly. "I meant to give it to you before, but I didn't think you'd take it."

I open the bag. It's stuffed with clothes.

Brand new *female* clothes.

I start pulling them out, stomach going tight as I get a better look at them.

"Where did you get these?" My flirtatious teasing utterly disappears as it hits me what this might mean. He could've left the cabin and I *missed* it. I have to ask: "*When* did you?"

"I bought them at the store when I got you that dress."

The dress I've been wearing for almost a fucking week. He's had clothes all along.

What?

Chase reaches up, scratching the back of his neck. If I didn't know better, I'd think he looked ashamed. But why would he? As long as he gets what he wants, why should he give a shit how his captive feels?

Any good feelings I developed for him when I found his wolf whimpering last night are gone. But then... then I notice something.

They're not my clothes or any other females. The only scent clinging to them is Chase's. They're clean at least, but they're also new. Like brand spanking, still has the tags on *new*. They're definitely not mine.

But they look like they are.

I have a t-shirt just like this one. Same color and everything. These jeans are the style I prefer. And that skirt... when I still believed I might be able to turn West's head and make him want me instead of Helene, I styled my hair, did my make-up, and wore a skirt that looks like that one to go see him at his cabin.

He didn't even let me inside.

As I marvel at what else is in this bag, Chase is talking somewhere over my head.

"I couldn't risk letting you go back to your pack to get your own clothes so I bought you some of the items I saw you in the most. I hope you like them."

Good going, Chase. Like I need the reminder that he was watching me long before he stole me away.

No underclothes in the bag, I notice. Why I am not surprised?

Still, I recognize what this is. It's a peace offering. I'm so sick of the silky red dress, I accept it.

"I'm going to the bathroom. Don't follow me."

He doesn't. I almost thought he would. Chase stays in the bedroom while I go to the bathroom. After I do my business, I decide to wear a pair of jeans and a yellow t-shirt that sets off my eyes. And if it shows off my nipples, too? Oh, well.

Once I'm dressed, I pat down my hips. How he got my exact size, I have no clue, but I feel so much better now that I'm out of that dress. Look better, too.

Chase seems to agree.

The moment I enter the room again, he immediately starts for me.

"What are you doing?" I don't back away. If I do, he'll only chase, and I kind of want to see what his intentions are. Especially since... "You've got that look in your eye again."

"What look?"

"The hungry one."

"That's because I am."

Holding my position, I gesture to the abandoned breakfast cooling on my plate. "Have mine."

He shakes his head roughly, his shaggy hair dancing as he prowls closer. "Not hungry for food."

Oh, boy. "Chase—"

His shake was rough, but when he closes the gap between us, his hands are gentle as he cups my cheeks with his palms.

"Don't be afraid, Quinn," he rumbles.

The heat of his breath fans the flyaways framing my face. I tilt my chin up. "I'm not."

Should I be? Oh, yeah. He's twice my size, a million times more dominant, and I can't allow myself to forget that he's a feral. Even so, it's been so long since a male looked at me like that. Longer since one touched me as if I was precious.

He brushes his nose against mine. "Good," he whispers before he slants his mouth over mine.

His lips are softer than I thought they would be. It's like his gentle touch. I expect the feral to always be rough, but he isn't. He's tentative, almost as if he's afraid I'm going to refuse his kiss.

Maybe I should. I don't. Instead, I part my lips and invite him inside.

Once he's sure of his welcome, Chase deepens the kiss.

Before I know it, his hands are at my waist. Slowly, he begins to skim up my side. His claws lightly scratch my skin. The tiny shock of pain makes me realize that he's slipped his hands beneath my shirt.

Do I mind?

I... I don't think I do. How can I? My hands are clinging to his back, pulling him against me.

I want *more*.

There's an awkwardness to his kiss that tells me that he's unpracticed. I guide him, stroking his tongue with mine, leading him so that it's more enjoyable for us both.

He breaks the kiss first. I get the vibe it's because he really doesn't know what he's doing and he needs a few seconds to recover before he goes in for another kiss.

That was my mistake. I gave a feral the benefit of the doubt—and that was after I willingly let him kiss me.

He buries his nose in the crook of my shoulder, right where it meets my throat. I'm used to this. Chase has this weird thing about taking my scent into his lungs. He hasn't done it since yesterday morning, and I figured he was making up for lost time.

Nope.

The light scratches on my side were erotic enough that I didn't stop him. But the way his fang drags across my neck like that? Or how it pierces my skin?

There's no way that was an accident.

Fucker *bit* me!

The hazy cloud of lust settling over me is gone in an instant. With one rush shove, I push Chase away from me. If he'd expected my reaction, I never would've been able to move his feet. Good thing he wasn't expecting it.

Chase slams against the door, rattling the whole damn frame. He drops, catching himself time to land in a crouch before he jumps back up to his feet.

I'm bristling with rage. "What were you thinking?"

"Quinn—"

Nope.

I can't believe it. I can't believe I let down my guard like that.

I'm a fucking *moron*.

My hand flies to my neck. When I find a trickle of blood there, I snarl, then show Chase the red slicking my finger. "Did you try to mark me?"

It wouldn't take. I'm already willing it to heal, so it's not like he left any damage. But he tried to, and that's all that matters to me right now.

"It was an accident," he says gruffly. His eyes are wild, his hands clenched into fists. His whole body vibrates, like he's dying to touch me again but the big, bad wolf knows better. "I never meant... Look, I told you. I want to *earn* you. I won't mark you until you ask me to. You have to believe me."

No I fucking *don't*.

Some alphas can tell when someone is lying. Deltas can't. What I wouldn't give for that ability right now because the expression he's pulling makes me want to believe that maybe—just maybe—he's telling me the truth. But why would he? I have to remember that he's proven again and again that the only thing that matters is that he gets his way.

Not this time.

I cover the scratch. Something warns me against

letting him see me heal it even as I snap back in the heat of my temper, "I will *never* want you to bite me."

I was right. Chase doesn't like that, not one bit.

It's as if a flip's been switched. His features twist, going from wounded to territorial in a heartbeat. "You're mine!"

This shit again?

"No. I'm not. And don't you yell at me like that." As he looms in front of me, I continue to stand my ground. Forming my own fist, I shoot out my pointer finger, jabbing him in his heaving chest. "Pro-tip, Chase? Females don't like males who bite them without permission and then yell at them when they get called out on it."

Thank the Luna that my words seem to sink in. He's the one who backs off. Chase is hanging his head, obviously holding onto his control by a thread.

He swallows roughly. I watch his Adam's apple bob with a pointed glare.

And then he sighs. "I need you with me, Quinn. I don't know how to be with females. You're the only one I've ever wanted... it was my wolf. My wolf told me to do it."

"Yeah? Well, tell your wolf that you can't just take me away from my pack and think that I'll jump at the chance to stay with a male I barely know." Or let him fucking *bite* me.

He dares to meet my angry gaze through the shaggy hair flopping forward into his determined face. "You'll get to know me in time."

Right. Like he learned all about me without me having any idea he was out there, watching. Too bad only one of us is an obsessed stalker, and it isn't me.

My hands go to my hips. "It's not that easy, Chase—"

"Why? Because of *him*?"

Did I think that he was holding onto his temper? His sanity? Yeah. That doesn't last.

Something crunches. It doesn't take long for me to realize it's Chase's bones. His shoulders widen, then hunch over, his fingers cracking as they begin to change into fucking *talons*.

He hasn't shifted to that beast all the way yet. It's close, though. His skin stretches, his cheekbones jutting out. His eyes have gone even wilder.

And all because he brought up West.

He doesn't use his name. He doesn't have to, and I'm not even sure if he knows it. When he was stalking me, he saw me with a male, and even as broken as he is, Chase would've been able to sense that West and I have a connection; everyone does, though my packmates pretend they can't. To Chase, the Beta of the Sylvan Pack is a target—because of me. If he thinks I'm meant to be his mate, then West is his rival. That's how ferals think. Everything is black and white.

Chase wants me.

West is, technically, my fated mate.

No West. No other male to claim Quinn. If his wolf is riding him as much as it seems he is, then there's one simple solution to his problem: eliminate the other male.

No.

"It's not about him," I say hurriedly. "It's about me and you. Leave him out of it."

Chase growls. My wolf yips. I clamp my jaw shut to keep from doing the same.

"You're trying to protect him from me." Well, yeah. Obviously. "*Don't*," he commands. "He doesn't deserve it."

That's where we'll have to disagree. West doesn't deserve to have a feral's rage directed at him all because he had the bad luck to be my fated mate.

"Stop this. I don't like the way you're acting."

I don't raise my voice, purposely staying as calm as possible as he continues to loom in front of me. I'm not afraid of him. Not really. If there's one thing I'm sure of right now it's that Chase won't hurt me. Now, if West suddenly appeared, he'd probably lunge for him, but I'm as safe as can be.

Still, I don't want him to completely snap. Right now, Chase is still with me. He's talking. He's not prowling around or smashing his fist into the wall. I have to keep him on the right side of his sanity or else I don't know what'll happen next.

Luna damn it. When did this become my responsibility? Just like this morning, I don't want to be in charge of him. I want to respond to his rising aggression because, as a delta, the alternative is submitting—and if he really was my mate, he wouldn't use his dominance against me. He'd understand that we're equals, and that, as his mate, I should come first for him.

That realization pisses me off even more; I shouldn't have to hold back because I'm afraid of setting him off more. He's still on the edge of going feral, and while I won't be the one who gives him a push, this is exactly why—despite his attempts at peace offerings earlier—I could never be a feral's mate.

With a wave at his still heaving bare chest, I tell him

in a firm yet gentle voice, "Take a step back, Chase. Get your shit together. You want me to be your mate? Here's another hint. This"—I wave again—"isn't attractive."

He throws his head back and roars.

I refuse to react. When the echo dies down, I raise my eyebrow at him. "That's not, either, tough guy."

Too far. I tried my best to reason with him, one shifter to another, and I think I went too far.

Chase's paw curls into a fist. "He doesn't want you." *Thud. Thud. Thud.* He beats himself in the chest. "I do!"

Oof. They're only words. Chase didn't hit me with his fists. Doesn't matter. I stumble back anyway, almost like he *did* strike me.

Wow. Just when I was beginning to think that he might not be so bad, he comes out with this bullshit.

Like I don't know that? Like I've spent the six months blissfully unaware that I was rejected? It's not a surprise to me that he knows—if Chase really did stalk me for nine months, there's no way he wouldn't—but did he have to throw it in my face like that?

At least he realizes it.

His hand falls to his side—and it is a hand again. The crazy gleam in his feral's bright golden eyes fades as his expression darkens. Sucking in a breath, he plants his feet, as if he wants to go to me but he accepts that he can't.

Bowing his head, chin to his chest, hair falling forward and covering his eyes, Chase rasps out, "I didn't mean that."

Yes. He did.

My laugh is hollow. "What? You're just telling me

something I already know. West doesn't want me. He's made that clear. Still a dick move rubbing it in. Is that what I'll have to look forward to if I stay? Should I be grateful that you decided to make me your captive? Is that it?"

His head jerks up again. There are red welts on his chest from where he smashed it with his fist. "No. I brought you here because I had to have you with me. I'm a selfish bastard, I know that, but I thought—"

"What? You thought that, just because my mate doesn't want me, I'd be happy to accept you as a... a... what? A consolation prize?"

"No!"

"Then what is it, Chase? Why me? I'm nobody."

He swoops in. Brave bastard, approaching a she-wolf who's on the edge herself. He's quick, too. Before I can dart out of his reach, he has me in another embrace.

His hand goes straight to my hair. His claws thread through the strands, stroking me softly as he murmurs, "You're somebody to me, Quinn. You always will be."

He says that now. I know from experience that a male will say anything to get a female on all fours. Why would this feral be any different?

"Yeah?" I say daringly. "Then prove it."

"I will. I vow it to the Luna. I'll do whatever I can. Give you everything I can. Everything you want."

If only I could believe that. "Let me go home. That's all I want."

Chase's hold on me tightens. "Everything but that."

Yeah. That's what I thought.

CHAPTER 9
PESTO

Thank the Luna for locks.

Oh, how the tables have turned. I went from being chained to a wall in Chase's basement to locking him out of the bedroom he gave me. When he realized that I needed some time to cool off, he left me alone. The second he was gone, I turned the lock.

He's gone for ten minutes. Maybe twenty. It wasn't enough time, and when I hear him padding back down the hall, I throw a nasty look at the closed door.

Chase tries to open it, muttering a curse under his breath when he discovers it's locked.

I smile, only because he can't see me through the door. When he rattles the knob, I school my face into my best pissed-off expression again.

"Let me in."

"No."

"Quinn—"

"Do I get to go home?"

Another rattle is my answer.

"Thought so. Until you decide to let me go, you can stay out there."

"This is my room."

I knew it!

"Too bad. You gave it to me. No take-backs. Sleep in the basement." I huff at the closed door. "Way I see it, it's your turn anyway."

"If that's what you want, I will. We need to talk first."

"No, thanks."

"Quinn. If you don't open this door, I'm coming in anyway."

"Go right ahead."

The knob turns again. With one quick jerk, he breaks the lock.

I should've known better than to dare him like that. Despite this being a shifter's cabin, there was no way any of the locks inside of here would be strong enough to withstand a determined male shifter.

He lets himself in. His eyes flicker over to the bed, but if he expected to find me waiting for him like I was before, he's sorely mistaken. I'm standing across from him, hands on my hips again, a warning on my face.

He scowls when he sees the food I still haven't touched. "You didn't eat your breakfast."

"I wasn't hungry."

"Be angry with me. Luna knows I deserve it. Kick me out of our room—"

"It's my room now," I remind him. "And I already did."

"If you need your space, I'll give it to you. But you will eat. I won't back down on this, Quinn. Kick me, scratch me, throw a sucker punch my way… that's fine. But don't go hungry because I fucked up again. Please."

I wish he was still the gruff, grunting wolf from a few days ago. When he talks to me like this, when he pleads…

"Why are you like this?"

His jaw goes tight. "Feral?"

"Confusing."

He opens his mouth, then closes it with a *click*, fangs hitting each other.

Good. I'm not done.

"I'm still a fucking prisoner here," I point out, "but you want to take care of me. You bought me clothes. You promise me things I want, things I can't have. I don't know what you're playing at, but it makes it harder for me to hate you for what you've done to me."

Chase's expression goes blank at my confession. After another moment when he just stares at me, unable to find the words, he finally nods. "I don't know. But I can't let you go. I'm sorry."

If only he really was. Maybe then I'd get to go back to Hickory after all.

I KNEW HE WAS INTELLIGENT. I MEAN, HE HAD TO BE. Somehow he was able to watch me for nine months without anyone knowing. Think about it. It wasn't just me he concealed himself from. He managed to evade the entire Sylvan Pack, including our Alpha and Beta, the entire time. It wasn't until he was ready to make his move to take me that Chase slipped up at all, and, honestly, I wouldn't put it past him to have done it on purpose for reasons only a feral would understand.

The wolfsbane helped. I'd gotten him to admit that he rubbed his wolf in a whole pile of the stuff before he approached our territory. It had covered up his scent. He didn't have any excuse when it came to his aura, though he did confess that it's only as strong as it is when his feral's close to breaking free. So long as he held back his wild side, it was easier for him to hide.

I asked him how he was able to do that. He refused to answer. He has a tendency to do that whenever I bring up his being feral.

I understand. Still, so much for *you can ask me anything, Quinn,* right?

He's smart, but he's also capable of learning. When I threaten to fling the plate of cold eggs and limp bacon at him like a freaking frisbee if he doesn't leave me the hell alone, he makes another strategic retreat. And, this time, he stays in the kitchen for the rest of the day.

I slam the door behind him. Lock's broken, so he can get back in any time he decides to. At least the loud noise makes me feel a bit better.

I stew for a little while, then begin to regret that I chose the bedroom to make my stand. If I kicked him out of the living room, I could've watched television to pass the time. There's nothing to do in here.

Figuring he lost any rights to privacy when he kidnapped me, I snoop through the room. That takes like two minutes. He has a closet full of jeans with maybe three or four t-shirts hanging off to the side. Nothing under the bed. He has a dresser, but that's empty, too, except for a sweater that looks suspiciously familiar.

I shake it out, scowling when I see the hunter green sweater I lost last spring. I'd forgotten it during one of my trips out in the woods. When I went back later to retrieve it, it was gone, and I thought one of the local wolves grabbed it for their den.

A wolf grabbed it all right. A big, black one.

Funny that he gave me an entire bag of new clothes and neglected to mention he had one of my old sweaters tucked in his dresser drawer.

That makes me angry again, and I pace around the room, cursing Chase and his heavy-handed belief that his desires trump mine. Who does he think he is anyway?

Ugh!

What makes it so much worse is that, around midday, the air begins to smell of food again. I can't quite place what the aroma is. It's a mixture of so many delicious scents that tease my hungry belly. I ended up eating the bacon in case I need some fuel later on, but that's nothing compared to a shifter's metabolism.

I'm hungry, and still pretty pissed, and I stay like that until Chase is knocking on the door, announcing that dinner is ready.

I've got two choices: I can either go hungry the rest of the night or suck it up to accept the food from Chase. He might think it's another gesture that proves I'm his, but I think of it as a necessary evil to keep my wolf strong.

I throw open the door, expecting him to have my plate ready. Not that I'm spoiled and he should. It's just that, since I've been here, that's how he's served me.

His hands are empty.

"Funny, Chase. What? Are you expecting me to apologize or something before I can eat? Because I'd rather starve."

"You know I won't let that happen." We've gotten past his early threats of holding me down and force-feeding me. The edge of his rough voice tells me that he doesn't need to threaten me again. I've been warned once. Next time, he'll just do it. "But, no. I've been thinking about earlier. I apologized, but you obviously didn't believe me. Words are cheap. I'll prove it. Come with me."

I almost refuse. He didn't use his dominance against me to order me to go with him, so I technically *could*. I've grown used to being around him, and him being a feral does something strange to my wolf. She doesn't react like he's an alpha. Despite his aura, she doesn't have the urge to submit to his like she does Bishop or even West.

I don't know what that means. Choosing not to examine it too closely, I think about telling him to fuck off —and that's when one of the food scents reaches me.

Holy shit. He has pesto out there. I can scent the basil and the garlic over the other aromas, and it sings to me.

Luna, I love pesto.

I shrug, trying not to drool. "I was getting hungry anyway."

***

It isn't just pesto.

I'm gaping at the circular wooden table he has stowed in the corner of his kitchen. Like, mouth open, eyes wide, nose twitching, full-on gaping. My wolf is up and bouncing around inside of my chest, eager to dig her snout into all that food.

Not gonna lie, so am I.

I can't believe it. My nose tells me that my eyes aren't lying, but I'm struggling to accept it.

Every single one of my favorite foods is laid out on his table.

I might be able to explain away some of it—I don't know anyone who doesn't enjoy a good spaghetti with pesto, or cheesy bread—but when you add the chicken enchiladas next to the venison steak, plus the meatball soup and a slice of caramel cheesecake... I can't pretend this isn't meant for me.

None of this stuff goes together, except for in my belly.

The clothes are one thing. Him telling me that he decided he wanted me nine months ago is another.

Realizing that Chase learned enough about me that he knows my favorite *foods*... that he spent all day cooking them for me as his way to apologize...

My stomach twists. I'm starving, and I'd chow down on every single one of those dishes, but I can't.

He... he really means it. He really wants to make me his mate.

This isn't just a meal or even an apology. It's a feast fit for a fucking proposal.

Food has a special meaning for shifters. Apart from how accepting a meal is the same thing as accepting a prospective mate's interest, it's part of our love language. It's also part of our community. In packs, shifters eat and talk together. It's a communal affair.

That's why it's been so hard for me lately. With West's rejection earning me the pity of every packmate in Hickory, I stopped eating with the others. When I couldn't face the others, I'd cook for myself in my cabin, always quick meals just to choke something down when my hunger outweighed the ache I felt at being ignored.

Chase isn't ignoring me. He's watching from the corner, his hip cocked against the stove as he waits on bated breath for my reaction.

I don't think he ever guessed I would burst into tears.

They're tears of frustration, and the first I've shed since he brought me here. Because this? This is proof that he won't be moved. He's going to keep me here with him. Unless I reach out to my pack and risk them facing off against a feral—because Luna knows he'll turn into the monster if I try to go—I'm stuck. He won't let me escape, and if by some miracle I do, he'll come after me.

And that's if the vampires don't get me first.

Chase pushes off of the range, stalking toward me. "Quinn? Are you… are you crying?"

I use my wrists to rub roughly at the tears. "It's nothing," I lie. "The food looks amazing."

"Fuck the food. You *are* crying. Come here—"

He moves to grab me.

I spin out of his reach, backing up until I hit the wall. It's instinctive. I just… I don't want him touching me right now. "I said I'm fine, Chase. Leave me alone."

"What's wrong?" He stops dead in his tracks. "What

did I do?" he demands, suddenly panicked. "How can I fix it? Tell me."

He can't, and I look away.

"I knew it. I'm doing this wrong. I've done it all wrong." Out of the corner of my eye, I watch as Chase runs his fingers through his hair, an anguished expression on his face. "I've fucked this up from the beginning."

He drops down into a crouch, cradling his head. "I had a plan. I was going to take this slow. It's just... a few months in, when I finally was ready to make my move, I followed you to your pack land. To the cabins, and the other wolves were there. I thought it would be easier on you if I said you were mine when you weren't alone. I didn't want to scare you, Quinn. But then I heard the rumors. About the Beta... I saw you with him. Your"—he takes a deep breath, then spits out the word—"*mate*. Approaching you, introducing myself... I couldn't wait, knowing someone else had a claim to you, even if they weren't following up on it. So I started to plan. I watched you. I watched him. I watched you watch him... and then, when I caught you two talking in the woods a couple of weeks ago, I knew... I had to do something."

I can't believe this. I can't believe this is happening. That Chase is actually being open and honest with me at last, and that he's confirming what I guessed all along: he *did* stalk me these last nine months. In the woods, in Hickory... he was there.

And I had no idea.

My mouth is suddenly dry. I don't know what to say or how to act. Am I scared, or is this what I've been waiting for? All I've wanted is to know *why*. Any maybe I still don't, not yet, but this is something.

I know that it really was *me* he was targeting.

"You took me." My words are soft. I'm daring him to deny it as I say, just a bit louder, "That's what you did."

"Yeah." He shakes his head in remorse, though the glimmer in his eyes when he looks up at me says he doesn't regret it one bit. "I took you." The glimmer dies. Anguish returns. "And now you hate me."

The pain in his voice cuts like a damn knife. Especially since the truth is that I don't actually hate Chase; his actions maybe, but not he male. He's too broken to hate. It wouldn't be fair.

I exhale roughly. "I don't hate you. Don't get me wrong," I add when his expression quickly shifts to one of hope, "I'm not your biggest fan right now. But I don't hate you."

I can't. Don't ask me why. He's certainly done enough to earn my hatred. I still can't hate him.

The hope fades. "I don't know what part of me led me to treat you like this. When you've done so much to help me without even being aware of it... I was selfish. I saw something I wanted. The idea another male had a claim to you made me crazed. I couldn't stop myself. I could blame it on being feral, but my wolf and human halves were in agreement. I had to have you, Quinn."

"But you knew about West." He made *that* clear. "You knew he rejected me. I might have been watching him"—Chase's cheeks go hollow as he sucks in a breath—"but you should've seen him watching Helene. We don't talk." As painful as it is to admit that, it's true. "I've had like ten conversations with West total since I found out who he was to me. That day in the woods you mention… it was a pity chat. Nothing more."

"And the day he warned you from going into the woods on your own?"

Ah. So he was spying on that conversation, too?

"You mean the day you kidnapped me?" I toss back.

The feral is a mess of emotions right now, barely hanging onto his control, but he has no shame as he nods. "Yes. That day."

"He was only doing his duty. Beta, remember?" And if I find out that he knew I had a stalker and never clued me in, I'm gonna go furry on his ass. One upside to his wolf being drawn to mine? It wouldn't necessarily be a challenge, would it? "Now, I'm not saying I want you back. It's just… he's my fated mate, but he's not *mine*. You acted like a creepy fucking stalker for nothing. You could've said 'hi'."

Chase slowly rises up from his crouch. His voice drops, imploring me. "Fate is a powerful thing," he tells me. "Everyone knows he can't have his omega. When he finally realizes that… when he accepts his fate… he'll turn to you. I thought that's what he was doing that day in the woods with the flower when you were talking. Didn't matter that it wasn't. My wolf needed you. I needed you. I had to bring you home with me."

"But why?" For days now we've danced around the topic. If Chase really wants me to believe that he picked me for some reason and not just because I was the only she-wolf he could get his claws on, he needs to explain himself. I have to ask: "Why me?"

"I didn't mean to go feral."

That doesn't answer my question at all. And, until I know *why me*, we're fated to go around in circles just like this.

"No one does," I say drolly. "But I don't care about that. You did this. You made these choices. I... I can't take this anymore, Chase. Be honest. What the hell do you want from me?"

I expect him to walk away. He does that. When I ask a question he doesn't like, it's time for him to leave. He always returns, as though he can't stay away, but he goes.

Not this time.

Instead of walking away, he takes a few careful steps toward me. Once he's within reach, towering over me, he says, "It started with your scent."

"**M**y scent?"

"When I become that… thing, I'm ruled by instinct. It's not my wolf in charge or my human half. It's something different. Something I can't control. If I have an urge, I act on it. If I'm hungry, I feed. If I feel threatened, I kill. And when I caught a scent on the breeze that had me going hard, all I could think about was getting the owner of it beneath me so that I could rut until I'd spent all my lusts."

I go still. He… he can't mean me, can he?

One look at him and it's clear. He does.

"I've never felt like that before," he continues. "I admit, I didn't fight the urge. I searched for the scent and I found a beautiful she-wolf sitting beneath a tree, playing with the flower in her hands. She was plucking it, singing a song under her breath…"

That does sound like me. Sometimes I would pick a flower, then play the old "he loves me, he loves me not" game as I tore off its petals. When I was younger, it would help me decide which male I would take out for a romp. Then the Luna picked me for West, and I stopped playing the game. It kind of loses its allure when you have to change the words to "he loves *her*, he loves me not".

"Are you telling me your feral side is what chose me?" I ask. "Not you. Not your wolf. But your feral beast?"

"All three of those are me, Quinn. We all want you. But being feral... I haven't been like this all that long," he admits. "Barely a year. It's still hard for me to understand what... *how* I ended up breaking in the first place."

It's the first time he's ever mentioned it himself. I'd have to be a fool to let the chance pass me by without saying anything.

I tilt my head just enough that I'm meeting his gaze. He can consider it a challenge if he wants, though I'm pretty sure he won't, as I ask him, "What happened?"

As if he purposely misunderstood me, he says, "I was a lone wolf first. I had my cabin here, but I spent more and more time in my fur. I should've known then that I wasn't right. I was too late, though. I changed into my other form for the first time and, after that, there was no going back. I'd never found a female that enticed the beast. I didn't know what would happen, and I was terrified."

Me, too. Just the idea of that hunched, patchy, snarling monster coming upon me when I was alone in the woods is pure nightmare fuel. The big, black wolf was bad enough.

"I couldn't stop him, though. At least, not when he had your scent." Chase pauses, then takes a hesitant step toward me, closing the meager gap between us. When I don't try to bolt past him, he takes another. He's slowly caging me in. We both know it. As long as he keeps talking, I'll allow it. "It was your voice. Your scent drew me to you, but then I heard your voice."

Look at that. Talking to myself in the woods might've saved me from being mounted by a feral. And all the times after that, too, most likely. Ha. To think I was worried my packmates might think West's rejection was making me lose my mind...

"My voice," I say, returning to the conversation. "That stopped you from trying to mate me then?"

"That's the truth of it. Something about you... hearing your voice calmed me down. It used to take hours for me to shift again. After hearing you sing, I still wanted to go to you, but I was a wolf again, not a monster. Mating was a want, not an uncontrollable need. I couldn't let myself hurt you." He moves into me, completely caging me in with one arm while laying the back of his other hand against my cheek. "I never will."

The funny thing is, I believe him. Even when I kneed him in his dick, then sucker-punched him, the most he did was wrap me up in his arms so that I couldn't lash out at him again.

"Nine months, Quinn. Whenever I had the chance, I ran from my cabin out to Hickory, hoping that I'd get the nerve to approach you. Every time I saw you from a distance, scenting you, hearing you... I got better. I almost introduced myself to you six months ago. But then..."

We both know why he didn't. Six months ago was when I found my fated mate—and it wasn't Chase.

This close, I can see how tight his jaw goes. A muscle

tics in his cheek, his eyes lighting up. Just the thought of West is bringing out the beast, even as Chase tries his hardest to hold him back.

He does. It's obviously rough, but as he stares unblinkingly into my tear-stained face, he does.

After a few moments, he shudders, then lets out a soft breath that warms my forehead. "It didn't change anything. You were still the only thing I looked forward to, the only thing that kept me sane. I found out about the other male after he already made his choice, and I worked toward taking you before he changed his mind."

He's so close to me, I can hardly move. When I shake my head just enough to disagree with him, my hair whispers against the wall at my back. "You don't have to worry about that. He won't."

"Don't be so sure about that."

I am. "He chose Helene. Our Omega. He isn't mine."

"You keep saying that. But let me tell you something, Quinn. A half bond can only last so long. I've seen it happen. One day he was going to wise up and he'd claim you. I would lose you before I ever had a chance to find out why you affect me like this. I couldn't let that happen. And every time I saw you together, I was more sure that I had to do what I was planning to do. My mind was made up, and not a moment too soon." Those golden eyes are gleaming with insanity. "You were together that morning. I was there. I heard him. He was trying to keep you from me. I had to keep you first."

Ah. He must be talking about the afternoon he took me, when West came over to warn me about the presence in the woods. After his subtle rejection, I can count the number of times we were together on maybe two hands.

So Chase really was there in Hickory that day, too?

I swear, if I ever get back, I'm going to have a word with Bishop about our shit security…

"I had a choice of my own. I could take you with me, or I could kill your male before he could claim you." At that confession—and the way I suck in my breath—Chase draws away from me. "I figured you'd prefer the first option. I don't want to hurt you. I fell in love with you that first day in the woods, and my feelings for you have only grown. You know I'm an alpha wolf. We're persistent, possessive bastards. I'm feral, too. I can't change that. You're the only one who can tame my beast, and I really am sorry. This isn't the way I wanted us to happen, but I can't change the past. I can only make up for it in the future.

"Stay with me, Quinn. Not because I chained you, or because you don't want to face the vampires. Stay with me because no male will ever treat you better than I will from this moment on."

He has such an intense look on his ruggedly handsome face that I can't come up with an answer for him right away.

I just stare back at him, but the more he meets my stare unblinkingly, the more I understand that he's absolutely serious.

I glance behind me at the food on the table. I fucking knew it. This totally is his version of a proposal, isn't it?

He's waiting for me to say something.

"Chase..." I sigh. "I can't promise you forever. If that's what you're asking me for, I can't do it."

"Then don't promise forever. Promise that you'll stay just a little bit longer. But you'll have to let me try to prove that I'm the male for you."

"How long would I have to stay?"

"The Luna will rise in a little less than three weeks. If I haven't convinced you to choose me by then, I'll let you go."

Chase might be a feral, but I've had the same thought since the beginning: he's a very intelligent feral.

I'm not saying I'm going to mate Chase. If I did that, I'm basically condoning how he's treated me from the moment I discovered him watching me nine months after he started. But the kiss did something to make me forget West if only for a few moments—something I never would've thought was possible before now—and lying down beside the black wolf had gone a little way to soothing something sharp and jagged inside of me.

He's broken. I'm broken. Maybe we can't fix each other, but hopefully we can't fall apart any more.

"And if I choose to go?"

"Then I'll just ask you to chain me up before you go. You'll be able to get away, and no matter what happens when I become that thing, he won't be able to get to you."

Fair enough.

"Okay. Until it's the next full moon, I'll stay with you."

It's not technically a lie. I have every intention of honoring my agreement—unless the perfect opportunity to escape presents itself.

Then all bets are off.

His lips split into a grin that turns him from ruggedly handsome to downright gorgeous. "Sit down. I'll grab the plates and utensils, and we can eat together."

Together. Oh, boy. It would be the first time, too.

Welp, I already agreed to this insanity. I might as well get a good meal out of it.

"Sure, but touch the pesto and you're losing a paw."

He chuckles as he moves past me toward the cupboard by the sink.

And I realize something. His chuckle? That was another first from Chase.

***

He wasn't kidding when he said he'd take any chance to prove to me that he was the right male for me. The food was just the beginning, and he's only playing hardball from there on out.

I'm ready for him.

Assuming I won't get to escape him, my new plan is to run out the clock while using my undeniable attraction to Chase to find a way to forget all about West. I only have to make it until the next full moon before he'll let me go back to Hickory. If I'm lucky, by then I'll have finally gotten over West. Let Helene have him. I'll find a mate of my own, bond with him, and my fated mate bond with West will be nothing but a bad memory.

That can't be Chase. No matter how much he believes that we belong together, he's still a feral alpha wolf.

Of course, if our goddess blesses him with a bonded

mate during the Luna Ceremony, that might be enough to keep him turning feral again...

That's just a guess. I don't know for sure. He tells me that, the closer we get, the more sane he feels, and I want to believe him. At the very least, he certainly seems like he's better than he was.

Even so, I'm not going to tease him because I don't know how his feral side will react; no matter how much he swears being around me calms his feral side, even he acknowledges that he's not whole, and I can't risk him turning on me. I won't let him fuck me, either. I haven't been with a male since I discovered West was my fated mate. I've finally admitted to myself that my days of casual sex are behind me, and the next time I let a male inside of me, it'll be because he's my forever mate.

I expect Chase to push me on that point. After all, I said I would give him until the next Luna to see if he can convince me that, even if we're not fated, we have some kind of tie between us.

To my surprise, he agrees that sex is off the table for now unless I'm the one who chooses to initiate it. Since I know that he's not the type of male who will mate just for the sake of the act, I won't do it. It might feel good for one night, but I have no doubt in my mind that he'll try to turn it into forever.

Luckily for me and my libido, it's not as easy as that. Say I forget myself for a moment and decide that Chase might be the perfect wolf to break my celibacy streak. Just having sex doesn't create a bond; otherwise I'd have at least ten mates of my own already. No. All matings have to be blessed by the Luna.

A bond can only be finalized on the night of the full moon, when the Luna is out. The couple has to mate—obviously—and they have to wear each others' mark. Some mates bite each other. Others use their claws. So long as they choose to keep it, the scars turn white. If the Luna accepts the mating, a bond snaps into place.

Don't want a bond? Don't fuck on the night of the full moon, and don't go crazy with your claws or your fangs. It's as simple as that when you're a low-ranking member of the pack.

Now, Chase is an alpha wolf, but he's not an Alpha. He doesn't have a pack; before me, he was a lone wolf. Only Alphas and their mates have to turn the Luna Ceremony into a spectacle for the rest of the pack. It's a way to welcome the female half of the Alpha couple into our tight-knit community, and to show every packmate that the Luna blesses their mating.

Of course, the rest of the ceremony takes place when the couple is alone, but the marks they each wear are a symbol of their lifelong mating.

Hey. Who needs wedding rings when a mating mark truly says *forever*?

Chase wears my bite on his upper arm. I haven't forgotten his reaction when he realized that I healed his bite on my neck. He truly wants to make me his mate. Sleeping with him when I have no intention of spending the rest of my life with a feral is just out of the question.

That's not the only boundary we set up.

We each have one that's non-negotiable. Chase refuses to talk about anything that happened to him before he first chanced upon me in Hickory nine months ago. I refuse to talk to him about West, and when he asks me in a puzzled tone how my fated mate could ever choose another over me, I add Helene to the list.

Once that's clear, our battle of wills is on.

He wants to prove he's the right male for me. I need him to understand that he doesn't have a chance.

And then he does something that is one hell of a blow to my resolve.

The bloody stink of hundreds of vampires permeates the woods outside of Chase's cabin.

Phew. I thought it was bad the other day when I ran face-first into the stench. My nose must've still been a little off because this is *worse*.

My wolf puts her paws over her snout. I do the same.

Chase chuckles. "You'll get used to it."

Yeah. Maybe if I chop my nose off.

Since he's watching my reaction closely, I reluctantly let go of it. Blowing air through my nostrils, trying to erase the stink, I settle on breathing through my mouth.

Better.

I toss my hair over my shoulder, looking around. My ears are cocked, searching for some sign that we're not alone. Unless I hear a footstep, there's a good chance a vampire could sneak up on me since relying on my nose is out. I'd never be able to pinpoint one vampire when they're all I smell.

I don't think anyone else is out here. Chase's senses

are much keener than mine; if there was, he never would've invited me to go out for a walk with him. He'd probably toss me in the basement if we had visitors.

Instead, with his hand planted on the small of my back, he guides me around the side of his cabin.

His palm is like a heated brand through my shirt. The first time he touched me like that, I slapped his hand off of me. Since then, I've gotten used to his casual touches. I promised I'd give him a chance to court me, to be my partner in the mating dance, and though I haven't let him kiss me again, I can tolerate a caress here or there.

It's been a couple of days since I gave him my word that I would stay. There are moments when he looks at me as if he can't believe I'm here; there are others when he's watching me darkly, already envisioning me walking away. I'm just glad he mentioned the chains. Something tells me that, despite *his* promise, I'll need them when I decide to go.

If I decide to go.

I've been gone from Hickory for more than a week now. Every day, I check on my bond with West. It's still there, though I'm finding it easier to block off. Where was this ability six months ago? It's almost like I suffered for nothing. Whatever happens with Chase, at least I know how I'll survive seeing West with Helene.

They say distance makes the heart grow fonder. For me, I've had the opposite effect. I don't know if it's because I've purposely blocked him so he can't find me, but the idea of the two of them together doesn't hurt me as much as it used to. It's getting easier and easier to push him out of my head the longer I'm out of Hickory.

Now I just need to find a way to push him out of my heart and soul—

I blink. It's an insane idea, and one that I've had a bunch of times since I made my deal with Chase. I couldn't believe I came up with it in the first place. The fact that it keeps popping up in my brain? Maybe... maybe I should try it.

I mean, hey, if putting enough distance between us has finally lessened the sting of West's rejection, what would an affair with another male do?

I could do worse than Chase. At least he's devoted to me. Sure, you could say *obsessed*, but that's not a bad thing for our kind of supe. When a shifter male threatens to challenge and kill a rival to claim a mate, it's considered romantic, as long as the she-wolf wants him back.

Do I want Chase?

I didn't. I swear I didn't.

I blame him. He said he would prove himself to me. So far, he's giving it a good go.

And all his efforts pale in comparison when he guides me around his cabin, down a dirt path that leads further into the trees that surround his home, and into a clearing filled with—

"Flowers," I breathe out.

He's at my back. I don't see him, but I can sense his heat as he moves into me. With one hand on my shoulder now, the other settles on my waist.

He sounds nervous as he says, "It's the Quinn Malone Memorial Garden."

"Memorial?" I echo. My words sound faint to my own ears. I'm too stunned by what I see. "But I'm not dead."

His husky chuckle sends a shiver down my spine. "Memorial because each one of these flowers reminds me of you. They're *my* memories."

"Oh."

What else can I say?

There are hundreds out here. Some are recognizable types—daisies, carnations, roses, tulips—while others are the wildflowers that spring up around Hickory. Those flowers are native to our land. Most of the others aren't. This is definitely someone's garden.

"I planted the first flowers after I found you. Those... the two bunches of roses over there, because your lips were red and your eyes were yellow. I thought they would be all, but I just... whenever my need for you got to be too much, I'd run from the edge of your pack land all the way back to my cabin. Some of these are ones I carried back between my fangs, roots attached. Others I bought from a human-owned florist down in Sacre Coeur."

Using his grip on my shoulder, he directs me to look at some pale pink posies. "You had a blouse that color on the day I planted those."

Again he moves me. He points at a yellow-petaled wildflower with a brown center. A brown-eyed Susan, one of the wildflowers that's shaped like a daisy, and is perfect for "he loves me, he loves me not". "You liked those. I saw you weave them in your hair sometimes. I tried to relocate those the most."

He did. Among the garden, I see at least twenty brown-eyed Susans that are everywhere in the woods surrounding Hickory.

Whoa. For the first time in a long time, I'm actually speechless.

Back home, West is known for bringing Helene a flower every time they meet as a token of his affection.

But Chase?

He gave me a whole garden.

Behind me, he's humming in anticipation. He's waiting for my reaction.

He desperately wants me to like what he's showing me.

You know, I should've guessed something was up when Chase pulled a worn, thin t-shirt over his head. It's a pale grey, cotton shirt, but it's been washed so many times, I can make out his pecs and his nipples and the dusting of hair at the top of his chest through the material.

It's the first time I've seen him wear one. I still don't have any shoes, and I'm beginning to think there isn't a force on Earth that'll get Chase to wear them, so we had headed out together in our bare feet. It's not so unusual. Shifters have thick calluses to protect our human feet while our wolves have pads. I could run without noticing the rocks or sticks, though you really appreciate a good boot when you accidentally step in a pile of shit someone left behind.

Trust me. I know.

And, sure, Mitchell said it was from a wild wolf lurking nearby, but I have my doubts about that...

The shirt was the first sign that something was up with Chase. The way he kept reaching for me, fiddling with my hair, absently stroking his fingers through the dark strands as if he needed to remind himself that I was still there was the second sign. It was like he was working himself up to something.

I guess he was. He finally invited me for a walk, and here we are.

I can't believe it. I don't know what to say.

So I don't say anything.

Spinning in his arms, I grip Chase's shirt, tugging him down so that his mouth is near mine. The material tears. I wince, but he doesn't seem to notice; if he does, he doesn't care. Now that our mouths are only a few inches apart, Chase swoops in, taking my lips with his.

Uh-uh. This kiss is mine.

I take control. Nudging him back with my nose, I tilt my chin so that I can suck his bottom lip between my teeth. I nibble it lightly, and when he groans, I slip my tongue into his mouth.

Chase shudders. His hands cup my ass, pulling me into him. I can feel the heat of his erection poking my lower belly and that just spurs me to kiss him harder.

When we finally break apart, he leans his forehead against mine, his hands on my shoulders bracing me.

"Reject him, Quinn. He doesn't deserve you. He doesn't deserve your heart."

"Do you?" I whisper, my voice as rough and ragged as his panted breaths.

"No," he says honestly, "not yet. But I won't give up until I do."

I press my hands against his chest. He doesn't realize that, with this garden, he pretty much has.

But reject him?

Reject West?

I feel like an idiot, but as often as I wished he would just put me out of my misery and finally cut the tie between us, I never realized that I could do the same. Probably because he's so much higher in the pack than me. Would it even take?

It did when the Wicked Wolf's mate rejected him, but she was an omega. They exist outside of the hierarchy of the pack for the most part. I'm just a delta.

Is it possible for me to reject the Beta?

I don't know. But it's definitely something to think about.

ANOTHER WEEK GOES BY, AND CHASE CONTINUES TO DO HIS best to take us deeper into the mating dance.

Luna help me, I let him.

At first, I had to keep reminding myself that this was never my choice. I didn't want to be here, and he basically conned me into staying for a couple of extra weeks. I did, making up every excuse to myself why I didn't try to find some way to escape, and it's been days since the idea even crossed my mind.

Eventually, I had to admit that I'm holding a grudge against something he can't help and I'm being just a little unfair. I still don't know what turned him feral, and courtesy of the boundaries we set, I don't ask.

He's done nothing but treat me like I'm the best thing that's happened to him. He's changed, too. He hasn't grunted in a week. He doesn't growl. The panicked look in his eyes when he walks into a room before he finds me there doesn't come as often lately.

He hasn't gone feral again, either. He insists it's because of me. It's a heady responsibility, but I've learned that a sane Chase is one I can't help but like.

I just... I guess I'm struggling with understanding why, of all females, he chose *me*.

If I'm being honest, if Chase showed up in Hickory in his skin, he probably could've had his pick of any of the single she-wolves there. Between his wolf being an alpha, his body looking like it was sculpted by one of the masters, and his eyes promising wicked things when they're not being used to threaten, no one could resist him. I certainly wouldn't have been able to.

Even knowing that he has his... issues, I don't think I can now.

The night after he showed me his garden, I invited Chase to sleep in the bed with me. I hadn't meant to do it. I've grown used to him sleeping on a blanket on the floor. He always fell asleep in his jeans. On two other occasions after the first time, I woke up to find his black wolf whimpering. Shifting to my wolf, I joined him on the floor.

He was always gone again when I woke up.

That night, right when he was about to make his bed on the floor, I cleared my throat, then patted the empty spot next to me.

I realized then that I trusted him, at least when it came to having him near while I was vulnerable. I didn't need to threaten his dick again. He would never touch me intimately without my permission.

Of course, when he joined me in bed and I pressed

my body into his side, Chase nearly choked on his breath when I willingly touched him. Emboldened by his reaction, I made sure it was okay if I touched him a little more.

He told me before to think of his cabin as mine. Same with his room.

That night, he added his body to the list.

I had free rein to explore it, and Luna did I. To be fair, after a couple of nights of me playing with Chase, I told him he could touch me, too.

He kissed me as if I'd given him some great gift. The way he stroked my belly before palming one of my tits was so reverential, I began to wonder how I was ever going to walk away from this male.

Plus, I'd finally gotten my hands on his dick. No way was I leaving until I got to take a ride on that sucker.

Did that mean I was thinking about taking him up on his offer? Staying with him forever and becoming his mate? I wasn't convinced just yet. Bonding with Chase would completely erase my tie to West, which would save me the trouble of figuring out if I can reject him instead, but then I'd be mated to him for life.

Was I ready for that?

No. And until I changed my mind—*if* I changed my mind—sex was still off the table.

For now, at least.

That's the problem with the Luna. Our goddess wants her wolves to take mates. She wants us to fuck. At its core, mating is about creating pups. It's about building families and continuing our species. In order to encourage shifters to procreate, something about the Luna appearing high in the sky turns a shifter's sex drive up to eleven.

Throw in a promise of a mate? It cranks up to twenty.

It's worse for males. At least, that's what I heard, though I take it with a grain of salt since it was usually my prospective lovers telling me that so I'd fuck them under the full moon. As long as I didn't let them mark me, it was just a good time, so it didn't matter.

Of course, after I found out West was my fated mate, I realized the need surrounding the Luna's arrival is pretty bad for females, too. I burned through a ton of batteries using a vibrator to keep me satisfied these last six months since I found it nearly impossible to turn to another male while West was still my Luna-given mate.

As a shifter, I know the Luna's cycle intimately. Already the need is clawing at me, and I still have six days to go until she's full. That means I have six days to make my decision because, if I do stay here, I'm going to fuck Chase. Already I feel like it's inevitable.

And though he vowed never to mark me until I agreed to let him, would he be able to control himself during mating? Or would his feral take over and, like he told me once before, decide to *rut* me until all of his lusts are spent and I'm his forever mate?

I don't know, but at least I have a few more days to figure it out.

CHAPTER 12
BETRAYAL

After breakfast, Chase leaves the cabin. We're running low on groceries, and since he insists on serving me at least three home-cooked meals a day, plus snacks, he needs to restock his supplies.

I discover where he gets everything from. Using the same truck that brought me from Hickory to Chase's territory, he drives into Sacre Coeur and loads up the bed with everything he might need for a few weeks at a time. He went through it all faster with me here, so he needs to head back earlier than he expected.

I offered to go. Not because I'm itching to visit a Fang City—I'm *not*—but because I figured Chase would never leave me on my own. He doesn't say it with words, but I can tell that he still expects me to vanish anytime he takes his eyes off of me.

If my choice is between being chained again or seeing where the vampires live, I'll take a ride into town.

Surprisingly, Chase doesn't choose either option. He doesn't want to risk me being around vamps, and he already said he'd never chain me up again. This might be some kind of test on his part, but he lets me stay in the cabin by myself.

It's lonely without him. I don't realize how much I've grown used to his aura brushing up against mine until he's out of the reach of my wolf.

He swears he'll only be gone for a couple of hours, max. When I get tired of waiting—and it's only been about twenty minutes or so—I decide to visit the garden out back. Chase made sure to let me know that it was close enough to the cabin that it was safe from any vamps who might be patrolling nearby so I could go there without him.

I lose track of how long I'm outside. Despite the vampire stink that, surprisingly, I *have* gotten a little more used to, my wolf preens being surrounded by nature. Having all of these flowers around me, it's like a little slice of home.

I have trees. I have wildflowers. For the first time in so long, I'm content again. I'm not hiding in the woods to avoid the pitying looks back in Hickory. I'm sitting in the grass because that's where I feel the most at peace.

The only thing that would make it better? Was if Chase was with me.

When I feel a prickle against the back of my neck, I know that he's home again. Since he doesn't know I'm out here—and after a trip to Sacre Coeur, he might not be able to sniff past the vampire stink to find me—I climb up from the grass, then jog back to the house.

I'm actually kind of surprised by how much I miss him, and how much I want to see him again. Just the thought of seeing what he brought back for me has me moving faster. He'd promised me a gift for leaving me behind, and if there's one thing I know about him, it'll be something meaningful.

I enter through the front door, expecting to find him waiting for me there. Nope. He's in here, I can sense him nearby, and I follow his aura to our bedroom.

Chase is pacing back and forth, muttering under his breath. So consumed by what he's doing, he doesn't even realize I've walked into the room until I call his name.

"Chase?"

"Quinn!" His head shoots up. A second later, he's lunging at me. "Where were you?"

He grabs my arm. It's not rough, but it's not a gentle caress, either.

What the hell?

I try to shake him off, immediately going on my guard. This isn't like the Chase I've come to know. "Let go of me."

He doesn't.

"You were gone. I couldn't scent you."

"Of course not. It stinks like fucking bloodsuckers out there, remember?"

His eyes are wild. I don't think he's listening to a word I say. His grip tightens. "I thought you left me."

"Why?" I shake my arm again, still trying to break out of his hold. I don't like the way he's looking at me right now. "You should've known better. I said I would stay. At least until the Luna appears again."

"You were lying to me."

I freeze. "What was that?"

Alphas know. It's just one more thing that makes them different than the other ranks of wolves. An alpha wolf instinctively senses when someone is lying to him.

I knew that. Not many shifters do, but the Alpha of the Sylvan Pack never hid that from the rest of us. Our old Alpha, Xavier, was open with that skill, too. Then, when he was younger, Bishop made a game of it among the shifters in our age group.

Chase is a born alpha. He might not have a pack, so he isn't a capital-a Alpha, but that doesn't change his rank. I guess... I just thought he didn't have the skill because he was feral. How many times have I lied to him? Whether on purpose or not, I must've done it a bunch of times. Did he ever call me out on it? No. So I thought he didn't know.

I was wrong.

I grit my teeth. I don't deny it, because he'll know that, too, but I do tug on his arm. "Does it matter? I'm still here. I stayed. Now, let go of me before I make you."

He does. Finally releasing me, he whirls away. I expect him to lash out, maybe punch the wall. He doesn't. He threads his fingers through his hair, leaving track marks with his claws, before he turns on me again.

"I need you, Quinn." His voice is soft. Broken. "When I thought you were gone... I don't think I can survive without you."

He might have to. "You barely know me."

The look he gives me just then calls me a liar without him saying the words.

He's right. Stalker or not, I have to admit he does know me.

The truth of just how much is in the clothes he bought me, everything in my size and close enough to my style that I probably would've picked out a bunch of those pieces myself. It's in the foods he prepares, and how often he serves me meals that are my favorites.

It's in the flowers out back that I was looking at just to be close to Chase while he was gone.

It's in the new pair of shoes laying on the bed, and the expensive shampoo and conditioner set I mentioned preferring in one of our conversations.

See. A meaningful gift, just like I thought, all because he *does* know me.

Just like I've gotten to know him.

His chest is heaving. At his side, he's fisted his hands. Chase is on the edge of his control, and all because he'd convinced himself that I left him.

I think about what he just said. I don't want someone to *need* me. I want them to love me. To *choose* me.

Maybe... maybe this is the best I'm going to get.

Back in the Sylvan Pack, I'll never be mate material. Not when the pack gossips will always whisper that I belong to West. The way that males like Tucker and Eddie proposition me for a quickie in the woods... that's all I'll ever be good for.

Chase isn't perfect. He has his flaws. I mean, for Luna's sake, he's a feral! And, sure, he hasn't gone off the deep end since my first night in his cabin. The threat that he might is always there.

Only one thing can tame a wild feral wolf: his mate.

It's something I've been trying to ignore for two weeks now. He's been so good since I've been here, so different, and he whispers at night it's because of me. It's like how he's convinced it was Fate's hand that had him running past Hickory the day he found me. Even then he knew I could calm him. If he claims me as his mate, I might just be able to tame him.

He wouldn't go feral again. It's a weight on my shoulders I don't need, so I've purposely avoided dwelling on that fact.

I can't now.

What if... what if I gave him what he wanted? Instead of waiting for him to take it, like how he took me from my home, I can offer it to him. It's not like he'd be my first. I mean, I've actually grown to like him which is more than I can say about some of the other males I've fucked.

This isn't a sudden impulse, either. While I was sitting near the garden, I kept thinking about it over and over again. Whether I want to be his mate or not is one thing. I definitely want to mate him at least once.

Why not now? Maybe it'll prove to Chase that there's a reason why I stayed.

I move into him. It takes all the courage I have, meeting his stare head-on and stepping close to an alpha that is bristling with unbridled emotion.

"Chase?"

He gulps. Something about the change in my tone has him watching me warily, though I can sense the lust and desire pouring off of him. He wants this as much as I do. More, actually.

"Yes?"

"Remember how we agreed you wouldn't even mention sex until I initiated it?"

His Adam's apple trembles. I watch it bob as he swallows roughly before grating out a very fierce, "I do."

"Well..." I open up my arms to him. "Consider this me initiating it."

That's all the permission I have to give him.

Chase falls on me. He buries his face in my hair, breathing deeply, before dropping his mouth to my neck. His hands are at my waist, holding me against him, though he leaves me a little room to work when I take a firm hold of his cock through his jeans.

Just like I expected, he's already hard. I'm ready for him, too. When he inhales deeply, then groans against my skin, I know he can tell. My arousal fills the room the same way his is a crackle in the air.

I flick open the button on his jeans with my free hand. He starts to suck at my neck, lapping at my skin, almost like he's tasting me. It feels so good, I tilt my head further, baring my throat to him in an instinctively submissive gesture.

My fingers reach for his zipper. His erection pulses against my palm.

His fangs sink into my neck.

I go motionless. It's a prey response, and one that pisses off this predator. But that's nothing compared to the realization of what Chase has just done. I initiated sex. I wanted to mate him. This was going to happen.

I had good intentions. And all that got shot to hell when he *bit* me.

This isn't a graze or a scratch. This isn't an accident. This is a male marking his female, making it so that every other shifter knows she's taken.

But he *promised* me...

Releasing Chase, my hands slam into his chest. I don't care that it's going to rip his fangs out of my neck. Using all of my sudden fury, I tap into my wolf and push him as far away from me as I possibly can.

He's strong. Too strong. Unlike the last time, I only get him a few feet away from me.

It's enough.

He freezes, like a deer caught in headlights. "Quinn, I... I don't know what came over me."

I do.

"You promised." My voice is low. It's full of agony and betrayal and rage. "You *promised*."

For a moment, I see the Chase I know. The horror that fills his expression, the remorse in the depths of his golden gaze. My blood dribbles down his chin, and he wipes it away with a shaky—

Paw.

Shit!

It all happens so fast after that. His body crunches, his fangs grow longer, and his eyes lose any semblance of rational thought. He darts out his tongue, lapping at my blood that stains his lips, before throwing his head back and howling.

It's a song of need. Of lust.

Of possession.

I know then that Chase is too far gone. The beast has taken him over, and I'm not his mate. Not really. He might wear my bite on his skin, but I just refused to let him mark me. He bit me before I even got his zipper down, so it's not like we had sex to take off the edge. Besides, without the Luna being out to bless any mating, a bond won't form.

He loves me, though. He told me so.

He said he'd never hurt me.

I hold out a hand. Like his paw, it's also shaking. "Chase? Can you hear me?"

The feral lowers himself into a crouch.

Shit. I take a step back.

He pounces.

I turn and run.

It was in the way he held his hunched body. A split second before he moved, I was already going. I bolt through the exit to the bedroom, pausing only long enough to throw the door closed in his face.

I expect him to follow right behind me and I'm not disappointed. From the smash that happens, then the crash, I'm pretty sure the feral ripped off the bedroom door before throwing it down the hall.

Crap, crap, crap.

Chase isn't thinking. That thing... that isn't my Chase. He told me before that, when he's completely feral, he loses any conscious thought. The beast runs on instinct and urges. After I flipped out on him for trying to mark me, leaving him with his button undone and his heavy erection pushing against his zipper, it doesn't take a genius to figure out what he's after.

Me. He wants me.

Fuck that.

I throw open the door that leads to the basement, thundering down the stairs. I don't bother being quiet. I *want* him to know where I've gone.

I won't let him touch me again. He'd never forgive himself if he did in this state. I don't think I could forgive him, either.

In that moment, I don't even know if I can get past him biting me after he promised he wouldn't.

He accused me of lying. Maybe that's true, maybe I did plan on escaping at the first chance I got, but I didn't. I stayed.

He lied to me. Well, turnabout is fair fucking play.

I duck into my old room in the basement. There's only enough time for me to throw myself in the corner hidden in shadows before Chase comes thundering after me. He races into the room, but I'm ready for him.

He's huge, but I've been underestimated my whole life. Just because I'm a regular old shifter, nothing special, everyone thinks that I need someone to take care of me. Screw that. I can take care of myself.

I throw my body at Chase. Knowing that I'll get only one shot at this, I aim for his knees.

The element of surprise is the only thing on my side. Chase would never expect me to attack him which just goes to show that maybe he doesn't know me as well as he likes to think he does. I'm still the same Quinn Malone that responded to a strange wolf encroaching on my territory by running first, then wheeling around to fight back.

That's what I do right now. To me, it's not fight or flight. It's a mixture of both.

I already ran. Time to throw down.

Or, better yet, throw the feral down.

Leading with my shoulder, I slam right into his knees. The force of my hit is enough to send the both of us flying across the room. Chase slams into the cinder block wall first, taking the brunt of the impact.

Just like I hoped.

When he's a feral, he can take a lot more damage than when he's in his skin or his fur. He's not invincible, though, and I made sure to hit him hard. Between me and the immovable cinder blocks, it's enough to stun even Chase. He collapses in a heap.

I make my move.

Running to the basement wasn't a mistake. Chase might've thought it was—with one high window and only one door, it was like heading straight toward a dead-end—but even in my panic and my sense of betrayal, I knew exactly what I was doing.

The chains are still down here. Even after he gave his word that he wouldn't use them on me again, he admitted he kept them in the basement in case I ever needed to use them on *him*.

Like, oh, maybe now?

There's no time to treat them with an extra layer of padding like he used to do for me. While the shackles are silver, and so is the length of the chain, the inside of the ankle cuff has been gilded. The gold doesn't completely shield the power of the silver—that's why Chase insisted on the fabric padding for me—but it'll offer him some protection.

It has to be enough. With my blood continuing to trickle down my chest, a stark reminder that Chase did this to himself, I grab the nearest shackle. Still open from the last time he unlocked it from me, I hurriedly attach it to the easiest part of Chase I can reach.

It's his wrist, and the shackle closes easily around it, snapping closed with an ominous *click*. It's looser than it would be on his ankle, but it's still tight enough to keep him in place.

My hand is already blistered from where I grabbed the shackle. I'd barely held it for five seconds, and the damage is almost enough to make me forget about the ache in my shoulder.

Almost.

Once he's trapped, I don't waste time hanging around. He was still huddled on the ground when I ran out on him, though the howl he lets out when he finally comes to again and sees what I've done shakes the whole fucking cabin as I dash up the stairs.

Welp, I think he just noticed that I trapped him in chains...

Good. Not only is this the payback I promised myself I'd get those rough days when all I knew was that I was a feral's captive, but only being chained by one shackle isn't that bad. Who knows? Maybe the sizzle and burn of the silver shackle will be a good enough reminder that, even if he believed I lied, so did he.

He said no pressure. He agreed to no sex unless I initiated it. And maybe I had, but I never once invited him to *mark* me. So what if he wears my bite on his skin like a brand he's earned? To me, that's not a mate mark. That's a battle scar from when he attacked me, nothing more.

I can still feel the sting of his fangs sinking into the point where my shoulder meets my neck. Using the one drop of energy I can spare, I focus on beginning to heal his bite.

Only then do I head for the front door. Without a second look back—or even a second thought—I rip it off the hinges, then dash out into the darkness.

The sound of the feral's furious roar chases after me.

Ignoring that is easy. He's in the basement, and it's not as loud as it could've been.

Ignoring the pang in my heart that hurts so much worse than Chase's bite?

Yeah. That one's a little bit harder...

CHAPTER 13
VAMPIRE

It's dusk. Not so dark out that I have to rely on my wolf's eyes to see, but the woods are gloomy. Unfriendly. The vampire stench doesn't help.

It surrounds me. Any resistance I built earlier is gone. The weight of the bloody aroma is heavy on my shoulders as I sprint through the trees.

I'm in my skin. I thought about letting my wolf take the lead, but since I have nothing but the clothes on my back to find my way home, I'd rather not run around butt-naked if I don't have to. Shifters don't mind nudity. Humans... they definitely do.

Of course, if it's the better option, I'll shift. For now, I'm moving at a quick clip, anger at Chase spurring to run faster. Now that it's his turn to be chained up, I know he can't come right after me, but he will eventually. I just have to be back in Hickory before he does.

Then, once I let Bishop know that he needs to train the pack patrol better, Chase will never get to me again.

And if I feel a pang at that thought, it's nothing. Just a stitch in my side from not having run in so long...

I pour on the speed, desperate to outrun the thoughts in my head. For some reason, every instinct inside of me is telling me to turn around. To go back to him.

Am I insane? Is Chase rubbing off on me? I always knew I was a broken she-wolf deep down, but this is nuts.

I can't go back. I left. I've made my choice. I have to deal with it.

Later, I'll blame what happens next on how I was more focused on what I left behind than where I was going—or who I might run into. By the time I realize that I can sense someone closing in on me from behind, and that they carry the stink of the undead with them, it's too late.

I try to escape my vampire pursuer anyway, silently chastising myself as I tear a path forward.

What were you thinking, Quinn? He warned you about the woods! He warned you that this was as much vamp land as it was his. Chase said I'd never survive it out here without him.

Luna damn it, I think he's right.

I'm flying through the trees. Vampires don't have wings, but somehow the corpse following me has kept up. Worse, he jumps out in front of me when I least expect it, as if I made a circle or something instead of fleeing straight.

Vampires are beautiful. It's just a fact of life. I've never heard of an ugly one since their supernatural looks have long been a lure for them to snare their human prey.

They need to feed, and they need to compel the non-supes to let them. Sure, they could just take the blood, but it's easier to return to a donor when they *want* you to feed on them. Good looks and charm go a long way to hide what monsters the bloodsuckers truly are.

The male who jumps out in front of me is no exception. His skin is perfectly creamy, without a single imperfection to mar it. His hair is golden blond, tousled in careless curls, with one stray curl falling forward, centered in the middle of his line-free forehead. His cheekbones are chiseled, his mouth full and sullen.

The pout becomes a smile when he sees me, panting and obviously afraid.

He's a vamp. I'm not an idiot.

I'm *terrified*.

"Look what we have here. Pretty little donor." His voice is eerily seductive. I shiver. "I caught your blood on the air. I already knew it was sweet, but you... this is my lucky day."

Are you kidding? Desperately ignoring the hungry look on his otherworldly features, I think about what he said? He could scent my blood? How—

It hits me. Chase's bite. I'm still wearing the blood on my skin from Chase's bite.

Damn it!

"I guess I never expected it to belong to such a female. Pretty enough to eat, you are. Such a shame you're one of *them*."

Them. A shifter. He knows what I am.

Worse? His eyes are red.

Ah, crap.

Every pup learns the rhyme: *When a vamp's eyes go red, run or you're dead.* Red eyes mean that a vampire is either a rogue—the vamp version of a feral—or in the throes of bloodlust.

I'm lost out here. Apart from this beautiful monster, I'm also alone. The air stinks of blood, but it's pouring off of the male standing right in front of me. He's already fed tonight.

Does that stop him from targeting me?

Not even a little.

I make it five running steps before he's on me. His arms wrap around me like steel bands, lifting me up off of the ground so that my neck is right at his mouth.

"It doesn't have to hurt," he tells me in undisguised glee. "For one of your kind, I'll make sure it does."

Sick bastard. His fangs sink into my neck like a pair of knives stabbing me. With his first pull, it's like fire has flooded my veins as he sucks my blood. I scream, hating myself that he got a reaction out of me, but it *hurts*.

Which is exactly his point.

Shifters aren't used to pain. We heal too fast, and even when we come into contact with silver—something that is deadly to us—it's bearable until it *isn't*. Suddenly, I completely understand why vampires are our ancient enemies. With their bite, they could bring even an alpha to their knees.

I'm no alpha. I'm a delta, and I'm about to fucking die in these woods in the arms of a vampire and there isn't a damn thing I can do about it.

I shouldn't have run. Almost delirious, I realize that, if

my fate was to be bitten tonight, there's only one male I want biting me.

Chase.

With the vampire's arms squeezing me tighter than an anaconda, his fangs digging deeper into my neck as he takes deep pulls that have me crying out in pain, I can't help but cling to the memory of Chase like a lifeline.

Even when he was a feral, he never turned on me. When he bit me, he was kind. Gentle. He lapped at my skin, marking me with a reverence we reserve for the Luna.

And while I had no choice but to leave him before he did something one of us would regret, I probably shouldn't have taken off so recklessly into the woods.

It hits me then. Really hits me. I'm about to die. This vampire is too strong. He's draining me right now. My wolf is almost feral herself, desperate to do anything to survive, but my human half is no match for him. And all I can think about is Chase.

It could've been so different. *We* could've been. So hung up on the idea of a fated mate, I thought I needed West. I don't. All my life, I've known that Fate—in the form of our goddess, the Luna—would have the final say when it comes to my life. That includes everything: my pack, my rank, even my forever mate.

I hate it. I always have. It's why I've rebelled since I was a pup. Whether it was taking to the woods to be alone, or accepting as many lovers as were willing to fuck me, or eating in my cabin while the rest of the pack was in the pack circle... *I* wanted to choose. I want my life to be *mine*.

It's why I fought so hard against Chase. No matter how much I felt for him and his situation, and Luna knows if things had been different, I probably would've wanted to jump him from the beginning... he chose me. I didn't choose him.

So why did I follow along with the idea of West being my fated mate for so long? That's not me. That's not Quinn Malone. For the last six months, I've been agreeing to something that I would've normally shot my middle finger at, wishing that West would give up the mate of his heart and fall in line because Fate said so.

Why would I want him to do that? I like West. We've always been friendly, and though I was drawn to him, I knew he belonged to Helene. That hadn't changed.

So why had I?

I've heard that your life flashes before your eyes when you're about to die. Not me. I see things oh so clearly, even as my vision begins to grow spotty.

I don't want West. I never did.

As for Chase...

I wish things had been different. At the very least, I wish we had made it to the Luna. I would've loved to know what decision I'd have gone with if I stayed.

My legs are weak. I suspect that I'm only on my feet because he's holding me up. The vampire is still feeding, and I don't know how much more blood I can stand to give him before I'm fully drained.

How will my feral react when he finds my lifeless body in his woods? He's already broken. I think this... this might shatter him.

I'm so sorry, Chase...

A familiar aura brushes up against me. For a second, I think this is delirium brought on by blood loss. I left him chained in the basement. No way he could've figured a way out already *and* tracked me down. It's impossible. It has to be.

But what if it's not?

If Chase is out there, I'm not going to just roll over and become this vampire's meal. I can't believe I submitted to him as much as I did. He's strong, sure, but I'm a fucking shifter. A Luna damned she-wolf.

With my last burst of strength, I tear my neck away from his fangs at the same time as I bury my elbows in his gut. The vampire—too complacent, and probably drunk on my blood—isn't expecting it. He grunts, and I rip myself out of his loose hold.

I break free, putting a good ten feet between us as my hand clamps over the brutal bite he left on my throat. Vamp bastard got the right vein because he tapped me like a fucking fountain. Hot blood is gushing past my fingers, pooling on my shoulders before dripping down my back.

I glare at him.

What a messy eater. I've never been this close to a vampire—before Chase, I've rarely even left pack land—but you'd think that a bloodsucker would know how to feed without having it stain his lips and dribble down his chin.

His red eyes are shining, almost like his irises are filled with blood. His grin widens, revealing his fangs. They're almost three inches long.

His voice has gone thick and throaty as he demands, "Give me more."

He doesn't do that weird super fast gliding thing like before when he first captured me. Instead, savoring my fear and my pain, he stalks toward me.

Asshole.

I stumble back, relying on the last of my wolf's strength to keep me moving. "No fucking way! Leave me alone, you freak!"

"I'm not a freak," he sniffs. Oh, great. I've offended one of the undead when I'm barely staying on my feet. "You are. And you're a trespasser here. Worse, you're a *dog*. I'd put you down for that crime alone, but your blood… it sings to me. I think I'll have another taste. If you're lucky, I won't drain you completely. Then maybe you can think of a way to convince me to keep you."

If I wasn't half-dead from the 'taste' he'd already taken, I'd snap out a kick to his legs, or maybe aim for the bulge those leather pants of his aren't doing anything to hide.

Some way to convince him? Yeah. It doesn't take a genius to figure out what the corpse is thinking. He might have a hate hard-on for shifters, but that won't stop him from sinking his fangs in my neck again or shoving his cock inside of me.

I'd rather fucking die.

The aura brushes against me again. It's like a caress, and one that bolsters me and my wolf. Deep inside of me, she throws back her head, singing a sweet song to her mate.

My bond with West is wide open. In a rush of panic

after I ran from Chase's cabin, I demolished the block I'd kept up these last couple of weeks. I wanted West to find me. I wanted my pack to know where I was. With Chase chained in the basement, I could finally escape—so long as I made it out of these woods. I wanted them to know I was alive.

And if anything happened to me? I wanted West to sense it so that the pack could stop wondering where I'd disappeared off to.

Is my wolf singing for West? No. He never could've made it from Hickory so soon, plus I haven't felt an answering tug from him since I opened it. That's not surprising—distance does play a factor in how a bond reacts between promised mates—but the wolf mine is calling to isn't a sleek grey wolf.

It's a big, black behemoth.

"Chase?" I whisper.

His aura pulses, so incredibly dominant that it nearly brings me to my knees.

It doesn't, though. It wouldn't. Alphas can make any other shifter submit, but not their mate. Instead, his aura lends me strength, and I put a few more feet between me and the vampire threat the second before I instinctively sense his approach.

He's here.

He's found me.

And though he's in his skin—and not his feral beast form, either—the look on his face is fierce and wild as he leaps into the woods, landing in a crouch that shows off his powerful torso.

"Get away from her," Chase snarls, spit flying as he

stares down the vampire. "She's no trespasser. She's my mate."

Maybe it's the blood loss after all, but my wolf definitely thinks so.

I don't know how he got here. Unless he kept a key to the chains in the pocket of his jeans or... or he swapped out the injection stores in the cylinder on his chain for a key instead... I don't know, but he's here, and I've never been more glad to see my feral in my life.

The vampire's whole demeanor changes. Chase is at his back, and he quickly palms his crotch before reacting.

Silly Quinn. I thought he was going to face off against my feral. Nope. As if he senses he needs some leverage, he flies toward me, putting me back in that iron-tight hold before I can blink.

Chase lets out a warning rumble.

The vampire smiles as he turns so that we're facing him—and Chase can see that he has an arm around my waist, his hand at my throat.

"Wilder. I didn't know she was yours."

Chase's last name is Wilder? Any other time I would've laughed at how fitting that was, but I'm half-drained. Barely standing. If it wasn't for the vampire still holding me close as though he's using me as a shield, I think I would've dropped already. Blood loss isn't as bad as a heavy dose of quicksilver—at least I can still tap into my poor, whimpering wolf—but it's a close second.

Chase circles him, growling softly under his breath.

The vampire moves in sync with him, dragging me as he goes. My head is feeling kind of woozy, but I'm still coherent enough to realize that my instinct was spot-on.

The vamp is using me to protect himself from my furious feral.

"You knew this was my land," Chase says at last. "You knew she carried my scent—"

"I never—"

"Don't deny it," growls Chase. "She sleeps in my bed. Lives in my cabin. I stroke her hair to soothe myself so don't you fucking insult me by pretending you didn't recognize that she belongs to me. And you *bit* her."

His soft chuckle tells me that the vamp's given up on pretending he's innocent in how he treated me. How can he? My blood's still flowing!

"You're right," he says, digging his fingers into the virgin side of my throat. It's better than him poking his bite, but not by much. "I did. And I'll do it again."

"You'll die first!"

The vampire pauses. "Is that a challenge? You dogs… you do so love a challenge. If it is, I accept. Last male standing gets the female for their own needs. What do you say, Wilder?"

I don't know what Chase is going to say, but I think the vampire is a moron.

This vampire might know enough about shifters to recognize me as one, but not enough to realize that you *never* come between a male wolf and the female he claims as his.

Good. He deserves whatever's coming to him when Chase rasps out, "I accept."

When the vampire sets me aside, promising to finish what we started as soon as he's done, it's all I can do not to laugh. He's signing his own death warrant and he doesn't even know it.

He opens his mouth, making sure Chase can see his long, pointy fangs. He flexes his fingers, his fingernails sharpening into claws. And then he grins.

Sick bastard.

Chase obviously agrees. His golden eyes flashing, he lets his feral beast out in a heartbeat. Bones crunch, deadly claws of his own unsheathe from his newly formed, furless paws, while fangs thicker than the vamp's —if not as long—jut from a crowded mouth.

He snarls, and the vampire flies at him. The sound their bodies make when they collide rattles the whole damn woods.

In reality, the fight doesn't last long. What seems like an eternity is probably only three or four minutes tops, but in a challenge? That *is* an eternity. I go light-headed from holding my breath in worry, silently cheering Chase on so that I don't distract him.

Did I think the air couldn't stink more of blood? I'm wrong. As soon as the two males collide, fangs flashing, claws slashing, bones crunching as they try to rip each other apart... the whole forest becomes covered in blood. The vamp stink grows worse, but Chase's blood joins it.

The scent of his blood makes my wolf insane. Only knowing that it's against pack law to interfere with a challenge keeps me on the edge of their battle. Even if a vampire isn't aware of our traditions, breaking them might be the one thing that Chase will never forgive me.

I can't help him.

Good thing that, nearing the end of the fight, I realize

that he doesn't need my help. He's as battered as the vamp, but Chase wants the win more. I almost wonder if he let the vampire get some nasty hits in just so he could maneuver him into a better position because, as soon as Chase locks his hands around the vampire's throat, his muscles bulge and he not only snaps the vampire's neck. He turns it into a stump!

The second the vampire is *dead* dead—and having your head ripped clean off your shoulders is a pretty good sign you're not gonna come back from that—Chase drops the head, kicks the body aside, then staggers toward me.

Right before he reaches me, he drops. Panic welling up inside of me, I throw myself down to my knees. He's on his, slumping forward, and through the patchy fur that covers his bare chest, all I see are gaping wounds and smears of blood.

Chase killed the vampire, but it hadn't been easy.

"Chase? Are you okay?"

At the sound of my frantic voice, the big idiot starts crawling on his knees toward me. His one hand is tucked to his torn-up chest, but he uses the other to gesture for me.

I hobble toward him.

He hooks his arm around me, pulling me against his body. Blood—the vampire's and Chase's—covers my clothes. I don't give a shit. I wrap my arms around his middle, just grateful we're both alive.

He's murmuring something into my hair. It's unintelligible over his choppy breathing. Before long, I realize he's not saying words, but making soothing sounds to calm the both of us. Bowing over my body, he laps at my ripped throat, cleaning out the vampire's mark on my skin. Half-feral, half-Chase, he's gentle as ever as he tends to me, mere seconds after ruthlessly decapitating a vampire.

Some girls like flowers. Luna knows I do. But to protect me? To keep me safe?

Is there anything sexier than that?

I want to tell him I'm sorry. That he shouldn't have bitten me, but that I shouldn't have run away. That I didn't truly believe he'd always come for me until he did.

I want to ask him how he found me.

But I don't. As I shift in his arms, deciding it's my turn to tend to his wounds, to make sure that my protector isn't too injured, I begin to notice all of the gouges, the claw marks, the scratches, and the bites that cover him.

Vampires are nasty fighters. They have claws and fangs, too, just like us shifters, but they can access them in their two-legged form in a way that most shifters can't. Alphas have more control over their bodies than regular wolves, but Chase didn't rely on his alpha side. He nearly went full-feral to fight that vamp, and he barely won.

Once I take stock of the wounds on his chest—some of them slowly beginning to close over—I see why the fight was as close as it was.

Picking up his hand, careful not to jostle it when he doesn't hide his wince, I stare down at it in horror.

"Holy shit, Chase! Did the vampire do this to you?"

"No." His voice is harsh. Choppy. He still answers me. "I did that."

His hand is mangled. *Chewed*. The bones are crushed.

The skin around his wrist is burned through, angry, red, and raw.

And I remember. The shackle.

The silver.

With a guilty pit forming in my belly, I admit that the silver explains the burns. But what about the rest of his hand?

My voice is a shaky whisper as I ask, "What did you do?"

"I needed to get out of the chains," he explains, as if attempting to gnaw off your own hand to get out of a shackle is the most rational thing in the world. "You were scared. I had to get to you."

I *was* scared. Terrified, actually, once I realized I had a vampire on my tail.

But how did he *know*?

My wolf yips, trying to get me to understand. I'm still feeling muddled. I have no idea what she's trying to tell me.

I'd opened up the bond I shared with West, hoping he might sense me on the other end and know that I was in trouble. That I needed help. With Chase in chains, I thought it was safe. He wouldn't be able to fight West, and I might be able to find the escape I've been looking for.

Only Chase found me first.

"How did you know?"

With his good hand, he pounds his bloody chest. "I felt you. In here."

"Like... like a bond?"

His eyes gleam, and I know that's exactly what he thinks it is.

"It's been there since the beginning," he says gruffly, daring me to argue. When I don't, he adds, "I told you. Fuck Fate. I chose you. My wolf did, too. Everything I am... everything I'll ever be... it's always been yours. I was just waiting for you to notice."

Oh, believe me.

I'm definitely noticing.

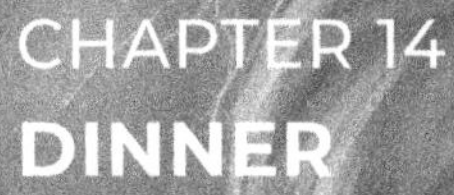

CHAPTER 14
DINNER

Chase doesn't have a phone in his cabin.

I already knew that. He made it clear when he removed my chains for the last time. A loner by choice even before he turned feral, he had no friends. No family. It was like pulling teeth to get him to admit as much—though I kind of guessed already—and he only did to point out the fact that he very rarely had contact with the outside world.

Translation: no one would hear me scream.

He has no one to call, so of course he doesn't have a phone; I don't, either, since mine is somewhere back in Hickory, I'm sure. To let Henry know that he had to kill the vampire that attacked us, Chase would have to head into Sacre Coeur and meet the leader of the Cadre at his office in person.

He heads out the morning after. He refuses to go until he's sure I'm completely healed, and I do the same for him. By the time he carries me back to the cabin, both of my bites are gone. Smartly, he doesn't mention the one he

177

gave me, only fussing over the one I got courtesy of the vamp.

Chase takes a little longer to heal. He really did a number on his hand, and that's not counting the injuries he got fighting a vampire hopped up on shifter blood. I made him take a shower so I could see how bad they were when the blood washed off. When I saw they were worse than I thought, I made him lie down.

My feral alpha was as submissive as a kitten. He went straight to bed, and I searched the bathroom for the salve he had that would speed up his healing. It was the jar he used when the silver of the chains burned my skin the time I tried to snap them. I figured, if it worked on silver, it might work on vampire bites, and it did.

Score one for Quinn.

By morning, he was healed up, too. There was no delaying it at that point. He had to go see Henry.

He assured me they have a good working relationship. I still don't quite understand why Chase would've chosen to live just off of a Fang City in the first place. At least, with the fang around his neck, I knew he would be safe when he meets with Henry.

I stayed behind. Of course I did. Chase wants to protect me, and there's no denying that I'm the one that vamp targeted. He doesn't want it to happen again. Neither do I.

That's why, after Chase sets out, I decide to stick inside of the cabin. I would've liked to visit the garden, but considering what happened the last time I did— Chase going feral, me going on the run, the vamp biting the shit out of my neck after Chase already had—it's probably a better bet to stay inside.

Chase wasn't sure how long he'd be. It all depended on Henry's busy schedule and when the Cadre leader could fit him in. He promised that, at the latest, he'd be home by dinner.

Taking him at his word, I figure out how I'm going to spend the day so I don't go crazy worrying about him telling the most powerful vampire nearby that he killed one of his.

I'm going to cook dinner.

Way I see it, it's my turn to feed him. I think of it as a thank you for saving my life, and if he wants to read more into it, well... he wouldn't be wrong.

The kitchen is stocked. The pantry is full. He has a freezer full of every kind of meat a shifter could want. I pick out a beef tenderloin, then grab a bag of potatoes to start peeling.

I'm not the quickest cook. I make a disaster in the kitchen, and it takes me twice as long because I try to clean up as I go. At least I'm sure it'll be somewhat tasty when it's done. Plus, Chase is a little later than I thought he'd be, so that gives me enough time to let the tenderloin rest when it's done.

I made mashed potatoes and asparagus as a side. I toasted pre-made rolls in the oven and left a crock of butter out to soften. I'm just setting the rolls down on the table with the rest of the food when I hear the front door to the cabin open.

The stink of vampire filters in first, though it's almost

immediately replaced by Chase's musk. His alpha aura reaches out to caress my skin, as if he's searching for me.

I give him a hand. "In the kitchen!"

Apart from looking exhausted, he's in one piece. I sniff. He doesn't have any blood on him.

That's a good sign.

"How did it go?"

"Henry understood. That's all that matters. Nolan came on my land and he targeted my mate." He pauses, waiting for me to argue with him. His eyes spark again when I don't. "We both know I had every right to kill him for biting you. He won't retaliate."

I blink. "Retaliate? Was that something that might've happened?"

He doesn't say anything. He just stares at the spread I have out on the table.

"Chase?"

"I... don't worry about it. Everything's fine."

If he says so. He's too preoccupied with the food. I'll just have to get more out of him later.

For now—

I wait for him to ask me about the meal. When he doesn't, I gesture for him to sit. "As you can see, I just finished cooking dinner for you." Not us, Chase. *You.* Hint, hint. "Sit with me. Let's eat. I mean, you've got to be hungry."

"I'm starved," Chase admits. He hesitates, and when he glances over at me, I swear I see hope burning in the depths of his golden eyes. "You cooked this? For me?"

"Yup." He's still standing there. "Aren't you going to eat?"

"Actually, I wanted to talk to you about something first."

"Oh." I try to hide my disappointment. I should've guessed cooking for him would lose any meaning after how many times I reminded him I was only eating because I had to. "Yeah. Sure. Food can wait."

Chase's gaze roves over my face. I don't know what he sees there, but it has him sitting down and reaching for the fork. With intense focus, he starts shoveling the food into his mouth.

I stifle a short giggle, irrationally pleased that he's tasting my food. "Slow down. You're going to choke."

"Can't," he says around a mouthful of potato. "It's too delicious."

"Eh. It's passable."

"You made this for me. I've never had better."

Oh. My cheeks warm as I flush in pleasure at his compliment.

Okay, then.

I join him at the table, taking a seat across from Chase. I go to make my own plate. Before I can grab it, he stops chewing and immediately takes the plate out of my hand. He's not rough, though he is determined to take it off of me, so I let him have it.

Chase swallows his mouthful, then starts piling food up on my plate. I watch as he picks the largest piece of tenderloin left on the serving dish before scooping out some mashed potatoes meticulously. He grabs one roll, thinks better of it, then reaches for one just a shade more golden brown.

No asparagus, I notice. I've given up wondering how

he knows when he does shit like this, but I *hate* asparagus. I only cooked it because it was in the fridge so I figured it was something Chase liked.

After placing the plate in front of me, he slides the rest of the asparagus onto his own plate. He eats it all.

As I eat like a normal shifter who isn't trying to gorge themself and get sick, Chase slows down. He matches my pace, the two of us having a companionable meal. I can still sense that he has something he wants to talk about, but he waits until we're both done with dinner, the dishes soaking in the sink, and the two of us sitting on the couch together before he mentions it again.

"Is it okay? Can we talk now?"

He looks so solemn, I can't help but tease him. "Hey… what's up with the long face? You're not breaking up with me, are you?"

Chase looks away.

What?

"Shit. I was kidding. What…" I move so that I'm standing in front of him. He still can't quite meet my eye. "Chase. Look at me."

A horrible suspicion slams into me as our eyes meet. My hand flies to my mouth. Between the gaps in my fingers, I say, "It happened, didn't it? When you went to the Fang City… you found your mate."

I always knew it wasn't me. I knew he had to have one out there.

Holy shit. Was it a vampire?

"I thought it was so weird that you'd want to live by vampires. I mean, it reeks, but you don't seem to mind it. I guess that would make total sense if you're supposed to be the mate of one of those fucking corpses. See! I knew it! All your talk of choosing me, of wanting me... you found her, didn't you? Is she pretty? Oh, Luna. And I fed you—"

Okay. I might've jumped the gun a little there. Chase's mouth had fallen open while I ranted, but since he didn't stop me, I kept on going. I probably wouldn't have stopped if it wasn't for the way that he finally breaks free of his sudden paralysis, hurrying toward me and placing his hands on my shoulders.

"Quinn."

"She's probably blonde, like Helene. With dainty little fangs and—"

"*Quinn.*"

I gulp. "What?"

"I didn't meet any other females, especially not a vamp one. And I'm not breaking up with you. You're mine. Until you walk away from me, you'll always be mine. That.. that's not what I wanted to talk about."

"Then what did you?"

He lets go of my shoulders, putting some space between us.

"Chase?"

"Look, I know I've fucked this up since day one. Every time I think I'm getting better, I inevitably screw up again. Like last night. I'm not doing it on purpose. Being an alpha... my wolf is strong enough to take what I want, and my feral side tells me I should. But I want you so bad that it means nothing if you're only here because I'm bigger than you or because I'm more dominant. You were right before. I'm not your mate. I'm only your captor."

He *was* my captor. That fact won't change.

But, when I was hiding from the vampire, it was Chase I thought of. It was Chase who I wanted to find me.

He said he would come after me. He did.

"You were," I begin, "but now—"

He gives his head a sharp shake. "I'm still feral. Last night proved that. I want to say I won't lose control again. I want to promise I won't bite you again. But I did that, and no matter how much I want you to trust me... to love me... to *choose* me... how can I expect you to do that when I can't even trust myself?"

"It's not you. It's the feral—"

"It's me. If you knew what made me like this..."

I take his hand in mine. "Then tell me. Help me understand."

Because he might've said he wasn't breaking up with me, but this ain't my first rodeo. This sounds like a text-book dumping speech.

It's not you, it's me...

Chase squeezes my fingers. And then, after a shuddering breath, he begins to speak.

I listen without a sound—or judgment.

"I was born into a small pack on the West Coast. The Wilder Pack. There were only ten of us, and I was the only one who was a true alpha from the time I was six. They couldn't let a six-year-old run the pack, obviously, so our Beta stepped up. My dad refused to leave our land, so we stayed. I always knew I'd take over when I got older, but power is a heady thing. Dane didn't want to give over control to me. He wanted to keep it. I let him. I was only fifteen. I didn't care. He did. He tried to push me from the pack, telling me a young alpha needed to see the world.

"I didn't know he was trying to get rid of me. He wanted me to leave. I left because it was Alpha's orders. At least... I told myself that because I didn't want to admit that my wolf was chafing against having to listen to a less dominant leader. It was better to be on my own."

I nod. I know exactly what he means. Almost everyone in the Sylvan Pack was more dominant than me, so maybe not that part, but being on my own? I was as much of a lone wolf as I could be while still staying a packmate.

Taking heart in my nod, Chase leads me over to the couch again. Once we're seated, he continues.

"I spent months away at a time, but I always went back. Until... one day, about a year later, they were all gone. No," he corrects, "not gone. *Dead*. My whole pack was wiped out by a single rogue vampire that stumbled on their territory." He pauses, then glances at the closed window. "He was from Sacre Coeur."

I gasp. "No."

"Yes. It took me three years to find him. All I had was his stink mingling with the blood of my family. Blood and death... it wasn't easy, but I was determined. I was nineteen when I tracked him to the Fang City, but I'd been a lone wolf all that time. I wasn't strong enough to fight him. So I bided my time, staking this land out as mine."

Still holding onto my hand as if it's a lifeline, he uses the other to gesture around him. "I built this cabin. Brick by brick, board by board. I had money. Everything that belonged to my old pack was mine, and I used it for my vengeance. I bought this land, so the vampires couldn't expand past their borders, and I built this cabin with the goal of one day finding a way past the vampires so that I could slaughter one of their own."

He says he was nineteen. The male in front of me is in his late twenties at least, if not his early thirties.

"Did you?" I whisper. For the young alpha he was, I desperately hope the answer is yes.

"No."

Damn it.

He sighs. "The Cadre knew I was here. They knew what I was doing. They let me build the cabin, and they allowed me to test their borders. I think... I think I amused Henry. That's a rarity to someone as old as he is, and because I did, he left me to it. He's a good judge of character, Henry. He knew I wanted revenge for something. He guessed I planned on attacking his city. He would've stopped me if I tried, but..."

His voice trails off. I can sense how much this is costing him, finally telling me the truth of his past, but as much as I need to hear this, he needs to say it.

So, with another squeeze, I wordlessly encourage Chase to continue.

He does.

"It was one vampire who destroyed my pack. A rogue who was good at pretending he was sane." Chase scoffs. "Kind of like me. He was responsible. Not the humans who live in the Fang City for supernatural protection. Not the vamps just living their lives. One male. I couldn't hurt the others. I just wanted *him*.

"Henry found out who I was hunting. I don't know

how, and I've never asked. It was a couple of years after I finished my cabin. I'd given up hope of finding my parents' murderer, but I stayed because I couldn't go back home. Then, one day, the leader of the Cadre showed up on my doorstep. Henry found the rogue, and he had him executed. He brought me his head, then he gave me his fang." Chase pats the vampire fang hanging off of his chain. "We made our deal that day. I got my revenge. If he wanted to share my territory, I was more than happy to. But…"

Somehow, I knew there would be a 'but'. "But?"

"But there was a problem. Henry killed Lucius for me. I got my revenge. I was satisfied. My wolf… wasn't."

"Oh."

"I thought losing my pack was the worst thing that could happen. I was wrong, Quinn. Do you know what really is? Apart from losing a mate, that is?"

I shake my head.

"Losing the last of my humanity."

And… there it is.

"That's how you became feral," I say, understanding the point of everything he just told me. "Your wolf didn't get to avenge his fallen packmates."

"I managed to stay sane up until about a year ago. It was fighting a losing battle. For years, I could feel my wolf twisting, changing, breaking. Eventually, my outside matched the way my wolf felt. After that, I could *only* feel when that… thing was in control. When that happened, I ran from here. I ran and I ran, and I didn't stop running until the time I passed the outer limits of a wolf territory and the most enticing scent stopped me in my tracks."

The whole time he was talking, Chase would only look at me for a split second before he glanced away. He stared at his lap. He stared at our joined hands. He looked over at the doorway to his cabin or watched the empty fire grate.

Just then he meets my eyes again. And, this time, he keeps his gaze on me.

"Rainwater," he whispers. "You smell like rainwater and hope. You smell like the home I lost, and the one I would've done everything to have again." His chest rises, then falls with the force of his exhale. "Even make you a feral's captive. And now you know it."

His expression says he believes that, now that he's told me his truth, I'll get up and leave him.

I tried. It didn't take.

Hey. I'm a shifter. I'll always see things differently. My wolf was smitten almost from the beginning. Chase won her over with his plotting, his dedication, his show of strength, and the way he proved that he could take care of me.

My human half took a little more convincing. But after I saw the garden... Yeah. I didn't stand a chance.

He was so sure he could convince me to stay. Damn it, he was right.

"Okay."

He leans back, taking in my whole face. "Okay?" he echoes.

I shrug. "Hey. You said to give you until the Luna. Just because you broke your vow, doesn't mean I'm going to break mine."

He opens his mouth.

"Me running from you doesn't count. You were feral, and I was pissed off from being bitten. Not either of our finest moments."

Chase exhales softly. "Do you mean it? Could you… do you think you might choose me? Someday?"

I'm still holding his hand. I lift up, pressing my lips to his heated skin, enjoying the way it makes my feral alpha rumble. "I think I might be able to do that."

CHAPTER 15
SANDALWOOD

Did I think that Chase seemed different in the days following him first bringing me to his cabin? That's nothing compared to the change that comes over him after I give him one last chance to prove himself.

At least, that's what he thinks he's doing. Me? I'm pretty much a done deal.

He chose me. As a wolf, a man, or some twisted combination of both with piss poor self-control, he wanted me. How could a she-wolf who desired nothing more than to be loved put up a fight against *that*?

He won me over slowly. A couple of weeks might not seem like slow to a non-shifter, but it is. We usually know our mates instinctively—whether they're given to us by the Luna or we choose them on our own—and if I hadn't been so hung up on West, maybe I would've seen what was right in front of me all along.

I fell for the broken male who lost everything, yet who could still touch me as though I was more than that.

The Luna is almost completely full. Four days until she's at her peak and any shifter couples could perform the Luna Ceremony and receive her blessing and a bond. Unless something goes terribly wrong between now and then, I might just be a mated she-wolf in a couple of more days.

Do I tell Chase that? Nah. Though I've basically gotten past his way of courting me in the beginning—he's a feral, and I finally understand that part of him will probably always be whether we have a bond or not—I still get a little pleasure making him squirm.

Besides, nothing ever goes right for me. I guess, deep down, I'm still waiting for something to go wrong.

Two days after the vampire attacked me, I'm afraid it does.

We're sitting in the living room. Though Chase has a television, he rarely uses it, and I kind of commandeered it over the last couple of weeks. He doesn't have internet or streaming services like we do back in Hickory—something I will be changing ASAP—but he gets a couple of basic cable channels.

It's after dinner. He's sitting on the couch, bare-chested as always, while I'm curled up into his side. The warmth of his skin does more to heat me up than the fire we lit earlier. It's cozy. Homey. My wolf is dozing, content to be so close to her mate, while I breathe in Chase's intoxicating musk.

I feel safe with him. Something I never would've believed after his ambush, but I do. He's my protector. I can let down my guard with him because I know that Chase never will.

So when his body goes hard and tight, stiffening beneath my cheek? I notice.

I glance up at him. His cheeks are hollowed. His nostrils are flaring.

His golden eyes have that warning gleam I know so well.

I sit up. "What's wrong?"

He doesn't deny it. Instead, placing one hand possessively on my thigh, he grates out one word: "Vampires."

"What?"

"I sense them. They're on our immediate territory." He narrows his gaze, concentrating. "At least two. I sense a female and a male, but there could be more. They're heading this way."

I'm not even a little surprised that he can tell. Bishop is like that, too. An Alpha imprints on their pack and his territory, all the more reason I still have trouble understanding how Chase was able to infiltrate Hickory without even Bishop knowing.

Then again, maybe he did. One of an Alpha's main jobs is to make sure their packmates are protected. If he sensed Chase stalking me and could tell that he was no danger to me, maybe he let him. Could be.

When it comes to Chase, though, I don't doubt his instincts. We might be a pack of two now, but he's lived on this land for almost twelve years. He knows every inch of it the same way that I could navigate the woods of Hickory blindfolded if I had to. If someone is trespassing out there, he'll know it.

He looks pissed, but not surprised.

"Were you expecting visitors?" I ask.

He shakes his head. "No. I talked to Henry. I told him what happened. Nolan attacked my mate. He forfeited his life when he bit you. Even if he hadn't challenged me, by vamp law, I could take his head."

Pack law is clear like that, too. I'd wondered if the vampires would be ticked off that Chase killed one of their own, but he assured me that that wasn't the case.

So what are vampires doing here?

When I ask Chase that, he squeezes my thigh, then rises up from the couch. "I don't know, but I'm going to find out. Stay inside the cabin. I'll be right back."

I nod. "You better, or I'm coming after you."

Despite the fierce look in his eyes, his lips curve. He loves it when I show concern for him, even if it's pretty much unnecessary.

With a stolen kiss to the top of my head, Chase heads out of the room. He disappears down the hall, returning less than a minute later. He's tugged on a t-shirt, pulling his necklace out so that the fang is on display. As always, he's barefoot, but he must have decided this meeting is important if he's gotten dressed.

Or maybe that's because I might've mentioned just how much I love his chest—and how a possessive she-wolf doesn't share. If there's a female out there, like he guessed, he wouldn't let her see what belongs to me.

And doesn't that just make me all warm and fuzzy inside?

After pausing to lay his hand on my shoulder, assuring me without words that he'll be safe, Chase heads out the front door. I feel his slipping aura and know that he's racing to meet the vampires before they make it to the cabin.

Like he said, he isn't gone long. Five minutes, maybe, and my wolf stops her pacing as she cocks her ear. I do the same. Chase isn't bothering to step lightly as he returns to the cabin.

I wonder why.

He pushes the front door in, waiting at the entrance. I run my gaze over him, exhaling when I see that he looks exactly the same as before. No bite marks, no slashes. I sniff softly, sampling the air. No more blood than the stench floating in through the open door.

He doesn't step inside. That's weird.

"Chase? Who was out there?"

"Giorgio and Louise." His brow furrows. "Cadre vamps."

"What did they want?"

"Henry needs to see me. He has something he has to tell me, but he couldn't come in person. He sent two of his top vamps to let me know. I'm supposed to head down to Sacre Coeur right now."

It's already dark. I can see the faint beams from the nearly-full Luna shining down behind him, silhouetting Chase.

"This late?" I ask.

"Yeah." He's frowning now. "I have to go. He knows what I am. He knows what kind of wolf I am, too. He didn't order me to see him. He asked. Cadre vamps don't ask. I have to go."

Following on the heels of Chase killing that Nolan vamp? He does. I know he does. He has a truce with

Henry, and the challenge didn't change that, but what if he ignores this request for a meeting?

"Do you want me to go with you?"

His jaw tightens. I know what his answer is going to be even before he says, "No. I need you to stay inside of the cabin. You'll be safe here, and I'll be back before you know it."

I get up from the couch. He's clutching the doorjamb with one hand, but the other reaches out toward me. He does that a lot. If my scent attracted him and my voice lulled his savage beast, the touch of my skin and the feel of my hair against him is enough to keep him in complete control.

Right now, I get the feeling he needs that.

I step into Chase. His free hand closes around me in a hug.

"I'll be safe." *I'm not leaving again.* "Will you be?"

His chin is resting on the top of my head so I feel it when he nods. "Of course. When I have my Quinn waiting for me, nothing can stop me from getting back to her. I told you when I first brought you home with me. I will always come for you, no matter what."

He did.

I used to think it was a threat. Now I know better. It's a promise.

I kiss the t-shirt material stretching between his sculpted pecs. "I'm holding you to that, Chase."

I'm nibbling on my thumbnail, tapping my foot against the floor as I wait for Chase to come back.

I won't go to bed without him. I could try, but it would be pointless. I have this growing sensation that something bad is about to happen. I'd rather stand in the living room, waiting for his eventual return.

The television is off. The noise was only bothering me before. The quiet is driving me crazy, too, but at least it can help me pick up on any sounds outside. Between that and Chase's alpha aura, I should be able to sense him when he's almost back.

An hour goes by, give or take. I don't know. Using his last trip to Sacre Coeur as a guide, it's nowhere near long enough for Chase to head into the Fang City, have an emergency meeting with the head of the Cadre, and come back.

So why do I hear soft footsteps approaching the cabin?

I go still. He told me that the vampires would never dare come this close to his house. The only reason Nolan was able to pounce on me in the first place was because I left Chase's immediate territory without a fang to protect me from the vampire's thirst.

My wolf is up, prowling around. She heard it, too, and she's growling softly under her breath.

And that's when a familiar scent breaks through the vampiric miasma outside. Despite the closed door and the shut windows, it finds me.

Sandalwood.

West.

It's impossible, but also undeniable. It's not just the

scent. Now that I've locked on it, it wraps around me, making my wolf stop in her tracks. It's not alone, either. A handful of other scents—all of them familiar—are mingled with his. Packmates. I can't decipher whose is whose, but I know them.

Am I hallucinating?

The doorknob turns. Without a knock, the door pushes in, and I'm standing in the perfect spot in the middle of the living room to see the males standing on the porch.

There are four of them, actually. One in the lead, three forming a triangle behind him. Tucker. Joey. Darrin.

And, of course, West.

"Quinn?" Like always, his voice is clipped, his expression closed-off and chilly. While relief comes from some of the other males out there, I don't sense any from West even as he says, "Thank the Luna. We found you."

My jaw drops. For a moment, I goggle at him, before I blink rapid-fire a couple of times.

Nope. He's still standing there on the porch in front of me.

I take a step back into the safety of the cabin. "West? What are you doing here?"

"Isn't it obvious? I've come for my mate."

"Your *what*?"

West looks around as he steps into the front room. The other three hang at his back. "Where is he? He's a smart male, I'll give him that. He hid his scent well in Hickory, and he covered up yours and his with the blood and death that surrounds these woods. It took us hours to track you, Quinn. Where is he? I want to face him."

He says face him. I know shifter males. He means *kill* him.

"You have to go," I say, barely able to hide my panic. "Before he sees you. You have to go."

"Not without you."

No.

I grab West's sleeve. The other three are his backup and, honestly, no real concern. I focus on the Beta. "Go. Now." I tug on his sleeve. "I'll stay. I'm fine. Go back to Hickory and let Bishop know not to worry about me."

Did I think that that would convince West? Maybe if I didn't sound like I was freaking out, it might've.

He disentangles his sleeve from my grip, announcing, "Look at her. She's too afraid to leave him." West pulls me into his arms, tucking me under his chin. His hand ghosts over my hair. "Ah, Quinn. What did that bastard do to you?"

I don't answer. I can't. He's not listening to me, and I'm still in shock that he's here. That he called me his mate.

He's touching me, too. I would've given anything a few weeks ago to know what it was like to find warmth in his arms, but now I feel nothing but an iciness in the pit of my stomach. My wolf is pacing back and forth, snapping her jaws, confused. She senses West's wolf, recognizes him as someone she should respect, someone she should want to be with, but he doesn't smell like *mate*.

Because he isn't Chase.

West takes my silence as confirmation that something bad did happen to me. And, maybe if he found me two weeks ago, I would've agreed. Being drugged, being chained... it sucked. But I understand why Chase did it.

He was desperate. He thought I was his mate. He would've done anything to keep me with him.

Wouldn't I have done the same if I was dominant enough to make a beta wolf mine?

If I could have chained West up to take him away from Helene, I would've. Now? I want to ask him why he's here. I'm not his mate. I'll never be his mate. He made that clear when he rejected me six months ago and let our bond grow jagged between us before I discovered how to cut him off myself.

Until I went ahead and opened it up while I was fleeing Chase...

Uh-oh.

No wonder they think he's done something to me. The bond was open when I was running, but I'd been angry then, only wanting to let my packmates know that I was alive and I was on my way home. It was still open, though, when the vampire attacked me.

Even if West kept his side of our bond closed, no way he could've missed my reaction to the pain as Nolan bit me, or how absolutely terrified I was when I thought the vamp was going to kill Chase.

He came. I don't know why, since every one of us knows I'm not his true mate, but he's here.

And he brought help.

There are four of them. West, Tucker, Joey, and Darrin. One beta and three deltas. None of them is an alpha wolf—thank the Luna that Bishop had to stay behind in Hickory when these four set out—but they're all part of the Sylvan Pack's inner circle. They're protectors, each one of them, and fierce fighters.

So is Chase. If he discovers that four of my old pack-mates came to his cabin to bring me home, there will be no holding his feral side back. Four on one odds aren't great, but I've seen him destroy a vampire. He could take them on. He might even win, which means that these four will die.

If they don't, Chase will.

I can't let that happen.

Pulling away from West, I clutch his shirt with trembling fingers. "West, you don't understand—"

"Sh. It's okay, sweetheart." *Sweetheart*? What the fuck? "You're safe now."

I was safe before.

"West, please—"

He ignores me. Chase... he would never, but West does.

Turning to the others, he's not just West anymore. He's the Beta of the Sylvan Pack as he gives them an order. "Take Quinn back to Hickory. I'll stay here and take care of the wolf."

What? No! This is exactly what I was afraid of all along. In the beginning, I didn't want the feral to destroy my fated mate for the sole crime of Fate giving him to me. Now? I don't want to see West die for the same reason. He never wanted me. I don't know why he's here now, but despite how my relationship with Chase has changed, I know he'll always see West as a rival until we have a mate bond between us.

The Luna is still four days out. We have an undeniable connection, sure, but it's nothing like the bond I share with West—and Chase knows it.

"He's a feral," I blurt out.

West exchanges a look with Tucker. Tucker nods, and West's cold, controlled expression cracks just enough to be noticeable.

"That explains everything," he says, more to the male wolves than to me. "Did he hurt you?" That one's for me. "Did he... force you?"

What?

"Are you asking if he fucked me?"

He blanches. He probably didn't expect me to put it out there like that. Clearing his throat, not quite meeting my eyes, he says, "Yes."

"He didn't." That's the truth. Chase is so desperate to make sure that he doesn't accidentally bite me again that the most we've done the last two days is kiss. "Not that it's any of your business, but he didn't."

West's grey eyes glimmer. They don't quite go shifter gold, but I see the emotion he's trying to hide before he says, "You're my promised mate, Quinn. My intended. It *is* my business."

No the fuck it isn't. One look at his handsome face, though, and I can tell it's not worth arguing with him over it. Something has happened since I was stolen from Hickory, but now is not the time to ask about it. With these four here, I can't risk Chase coming back to find our unwanted visitors.

I have to leave with them. I'm one delta she-wolf facing off against four of her much more dominant packmates. Even if West wasn't the Beta, I would never be able to refuse them if they insisted on me walking out of that door.

The most I can do is get out before Chase challenges them. Because he will. I know he will.

I can't let that happen.

I'm no damsel in distress. I never have been. Even when Chase had me chained up in the basement—something I will never, ever tell these wolves since they already expect the worst—I didn't shy away from him. I distinctly remember threatening to rip off his dick if he got any sick ideas in his head.

But West is used to an omega female. If Helene had been taken captive by a feral, how would she act?

I throw myself back at West, wrapping my arms around his waist. He stiffens for a moment before closing his arms around me.

Purposely putting a tremble in my voice, I whisper, "Don't leave me, West. Don't stay behind. I don't want any of you to. You came to bring me back to Hickory. Let's go. Let's go now, all of us."

West sucks in a breath.

Did it work? Luna, please... please please please let it have worked.

"Of course, my mate. If that's what you want."

Yes!

"It is." I sniffle for good measure. "I'm ready."

"You heard her. Come on. Let's get her out of here before that feral monster returns for her again."

I'm not his mate. The way West so readily gives in to my theatrics... I know then and there that I'm not his mate, no matter what he's saying now. Because, as a dominant shifter male, no way in hell would he walk away from challenging Chase. If he thought of me as his, he would make the feral pay for what he did. His own wolf would need it otherwise he would never be satisfied.

Just like how Chase's wolf needed vengeance on the rogue that decimated his pack, West's should hunger for revenge on the feral who stole his mate away from him.

But he doesn't want it. Despite his words, he's not here because I'm his mate. He's here because he feels like he should be, and as the Beta, it's his *duty*.

Good. Because I'm not his mate, either.

Not anymore.

Now I just have to hope that Chase really meant it when he said he would always come for me.

And that he doesn't take it as the ultimate betrayal when he walks into the cabin, discovers I'm gone, and inevitably recognizes one of the male scents lingering in his space as West's.

I don't know why I thought they'd come on foot. I mean, I knew that Chase had used a truck to travel from Hickory to just outside of Sacre Coeur. Considering the last my packmates knew was that I was missing, then I was running, then I was hurt, and finally terrified, they had no idea what they were going to find when West followed his half of our bond to me.

Especially since I threw up a block as soon as I remembered to. For all they knew, closing it off meant I'd succumbed. No wonder they all looked at me like they'd seen a ghost when the door flew open and I was standing in the middle of the room.

Joey and Darrin are murmuring to each other. With West hurrying me through the woods, Tucker taking the lead to clear the path, I guess they thought that their bringing up the rear meant that I couldn't hear them.

They're wrong.

I can pick up their concerns for me. None of them are alphas so they can't tell what part of what I said was true and what was a lie. With the exception of West, I've slept with every other male here. It was no big deal at the time, and I don't regret it one bit. Still, knowing how free I used to be with my affection, they both doubt that my feral hasn't spent the last two-plus weeks screwing me senseless.

It doesn't help that I carry his scent on me. On my skin, on my clothes, on my hair... there's no denying that he's touched me and I've touched him. For Luna's sake, Chase and I sleep in the same bed. I was living in his cabin. Of course I smell like him!

Before, my packmates pitied me because they knew my fated mate rejected me. Now they feel sorry for me because they're sure I've been a feral's chew toy since I've been missing.

Let them think what they want. I've never really cared what other wolves thought about me before, and after the last six months, I've developed a hard shell. So long as we get out of here before someone gets hurt, I don't care. I'll go back to Hickory like they want, I'll explain everything to Bishop, and then I'm gone. If Chase doesn't come for me first, I'm going back to him.

And not just because I promised I'd stay until the next full moon...

They came by car. I'm squeezed between West and Joey in the backseat, with Tucker and Darrin up front. Smart. I've seen Darrin drive before. Guy's got a lead foot and a need to find adrenaline wherever he can. He drives like we're invincible instead of simply supernatural.

We're back on pack land before midnight.

I can't wait to hop out of the car. Being around four

male shifters has rubbed my wolf so raw, I have to keep my teeth gritted to keep her snarls from escaping me. What used to signal *safe* to me is a big, honking neon *danger* sign. They're too close and it's almost all I can do to resist the urge to unsheathe my tiny claws and slash at them to get them to back away.

West... he's too close. He's not quite touching me anymore, though this is the closest we've been since we recognized the mating bond springing up between us. This nearness has my stomach flip-flopping—and not in the good way.

When Joey starts to ask me for details about what happened with the feral, West silences him with a look. Heeding the Beta, Joey shuts up, but I know he's not only just curious. He's dying to know what happened. They all are. But West is the highest-ranked shifter in the car and they follow his lead.

It's an awkward, quiet ride back. I almost scream out loud just to break up the tension. The only reason I don't is because my packmates—all of them except West, that is—are watching me closely as if they expect me to do just that. They expect me to break.

I just want to go to sleep, wake up, and discover I'm curled up next to Chase.

Before, all I wanted was to get away from him. I was dying to get back to Hickory, even though I knew West wouldn't be waiting for me. Now he's here, he's bringing me home, he's calling me his *mate*... and I just want to be back in the cabin in the woods, with my garden and my male.

West didn't bring me a flower, I realize. I was missing

for just about three weeks and he showed up like my knight in furry armor—and he didn't bring me a flower.

If I was Helene, he would've.

Surprisingly, that realization... it doesn't hurt anymore. It's just fact. He can call me his mate all he wants, but I know where his heart truly lies. It's where it always has been: with a beautiful omega she-wolf who I was jealous of for way too long.

Which makes my decision to skip out on my old pack as soon as possible a sound one.

The Sylvan Pack is based in the woods; it's how we got our name after all. The original pack didn't go for grandiose names. We live in the woods, we're the Sylvan Pack. The majority of our forest is made up of hickory trees? Boom. Our community is known as Hickory. The heart of pack land is in the center of the circle where our ancestors first built their cabins? It's the pack circle.

On the edge of our land, on the side closest to the local human town, is where the pack council keeps the cars we all share. Fittingly enough, it's the pack garage, and Darrin drives us there. Once we all hop out of the car —and I mean that literally, I'm so ready to get away from their auras—we jog the rest of the way back to Hickory. I have two males on each side, as if they expect me to be attacked again.

Yeah, right. First of all, if Chase attacks anyone, it's not going to be me. Secondly, even if he's made it back to the cabin, I'm hours ahead of him. I don't expect him to drive. Knowing him the way I do, he'll go feral and run the entire way here.

I just hope I can intercept him in time before he decides to challenge my whole pack.

Four on one… I give Chase the edge. Dozens on one? With Bishop involved in the fight because, technically, I'm still one of his? And with West suddenly insisting on calling me his mate?

My feral is strong. He won't survive that.

I can't let anything happen to him. I *won't* let anything happen to him.

Too bad it's not going to be my choice.

All I want in life is to get to choose. When we cross into the inner border of Sylvan Pack territory, I move a few steps ahead, running in the direction of my cabin. As much as I wish I was still with Chase, I miss my home. I miss my stuff. Maybe… maybe this was a blessing in disguise. While I'm here, I can pack up everything I own so I can bring it back to Chase's cabin. Really make the place our home.

West moves ahead of me. Shaking his head, he tells me, "Not there, Quinn. Alpha wants to see us."

At that, the other wolves break off from me and West. Now that they're back, they have cabins of their own to go to, and they did what they were instructed to do. They brought me back to Hickory.

Seems like it was West's job to bring me before Bishop.

The porch light is on in the Alpha cabin. We don't enter through the front, though. That part of the cabin is saved for Bishop and Sofia, plus the pups they'll have together one day. As a packmate, I'm allowed to visit Bishop at any point during the day—when he's home—

and when that light is on at night, but only if I approach the back of his cabin where he keeps the den.

In a shifter pack, the Alpha's den is a safe place. We can bring any concerns to the Alpha there, knowing that he'll listen to what we have to say. Pack councils have their meets here, too, and if a she-wolf wants to talk to our Alpha female, Sofia is known to make the best cappuccino ever as we chit chat by the fireplace.

Tonight, Sofia is standing beside her mate as West opens the always unlocked door to the den before ushering me inside.

She smiles when she sees me, relief flooding her softly rounded face. "Quinn... I'm so glad you're home. We were so worried about you. Weren't we, baby?"

The Alpha nods.

Bishop Dupuis is the opposite of his sister. While Helene is fair-skinned, slender, blonde, and beautiful, Bishop is a hulking, tanned male with dark brown hair, a full beard, and a hard look in his dark gold eyes.

He's also a male of few words. Chase might've grunted a lot while he was struggling to keep his hold on his feral side, but Bishop? He's the big, strong, silent type. Before Sofia mated him—when he was still the future Alpha instead of the leader of our pack—West usually did the talking for him. Despite Bishop being five years older than West, they've been best friends for as far back as I can remember, and West was Bishop's right-hand wolf long before he was named Beta.

I always thought it was interesting that West always knew what Bishop was thinking. Just then, as the two males look at each other, I get the feeling it goes both ways.

West lets out a breath. "You were right. The prints we found belonged to a feral. He's the one who took Quinn."

Bishop frowns.

Sofia lays her hand on his forearm. Her pretty hazel eyes flicker over my face. "Oh my Luna... are you okay? I can wake up Ginnie, if you want. She can check you over, if you need her to."

Ginnie is the pack healer. I shake my head. "I'm fine. I just... if it's okay, I'd really rather go to my cabin. It's been a long night. Maybe we can talk again tomorrow?"

Bishop furrows his brow. His alpha aura slams into me like a gust of wind during a thunderstorm. I almost stumble.

Wow. I forgot what it was like to be around an alpha who has no problem using his dominance against me. I hadn't even dared to meet Bishop's eyes—I was focusing on his forehead, instead, so he didn't take any accidental eye contact as an inadvertent challenge—but the urge to bare my throat is so strong, I cock my head to the side, letting my sheet of hair fall over my shoulder.

Sofia slaps Bishop's arm. It's more of a gentle love tap, but it does the job. He reels in his aura enough that I can straighten again.

West hasn't moved. He's just standing there, like he's a soldier at attention.

Then again, he's the Beta. That's kind of his job.

Bishop jerks his chin at West.

He nods.

Sofia helpfully translates for me. "I think that's a great idea. West can bring you back to your cabin, Quinn, so you can get some rest. If you feel up to it, we can talk tomorrow."

Fingers crossed I'm gone by tomorrow.

I don't say that, though. I don't say anything that Bishop can tell is a lie.

So I just nod. "Thank you."

WEST FOLLOWED ME THE ENTIRE WAY HOME.

I couldn't shake him. No matter what I said or did, he refused to leave my side. He didn't throw the *m*-word around again, but he made it clear: Bishop and Sofia thought he should stay by me for the time being, so that's what he was going to do.

I drew the line at inviting him inside of my cabin. The Alpha couple didn't say that I had to, and it's a relief to bid him good night before closing the door in his face.

Bet he never expected *that*, huh?

The next morning, I meet with Bishop again. West knocks on my door, bright and early, to tell me that the Alpha wants to see me. He walks me over, then leaves me at the den, mumbling something about returning for me later.

That throws me. Not only doesn't West *not* mumble, but since when do I need a freaking bodyguard while in Hickory? Do they know that Chase will come after me again? That it wasn't a fluke he took me in the first place?

Or is something going on with West that I just don't understand?

Hoping it's the second one, I let myself into the den where Bishop is waiting for me.

Sofia had gone with Ginnie to check on Kara's twins —who were born while I was gone—so she misses the meeting. Fun for me, right? Without his mate to speak for him, I get to have a heart-to-heart with the Alpha of the Sylvan Pack.

It isn't so bad. He apologizes for letting Chase get that close to me in the first place, and when I point-blank ask him if he knew there was a shifter watching me, his only answer is, "I didn't know he was a feral or I would've stopped him before he took you."

Alphas. They do what they think is best for the pack, and he begrudgingly admits that he hoped I might reciprocate the strange shifter's attraction to me. He understood that I was his Beta's fated mate—something he respects since Sofia is his—but his parents were a chosen mating. He knew firsthand that they worked out, just like he knew that I'd never be happy with West.

It's weird. He makes it a point to tell me that. Not that West will never want me—which I already knew—but that I won't be happy settling with his best friend.

And it's not like he's trying to get me out of the picture so that West and Helene can finally be together. I asked. I have no shame, and it was so strange to have a one-on-one conversation with Bishop, I just went for it.

No. Helene is still promised to Rafael of the Gravetail Pack.

And West? Up until he came running to Bishop with the news that he finally felt me on the other side of his bond, he was still hoping that Helene would change her mind and choose him.

That's when he told Bishop that, if they found me alive and brought me back to Hickory, he would make me his forever mate as soon as I was willing to perform the Luna Ceremony with him.

That... that brought our little chat to a screeching halt. I didn't believe him. Bishop's my Alpha, and I almost accused him of being full of shit. If he could keep something like a strange wolf stalking me for nine months from me for all that time because he thought it was for the best, who knows what his motives are now?

Turns out? He was telling the truth.

Know how I know?

That night, after I managed to slip out of the Alpha's den on my own, heading out to my favorite spot in the woods, then dashing back to my cabin when I smelled sandalwood on the breeze searching for me, West finally tracked me down.

And it's not like he didn't know where I'd be. Since my forcible return last night, I've had more eyes on me than ever before. Each and every one of my packmates is dying with curiosity over my abduction, plus the patrollers are watching me so closely, it's like they expect Chase to show up in the middle of Hickory to claim me or something.

He hasn't yet. I try not to let it bother me that it's been twenty-four hours since I've seen him last—more than enough time for him to finish his business with Henry, discover I'm gone, then come for me—and there's still no sign of him.

I'd had high hopes when I went out into the grove. I know his scent now. Even if he rolled around in a tub full of wolfsbane, it doesn't matter. I'd recognize him anywhere.

But he hasn't come for me yet.

West did, though.

When I peek out of my window and see him on my doorstep, I almost want to call out, "Nobody's home." It would be pointless, since his wolf would've told him I'm inside even before my voice would've confirmed it, but I don't want to see him right now.

I also don't think I have a choice.

Pulling open the door, I cock my hip against it, barring him from coming inside. "West. I thought you didn't have to watch me when I was safe inside of my cabin."

A flush rises high on his tanned cheeks. Bulls-eye. I knew Bishop had them keeping a close eye on me.

"Can I come in?"

I pretend to think about it for a moment. "I don't think that's a good idea," I say honestly. "Why don't you tell me what you want out here first?"

He clears his throat. "Very well. I've come to ask you if you'll accept me as your forever mate? The Luna chose us for each other, and I know I... might not have reacted to that news as I should've, but I did a lot of thinking while you were gone." Gone, he says. Not missing. Not abducted. For Luna's sake, he sounds as if I was on a three-hour cruise or something, not living with a feral for three weeks. "I shouldn't have tried to go against Fate. The Luna rises in three days. Will you have me then?"

I can't help myself. I laugh.

A month ago, I would've done anything to have Weston Reed standing in front of me, asking to be my mate.

But that was a month ago.

"No," I tell him when I can finally stifle my laugh. "Of course not."

I don't think he could've been more stunned if I shifted on the spot and my wolf went for his cock with her teeth. "What?" It's not a stammer, but it's pretty close. "You're refusing me?"

If that's what he wants to call it. "Uh, yeah."

"Why?"

Why? Is he fucking serious? "Um, maybe because you spent six months ignoring me? Rejecting me? That ring a bell?"

A flash of shame shatters his composure. It breaks my heart for him.

"West," I begin.

"No. You're right. I shouldn't have done that. If anything, I should've released you from the bond as soon as I knew I couldn't go through with finalizing one with any other female."

Couldn't. Not wouldn't. Just like I knew all along... he didn't have a choice any more than I did. Only his choice was about giving up on his heart's mate while I just wanted to get out from under the thumb of Fate.

We both did, I guess.

And it wasn't me. Any other female unlucky enough to get between the Beta and the female he really wanted... she would've been treated the same way.

Good thing I'm Quinn Malone. It sucked, but I dealt with it. If I hadn't been paired with a male who didn't want me, would I ever have been free to fall for Chase? Probably not.

In a weird way, he actually did me a favor.

It's time I do one for him.

I clear my throat. "Weston Reed?"

His grey eyes flash golden. I think he knows what's coming. "Yes?"

I take a deep breath. "I reject you."

The bond snaps. Just like that. No muss. No fuss. It's just... *gone*.

West exhales softly. "Thank you, Quinn."

I wink at him. "No problem. Honestly, if it had occurred to me sooner, I probably would've done it before. I guess... I guess I just didn't think it was right for a delta to reject the *Beta* of the pack."

He snorts. I haven't heard him do that in years. "Please. Everyone knows that the hierarchy is bullshit half the time. Sure, Bishop is in charge, but the rest of us? It doesn't mean anything. Even the smallest delta can be strong. Look at you. You survived a feral."

As if on cue, a howl splits the night's sky. It sounds closer than the source probably is, and if I was inside my cabin with the door closed, I don't know if I would've heard it as loudly as I do, but it stops me before I respond to West's comment with a retort.

That's okay. I forgot what I was going to say anyway.

Because that howl? I *know* that howl.

Chase.

He's here.

West's head whips around. "What the fuck was that?"

Ah. There's the West I remember. Not the cold-hearted Beta who pretended I wasn't there and who spoke so prim and proper, but the guy who was handsome and funny, and who cursed like a drunken sailor when it suited him.

He would never be a good mate to me. Hopefully, one day, he'll find someone to make him forget Helene the way that I found Chase.

The echo of his howl makes my heart thump fast and, I kid you not, my panties damp.

That was a possessive howl. His wolf is shouting, *Mine.*

And he's here for me.

I grin. "It's my mate."

CHAPTER 17
MATE

Based on his howl, I can tell what direction he's coming in from. I don't even think. I just bolt out the door.

West is *quick*, damn it. He lashes out his hand, snagging me by the wrist before I've made it two steps past my doorway.

"Quinn, wait—"

No waiting. I have a feral out there who doesn't know what happened to me. Can Chase catch my scent from that far? I'm not sure. Considering he's heading toward the clearing where I've spent so much time, he should be able to tell that the most recent layer of my scent is from this morning and not three weeks ago.

Then again, I'm pretty sure his feral side will be in charge.

Will the beast be rational? Doubt it.

Will he tear past the hickories and the wildflowers, racing for the heart of pack land where my cabin is? Probably.

Will he challenge any wolf he sees?

Oh, yeah. You can bet on it.

I have to go. I'm the only one in the Sylvan Pack who can calm this raging feral. If he scents me, if he sees me, if he hears my voice... I can keep anyone from being hurt tonight.

I absolutely refuse to let anyone get hurt because of me.

"I love him," I blurt out. It's the truth, too. I love Chase, and if anything happens to him, I'll never forgive myself. "Let me go!"

West does.

"I'll lead him away from the pack," I yell back, already running toward the trees. "Don't let Bishop send anyone to hurt him!"

Does he hear me? I don't know. Will he listen? I'd like to think so.

Will I do whatever I can to save Chase?

Yup.

I run. Out of Hickory and through the woods, I sprint. As soon as I make it to the edge of our immediate territory, I shift. My wolf will give me more speed and I'll need it if I want to get ahead of Chase and guide him to a spot where it's safe for us to reunite.

If there's one thing I know, it's this: if I run, Chase will come after me. He doesn't just ambush. He pursues.

And I'm counting on him to.

I know when he picks up on my scent and realizes that I'm nearby. His howl turns into a mournful whine, then an echoing roar. If I wasn't absolutely one hundred percent sure that he would never hurt me no matter what form he took, I might've dashed back to Hickory and prayed that my packmates would protect me.

But I don't. I keep running, and when the big, black wolf suddenly appears behind me, I push my wolf to go faster.

He lunges for me.

I zig.

He snarls.

I zag.

He doesn't give up. There's no reason to. As if the primal part of our wolfy brains has taken over both of us, we continue the chase.

He's never that far behind me, and though I could lose him easily if I wanted to since I know the woods outside of Hickory far better than he does, I don't *want* to lose him.

He still needs to feel like he earned me, and I need to make sure we're as far away from pack land as possible.

Then we'll both get what we desire.

When I feel like we've put enough distance between us and Hickory, I pretend to stumble over a rabbit hole I could've easily avoided. It gives Chase the chance to overtake me and he does.

Yes.

He catches me, tackling my wolf to the ground just like I thought he would. I land in my fur, taking the hit a lot easier than if I was in my skin. Chase lands on my back. With his instincts riding him hard, I know he'll go for my scruff.

I shift. No wolf, no scruff. All I am is a willing female who got mega turned on during the chase, and as soon as my arousal hits him, I'm betting he shifts, too.

If he doesn't, I'm screwed. Well, no. The opposite, actually. Shifters don't mate in their fur, and if I'm in my skin, Chase will either shift with me or his wolf will back off.

Of course, there's a third option. He might turn into that beast form where he can barely speak and he's ruled by his urges. On the plus side, I know from firsthand experience that, as a feral, he's two-legged with a cock that grows hard.

Is it a technicality?

Maybe.

Will I let him fuck me?

I think I might.

He's still Chase after all, and I have to believe that, even as a feral, he loves me enough to be gentle.

When I feel the pulse of his shift on my bare skin, I can't bring myself to turn around just yet.

"Quinn... Oh, Luna... *Quinn*. I thought you were gone. I thought you left me."

His voice is broken, but it's human.

I glance behind me. I have to. Know what I find? A very naked, very *aroused* Chase is on his knees behind me, clinging to my thighs, holding onto me so he can keep me from running from him again.

Good thing I have no intention of doing that.

He chased me. He caught me.

He won.

"I would never," I tell him, reaching back to stroke whatever part of him I can find. I touch his forearm, and he jolts. "I want you to know that. What happened… what you think happened… it didn't. I didn't want to leave. I was coming back to you. I just… you said you'd always come for me. I was waiting."

"I'm here." He sounds a little calmer. Like being near me is enough to soothe his beast—and it is, isn't it? "I will always come. Choose your male, I'll still follow you. Because I chose you and I can't let you go."

"Then don't."

"What?"

I wiggle my ass, just in case he didn't notice that we're both completely naked. "I don't just want you to hold on tight. I want you to get as close to me as possible. Take me. Claim me. Make me yours, and then you'll know that, no matter what, I *want* you to chase me."

You know, I thought I'd have to work harder to convince him. Nope. As soon as I wiggled my ass at him, he was already mounting me from behind.

"I'm sorry, Quinn. I can't… I have to."

"That's fine, baby. I want you to."

"It's that *thing* in me. I can't fight him—"

And… that's where we have a problem.

I immediately drop to my belly.

Chase lowers himself down, too. I can see his arms bend from my angle, and I scoot out from under him before he can pin me on the grass.

"Quinn?" His voice is a confused grunt. He's winning the battle against his feral side, but I don't think he'll be completely victorious until he finally feels like he's claimed what is his. "I thought…"

Good thing I'm ready to help him with that.

Only... we're in this together. I never want Chase to look back on our first mating and regret it. If he mounts me from behind while blaming his feral side, he won't see my face. He won't know that I want this as much as he does. That even if his instincts are hard to ignore, I don't want him to ignore them.

There's only one thing to do about that.

Using the tip of my foot, I push him back. He's on his knees, cock pointing straight up at the sky. It's even more impressive when I have him this way.

Oh, I'm going to enjoy this.

Looping my arms over his shoulders, I climb up on his thick thighs. My intentions are obvious. There's no denying what I'm about to do.

So that he never doubts that we're in this together, I need to claim *him*.

But he's an alpha. A feral. Some males can be touchy when a female takes them like this instead of her assuming the usual face-down, ass-up position.

Just in case, I check with him. "This okay?"

"The only female I've ever wanted is sitting on top of me. We ain't got a stitch of clothing on between us. Her arousal is making me dizzy, and it's all because of me." He pauses, suddenly unsure. "It is for me, right?"

I nod.

He shudders. "It's more than okay, Quinn. I'm yours. I've always been yours. If this is what you want to do, that's fine with me. I just... I need to know you're mine."

I climb off of him. For a split second, his face twists in an expression I can't quite see even beneath the moon-light, it's that dark, but he gets control an instant later. He obviously thought I was rejecting him, but if that's what I want, he'll let me.

Look at that. My feral finally learned to let me make decisions on my own.

Good boy.

I jerk my chin at him. "I am. Now get on your back."

He looks puzzled but he doesn't even question me. He immediately lays flat on his back.

It's not the full moon. The Luna won't be out for three more nights. Though I called him my mate to West—and Chase is, now that I've finally released West from the bond I clung to for way too long—he won't really be mine until we perform the Luna Ceremony.

Does that mean I plan on waiting?

Not even a little.

While he watches me closely, I get down and straddle him until the weeping head of his cock is pointing straight up at my pussy. An inch, maybe two separates the tip from my entrance. I have one hand on his chest, bracing my weight as I rise up on the balls of my feet so that I'm crouching over him.

I've seen his chest heaving before. I've seen him out of control. I've seen him go absolutely still.

Somehow, Chase is doing all three at the same time. It's like he's waiting for me to change my mind, climb off of him again, and sashay away back to my pack.

"You're mine," I tell him, lowering myself just enough that the head of his cock brushes against me. "I'm yours. The Luna can bless our mating another time. Tonight, I make you my mate. And you can't stop me."

"I never would."

"Good."

I'm so fucking wet, he slides right off of me, though his audible moan makes me eager to let him feel that sensation again. I put my weight against him, pressing his impressive length against his taut belly. Sliding back and forth, I make sure to spread my wetness all over every bit of his hot and heavy cock.

Chase's eyes are glowing in the darkness. He slams his head back against the dirt, clutching the grass with his fists. I realize that he's trying his best to stay still only to hurt himself when it gets too much. I can't have that. He needs to feel as good as I do, and though pleasure sometimes is so intense it can be painful, I don't want him banging his head.

"Stay still," I tell him, my voice coming out throaty. I press down on his cock again, making sure he can feel my heat. Chase moans, and I grin. He didn't move at all.

Good.

As a reward, I reach down, taking each of his hands in one of mine. I use my thumbs to knock loose any stray blades of grass he yanked out, then press his searing palms to my aching tits.

"If you need something to hold onto," I purr, "why don't you give these a try?"

"Luna, Quinn... you're so fucking *soft*."

"Mm. You like that?"

He bobs his head, his fingers roving over each of my breasts. "Very much, yes."

I lift myself up off of him, careful to make sure he doesn't lose his grip. I shouldn't have been worried. He's not letting go of my tits for anything.

"Maybe you'll like this better," I tell him, reaching between our bodies again. I'm soaked, his cock is slick with my wetness, and as I angle him so that he's lodged firmly inside of me, gravity takes over and slowly, slowly I sink down on top of him.

Once I'm fully seated, our groins touching, I take a second to adjust to the fullness of Chase inside of me and *squeeze*.

He just about chokes.

"How was that?"

"Unh... yes. This... this is very good, too."

I wink at him. "Got one more trick for you, tough guy. You think you can keep up?"

"I think you're trying to get your revenge and kill me, baby, because I don't know if I'm going to survive what else you've got in store for me. But, Luna, what a way to go..." A bead of sweat forms on his brow. "Try your worst."

Oh, I'm in trouble. A male who is playful during sex? That's my *dream*. Add that to a cock that stretches me out in all the right places?

I already planned on keeping Chase. Now I dare anyone to try to take him away from me.

Bracing my hands on his sculpted torso, I push against him, using the leverage to rise up off of his dick. Not entirely, though. Just to the point where it's only his head still inside. With a chuckle, I tell him, "Remember that you said that," before I let my full weight fall back on top of him.

Chase screams.

"Good?" I ask, double-checking.

"Do that again and I'll give you whatever you want."

How can a girl resist? "Okay."

He doesn't scream this time, though he does moan. I like it so much that I pick up the pace so that he'll do it again. Before long, I develop a rhythm that has Chase knocking his head against the ground once more. He stops when I slow down, though he keeps his hands right where I put them no matter how fast I ride him.

I don't think he's blinking. It's like he wants to witness every time I bounce up and down on his cock, so he's watching me closely, taking it all in. I think I'm doing the same. His look of awe mingled with the sounds I'm tearing out of him is doing one hell of a number on my ego. It's never been so boosted.

I've never felt so worshipped before, either. It's a heady feeling, only surpassed by the look of wonder and despair that flashes across his face when he realizes he's about to come.

"I... I don't think I can last much longer," Chase grunts, kneading my tits with so much force, I'm just about there with him.

"Stay with me just a few more seconds," I tell him. "Almost... almost there."

He nods, as if his words are failing him. Like all of his concentration is on doing what I asked.

He's an alpha who will take commands from this delta, in a moment where things like rankings and dominance don't exist, and I've never felt more powerful.

Still riding him, moving as fast as my hips will allow to increase the friction against my clit rubbing against his groin, I let go. It's harder to keep such close contact without me grabbing onto his waist, but I need my hands.

I doubt Chase agrees since I use them to shove him off of my tits.

"Hey!"

"Sit up, Chase," I tell him. My words come out choppy. He says he's close. Well, so am I. "Grab my lower back so that you're sitting up and I'm still on your lap."

Does he know what I'm doing? Maybe. His brow is creased, though maybe that's because I'm still working his dick. I squeeze my inner muscles to punctuate my directions, breaking him from his notably stunned spell.

Shifting his upper body, rising up so that he's sitting, I let out a squeal. This new position hits me at a different angle that has my orgasm coming on fast.

But first—

I swoop my hair over one shoulder, then tilt my head to that side. "When you're ready to go," I tell him, "let yourself go. But this is it, Chase. This is your chance. If you want to bite me, I'm ready. If you don't—"

I don't know why I thought he might refuse. I haven't even finished the alternative before he strikes like a damn rattlesnake, biting me at the point where my shoulder meets my neck.

It stings for a second, but I expected that. I mean, he's bitten me before, and that was nothing compared to a vampire making me his dessert. There's something different in this bite, though. Maybe because I know it's for real, that I'm keeping this one, that it will forever be a sign of the love I have for this male... it's different.

And I immediately start coming from the force of it.

I'm not the only one. Removing his teeth gently so that I have a perfect mark instead of a tear, Chase holds on just long enough before he starts bucking up in me wildly, shouting my name to the sky as he finds his release.

That's okay, I'm yelling, too.

Good thing I led him on a chase out of Hickory, I think as I start to come down from the height of pleasure. With the both of us being screamers, none of the pack would get any sleep tonight...

I WAS READY TO SPEND THE REST OF THE NIGHT RIGHT where we landed. With Chase curving his body around me, my beloved hickories arcing high over our heads, I've never been so content. We're not on pack land, so I thought it would be fine.

And that's when Chase takes my hand in his.

Thinking he's just insatiable, I expect him to place my palm on his cock. With him being the big spoon and me the little one, there's no missing the fact that he's already recovered from our first momentous claiming—and the second.

I'm still humming inside of my skin. My wolf preens that Chase is choosing us again already. With him buried to the hilt inside of me, it's the one time both halves of me can enjoy this magnificent male. She's game. I'm a little sore—six months of celibacy will do that to a girl—but I don't mind. If he wants to mount me again, he's more than welcome to.

Or I can mount him again. That was fun.

Mm. Maybe he can take me while we're both on our sides and that way I can fall asleep as soon as my next orgasm crashes over me...

I'm just about to ask what he thinks when he moves my hand. It isn't down toward his erection, though, like I expected. Instead, he brings it up to his nose, then takes a deep sniff that has him growling under his breath.

Uh-oh.

How could I have forgotten?

"You smell like *him*."

Him. Right.

West.

Crap.

"He grabbed my hand. That's all, Chase."

He sniffs again. Starting at my palm, he trails his nose all the way to my armpit. Probably not the most pleasant for him after all the sweating I just did, but I guess I pass tonight's sniff test because he starts grinding his cock against my ass. I can't tell if it's an involuntary reaction because my scent turns him on or his way to initiate sex so that he can get more of his scent on me to replace the one spot on me that West touched.

Considering he's jerked my hand higher, burying it into his sweat-soaked hair, covering me with his scent as he slips his cock between the cleft of my ass, I'm going with that second one.

I widen my legs just a little in open invitation.

He stops. Damn it. He was getting so *close.*

"Chase."

"You said he grabbed you. Why did he grab you?"

Single-minded male. I should've known.

Fighting back a frustrated sigh, I admit, "He tried to stop me from going to you when I heard your howl. I wasn't going to let him stop me, and when he realized I was going to you no matter what, he let go. I didn't have to break his hand or anything."

I thought that would appease him. At the very least, he seems pleased to hear how desperate I was to get to him. He starts rocking again, slower this time, as he grates out, "No one keeps us apart. Next time I see him, I'll kill him."

I'm not surprised. Can't let him kill my ex-almost mate, but I'm not surprised that that was his reaction.

I wonder... will a quick handjob distract my murderous mate? It'll kill two birds with one stone: transferring the overpowering musk of his innate scent to my hand while also making him feel good. Then we can forget all about killing West.

Hmm.

Won't know until I've tried.

Jerking my hand out of his loose hold, I reach all the way down, taking firm command of his cock. He immediately starts moving again, thrusting into the circle I form with my thumb and my forefinger.

"Quinn..." He's panting. "If you think... unh... you can control me... oh... with sex..." He shudders, and though I can't see what's going on behind me, I feel it when his come spurts out, getting on my hand. He falls forward, one hand landing on my hip in a possessive brand. "You're absolutely fucking right."

With my back to him, I don't have to hide my smile. "Don't kill him, Chase. For me?"

He stiffens. Unfortunately for my libido, it's the rest of his body this time, not his cock. "Because you still love him?"

I snort. "Please. I never loved West. Not like that. I never got the chance to. He's loved Helene for like ten years now. He was my friend, and, sure, the Luna thought he should be my mate, but that didn't mean I loved him. I just figured I might in time."

"But you don't?"

Letting go of him, I spin in the grass, moving so that we're facing each other. His hand fell when I moved. As soon as my position changed, he put it right back there. It's almost as if he can't let go of me for a single second.

I look into his bright gold eyes and I know it's true.

Just like I know how to soothe his worries.

"How can I love him?" I nip his bottom lip. "Mating is for life, Chase. I rejected the bond I have with West—"

"You did?"

I nod. "Yup. And you know why?"

He swallows roughly. He shakes his head.

Luna save me from overly thick males.

"Because I love you. I choose *you*. You asked me if I could. Well, I did when I rode your cock. Remember? Like an hour ago?"

Chase rumbles deep in his chest. "I remember."

I raise my scarred eyebrow at him. "You sure? 'Cause, if you want, I can refresh your memory."

This close, it's my belly that notices it when his dick starts stirring again. It twitches, then leaps, prodding me just above the curls that cover my pussy. If I didn't know any better, I'd think the damn thing has a mind of its own, already seeking my entrance.

Not that I mind. And when Chase takes me up on my teasing offer, lifting me up and guiding his length back inside of me, I give myself a mental high-five for coming up with this plan to distract him.

It won't last, though. So I snapped my bond with West earlier tonight. I told Chase the truth: that I love him. That I chose *him*. I have his mark on my skin. Even now I can feel the itch of it turning to a scar that I'll never erase.

But until we're fully bonded, he'll think of West and his wolf as a rival. Even though we're not in Hickory, we're close enough.

West is *too* close.

I don't want to risk Chase going feral again. And though the idea of wearing him out through copious amounts of mind-blowing sex has a certain appeal, I gotta sleep some time. And while I trust him when it comes to me and my safety, it would be cruel of me to insist on staying nearby the Sylvan Pack when it would make things so much harder for Chase.

Especially since we have a perfectly good cabin waiting for us.

I ride Chase again until we're both falling apart in each others' arms. Then, at my urging, we shift. Kind of have to. Chase ran all this way as a big, black wolf, and my clothes are scattered ruins somewhere on the edge of Hickory.

One day soon I'll have to go back to clean my old cabin out; I want my stuff and I won't leave any of it behind for good. Maybe once we're fully mated and I can bring Chase with me to show my feral mate off to the rest of the pack, I will.

For now, with both of us in our fur, we head in the direction of Sacre Coeur.

We've got a long night of running ahead of us. At least we're going home together.

CHAPTER 18
CHOOSE

Three nights later, I'm standing on the front porch of our cabin when Chase sneaks up behind me. He makes not a single sound as he approaches. He doesn't need to. I've always been able to sense him. It's just... now more than ever.

He rests his palms on my shoulders, moving his head so that his beautiful mouth is right next to my ear. "What are you looking at, my Quinn?" he murmurs.

As if he has to ask. But since he did so nicely, I point up at the sky.

The Luna shines down on the forest in front of us.

His grip tightens on me. It doesn't hurt; he vowed he'd never hurt me, and I believe him implicitly. In fact, when Chase loses just enough control that the points of his sudden claws dig into my shoulders, it's all I can do not to let out an audible moan.

After I accepted his bite that night outside of Hickory, I'm not worried about him marking me anymore. Not while I'm the proud owner of twin crescent-shaped fang marks that created a beautiful silvery-white scar at the point where my shoulder meets my neck.

Once the Luna blesses our mating tonight, the mark will turn pure white. Our bond will forever be unbreakable.

Chase Wilder will be mine forever.

For the last two days, ever since we returned to the cabin, we've hardly been off of each other. It's like Chase needs to be constantly assured that I'm open to him whenever he wants me to be, and I already knew that it got me off to be desired. All he has to do is growl softly, whispering how much he wants me—*wants* me, not *needs* me—and I'm already growing damp and ready for him.

Today was different. As if we knew what was coming, we managed to stay apart from the moment we woke up in bed together. Chase took a drive into Sacre Coeur to buy more supplies when he found his control failing. I cooked him another meal that he devoured while eating me up with that hungry look of his.

We watched some television, both of us sneaking peeks toward the window, waiting for the Luna to rise.

Chase doesn't keep the shades drawn anymore. The windows stay shut—I don't think I'll ever get used to *eau de vampire* wafting past my nose like that—but he doesn't mind letting in the sun now that I'm here with him. It was his feral side that was sensitive to the sunlight, but the longer we're together, the easier it is for him to restrain his beastly side.

I thought mating him would make him a former feral. I asked him when he first made it back to the cabin, but

Chase admitted that he still felt the urges. He said it with defeat, as if he thought that I might change my mind about staying with him if he couldn't shake that part of him.

Silly feral. To prove to him just how unfounded his fears were, I dragged him into the shower so that we could rinse off after our long run, then I sank down on my knees in front of him to worship his cock.

Yeah. He doesn't doubt that I'm hot for him anymore.

At least, I thought so, until he says in a hesitant voice, "Are you sure about this?"

Oh, Chase. He's not going to stop worrying until the Luna Ceremony is done and we're forever mates. Then again, this male will probably worry for the rest of our long lives together.

That's fine. I'm up for the challenge.

Does that mean I'm going to make it easy for him, though?

Ha. Not a chance.

I swivel my head on my neck, giving him an incredulous expression. "Luna knows I am. What about you? You want to call this off, let me know." I twitch my lips, going from incredulous to teasing. "I might be able to find another male to do this with tonight."

Chase lowers his hands from my shoulders to my waist. When I first met him, a tease like that would've triggered his feral side. He would've shouted that I was his, maybe even thrown a couple of punches at a cinder block wall.

The new and improved Chase?

Fucker *tickles* me.

I squirm. I've always been incredibly ticklish, something he learned early on when we first started to play with each others' bodies. Lately, it's his secret weapon. He tickles me and I wiggle, and eventually he gets me in a new position that he can enjoy. Once I'm full of him, pleasure usually replaces my ticklishness, so we both end up winning.

Too bad we're not naked—yet. All I can do is try to avoid his questing fingers, curling up as I turn into Chase, giggling against his bare chest.

"Okay, okay. You win."

He drops his lips to my mark, pressing an open-mouth kiss there. "You gonna threaten me with another male, Quinn?"

"Well—"

He tickles me again.

I squeal and bite his nearest ab.

Chase shudders, all playfulness gone.

His aura grows thick with arousal. He was already hard when he approached me—I could feel his cock pushing through his jeans as he stepped up to my back— but this is different. He already wears my mark. I got him to admit that he was pleased when I fought back the day I met him because he got to keep the scar to prove that, no matter why I'd done it, I marked him.

Of course, I wanted to give him a mark that didn't represent me trying to flee from my captor. I did that last night, taking a chunk out of that gorgeous tight ass of his. I'd waited until he'd finished to roll him over, massaging his cheek before I bit it, leaving a mating mark that was just for the two of us.

Courtesy of a shifter's amazing recovery time, he was already erect by the time I chose my spot. Probably because of the massaging, or because I point-bank told him his ass was mine and I was marking it so he always remembered that.

Poor guy. I don't know if I was his first lover. I never asked, and he pointedly refuses to ask me about any of my previous males. We chose each other. That was all that counted. We didn't have to be the first, just the last. Either way, he's definitely out of practice. It doesn't take much for me to make him go off, and he just about *exploded* when I marked him.

Fair enough. I don't think I've ever come so hard in my life as when he bit me that night in Hickory.

Tonight's the night of the full moon. Lust and promise and *forever* are hovering just out of our reach. To make what we have final, all he has to do is claim me beneath the moon. That doesn't necessarily mean out in the wild —in our bedroom would work just as well—but we're shifters.

Why shouldn't we claim each other wearing nothing but the moonlight on our skin?

"Do you have your necklace?" he asks me.

I know exactly what he means.

It was a gift from Henry to Chase in celebration of our mating. He'd claimed me as his in front of Nolan, and later told the head of the Cadre the same thing: that I was his mate. Mates are sacred to all supes, shifter or vamp. As a sign of an apology on behalf of the Cadre, Henry had one of his vampires retrieve Nolan's severed head. He broke off one of his fangs and had a necklace made for me.

Giving it to Chase as a peace offering wasn't the only reason why Henry had sent those two Cadre vamps up to our cabin. While doing their patrol, they reported seeing four unfamiliar wolves running in a diamond formation. They told Henry who called Chase down to see if he knew anything about that.

Of course, he didn't. He had no idea that West, Joey, Tucker, and Darrin had followed West's bond to the area and were searching for some sign of me. He's smart, though. Putting two and two together, he took the necklace from Henry, thanked him for the heads up, and arrived back at the cabin just in time to miss us leaving.

I found out why it took him so long to come after me. He actually put himself back in the chains for the night so that he didn't show up at Hickory and slaughter the four males—and the rest of the pack if he had to—to get to me.

See? I knew I had good reason to worry. But, on the plus side, my feral's getting better and better. Even Chase admitted that the old him would've followed his instincts and gone after me. The new Chase? He knew that I'd never get over him hurting one of my pack-mates. He waited until the urge to attack became a determination to get his mate back before he came for me.

And, Luna, am I glad he did...

With the necklace, he doesn't have to worry about another vampire bothering me if I go anywhere in our territory without him. He's even willing to bring me to visit Sacre Coeur now that I have a fang that's an added layer of protection.

As for shifter rivals, he has none. Any wolf who might be interested would look the other way as soon as they saw the mating mark on my neck. After tonight, it'll show every other male that I'm a happily bonded she-wolf.

I can't freaking wait. Dipping beneath my shirt—one of a set of cheap tees that Chase bought for me when I complained I was going through my new clothes too quickly—I snag the golden chain, lifting it up so he can see the fang hanging there. It's charmed, too, just like his. When I go from my skin to my fur, my clothes might be destroyed if I don't strip first, but I'll have the necklace wherever I go.

"You ready, Quinn?"

Excitement floods through me at the way his deep voice dropped.

Breathlessly, I nod.

His eyes flash. "*Run.*"

It's instinctive. My feral growls for me to run and I don't even stop to tear off my shirt or shuck my jeans. I shift on the spot, letting the tatters of another outfit rain down behind me. My wolf is already streaking away from him, my tail going horizontal at my speed.

My mate lives up to his name. I run. He chases.

But I'm as eager to make him mine as he is, so while the chase is fun, so is what happens after it's done.

Together, we sprawl out under the moonlight as Chase claims me for once and for all.

Look at that. I started out the feral's captive. Now I'm the feral's mate.

No.

As our bond snaps into place, the Luna bathing us both in her silver glow, I dig my claws into his back as he empties himself inside of me. And I think to myself, this feral alpha is *Quinn's* chosen mate.

For the first time in my life, I finally got to choose.

EPILOGUE

WEST

It doesn't matter how far away Quinn is from me, or that she released me from our bond when she rejected me three nights ago. Whether she stayed in Hickory or she followed her heart to that small cabin outside of the Fang City... it doesn't matter. When she performs the Luna Ceremony with that feral of hers, I still feel an echo of it.

I expected it to be a relief. One of the many weights off of my shoulders. In a way, it is. For the first time since I met her golden gaze across the crowd that fateful day, I don't have my wolf torn between circling the dark-haired delta and lying down at Helene's feet, offering his throat up to her, begging for her to show me a lick of attention.

In other ways, it's like I'm a failure. A complete fuck-up. The Luna meant for me to make Quinn mine, but I couldn't. Not while Helene owned every inch of my heart and soul already.

I've loved her since I was a pup, too young to understand the yearning I felt for her. This isn't fate. It isn't ordained by our goddess. This is just a male knowing in an instant that he's found his female.

But she isn't mine. Helene is promised to another, and when her alpha mate comes calling, I know she'll go. She believes it's her duty, that no matter how she might feel for me, she'll become an alpha's mate.

Unless... unless she becomes a beta's bride.

My love for her is the biggest open secret in the pack. It's the same reason why I never had to outright reject Quinn, turning her into an outcast; unfortunately, I did anyway. She always knew she'd only have half a male at best if we went through with our mating. She'd own my body, and my wolf would be the perfect mate to hers, but could I ever love her as much as Helene?

No. It was harsh, but reality, and when I accepted that, I knew I could never accept Quinn as mine.

For nine years I believed that Helene would always be. I imprinted on her with our first kiss, and I waited for the day the Luna would inevitably mark us as fated mates. For alphas, the Luna usually blesses them with the name of their mate during the Alpha Ceremony; sometimes they learn it as a future Alpha, like Rafael did. As a beta, I just thought I had to wait until I came of age.

Didn't work like that. I was twenty-seven before I heard the Luna's whispers, but it wasn't Helene's name echoing in my ears.

And it wasn't Helene that my body responded to in that moment like it had a thousand times before.

When my cock went hard for Quinn the first time, it

was an utter betrayal. By then, I already knew that Helene was promised to Rafael, but I'd resigned myself to waiting for her to wake up and choose me. To love *me*.

To claim me the same way I would've killed to make her mine...

Wolves have a reputation of mating for life. Fuck if I know if that's true or not, but shifters? We do. Once you perform the Luna Ceremony, have claiming sex, and leave a mark, the only way out is death. Even then, if I thought all I had to do was wait out her mating and challenge Rafael, I might. But a mate bond doesn't necessarily snap after death, and most mates don't survive it when theirs died.

If I challenge Rafael and win, I might lose Helene anyway.

As if I have her now...

She loves me. Though she hasn't said the words back to me since we were twenty-four and foolishly oblivious to the way life works in a pack, Helene *is* my life. She loves me, but she won't betray the promises she already made. She won't betray the Sylvan Pack and the alliance we have with Gravetail.

She loves me, but she'll never betray Bishop—

"*Fuck!*"

The curse bursts out of me. At the same time my fingernails lengthen and thicken, my claws unsheathing. My shoulders hunch, fangs burning my gums, begging to turn the canines into something sharper, something more fierce and wild and untamable.

Just then I understand what might drive an honorable

male to become feral. The weight is lifted, but all that does is remind me that I'm still suffering.

At least Quinn isn't anymore.

She's set me free. No challenges—though her feral would've if she hadn't gone to him before he reached pack land—and no regrets. I gave up on the life we might've had the second I realized that I still loved Helene more than I was willing to bend and accept a fated mate bond. Quinn chose her mate, and though some part of me will forever wonder *what-if,* the way she laughed at me when I offered to bond with her was the right move.

We were fated, but she wasn't mine. I didn't choose Quinn—I chose Helene. I'll always choose her.

Once upon a time I thought she chose me, too. And it doesn't matter that I know why she won't.

I still turn into a fucking wrecking ball as I take out all of my frustration, my fury, my *need* on the tree in front of me. I scratch and I claw, shredding the bark until I reach the pulpy inside. The behemoth shakes under my attack, but I keep on going until I've turned my claws into nubs, blood trickling down my fingers, pooling in the lines of my ripped-open palms.

Sweat drips from my brow, stinging my eyes. I need the pain. Without it, I feel the ache of Helene's continued rejection, plus the emptiness where Quinn used to reside in my chest. She deserves her happiness. If I accepted our bond—if she fucking settled with me like I asked her to—she would've been as miserable as I am. As possible as it was, I did love her. I wanted what was best for her.

It just... it wasn't me, damn it. It would never be me.

I keep going. The hickory can take it. It's covered with gouges from all the other times I just couldn't keep control, and though it shudders, it'll be here the next time I need an outlet for my grief.

It's the only one I have.

My claws will heal. So will my fingers and my palms. Using my forearm to knock back a loose strand of hair, swiping the sweat slicking my forehead, I fold my fists, pummeling the other side of the tree. Flesh tears. Blood sprays. A drop lands on my lip and I lick it, savoring the tang.

More.

If any of my packmates saw me like this, they'd be running to Bishop. Alphas are the only ranks in a structured wolf pack that are allowed to momentarily lose control like this. With all the aggression built into their bodies, if they didn't blow off steam from time to time, they'd explode. Betas... we're the righthand wolves. The calm and steadying ones. Those responsible for bringing our Alpha back from the brink for the good of the pack.

Mates do that, too, but Luna knows I don't have one. Rejected by one, loved then released by the other, the only thing that calms me is knowing that my chosen mate loved me once.

I swear to our cruel goddess, she loves me still.

Helene refuses to say the words. From the moment it became obvious to the pack that Quinn was my fated mate, she stopped me from telling her the same. We were both meant for others, she whispered the night she tried to tell me goodbye, and it was better that we leave it at that.

Better? I'd asked. Better for fucking *who*?

Not me. And when I saw the regret in her pale yellow eyes, I knew that Helene was as trapped in the idea of a fated mating as I was. Only, I loved her enough that I made a conscious decision to reject Quinn, leaving her free to choose her feral.

If only my female would choose me, I could make her that happy. I know I could.

There's still time. Glancing down at my hands, my chest heaving as I struggle to get my control back, I see that my shifter healing has already started to kick in. The smaller cuts have closed over, the larger gashes beginning to clot. Dried blood has left my hands sticky. I quickly wipe them on the flattened grass, trying to get rid of some of it. My packmates will still scent it on me, but we're shifters. Blood usually comes with the territory.

Rising up, I run my ruined fingers through my sweat-soaked hair. I shove it out of my face, tilting my head up to look at the sun streaming through the trees, the early light of dawn shining on me. The Luna must've swapped places with it while I was getting some of that out of my system.

It's morning now.

My wolf is hungry. My stomach is twisted—it usually is—but I'm not an idiot. I need food, and I also need to show my face around the pack so that they know their Beta isn't suffering from losing his mate. It doesn't matter that I ache for Helene, or that I was happy for Quinn to choose another male instead. Shifters live and die by the grace of the Luna, and if the Luna blesses us with a mate, we're not supposed to disagree. It's one thing to choose a mate before we find the one meant for us, but to reject them for another? The way my packmates see it now, Quinn rejected me for her feral.

Good. Though I know I came off like I couldn't give a shit about Quinn's feelings, I did. I'd rather be the rejected Beta than the prick who kicked a poor delta while she was down. I can take the hit. For a while, she had to, but if I could've made any other choice—if I could've turned my fucking heart off and put Helene behind me—I would have. But I couldn't, and I have to live with that.

That's my choice.

Bleeding for Helene? I'll do it gladly.

Waiting on the sidelines, hoping against hope that maybe she'll see me again?

If that's what it takes.

I exhale. It's rough, a full-body shake, and then I'm West again. I'm the Beta of the Sylvan Pack. I'm Luna-damned untouchable, answering to only two others: my Alpha and my heart.

Glancing around, avoiding the added destruction to my tree now that the urge to hurt has been sated for the moment, I tap into my wolf and look out into the distance. Shimmering with dew, I see a flower that would look perfect nestled in Helene's beautiful blonde hair.

I can't say I love her. She won't let me.

But I can show her.

Loping past the closely grown trees, I pluck the flower from the dirt, then twirl the stem between two blood-stained fingers. My claws are halfway regenerated, and by the time I stop by Helene's cabin on the way to meet with Bishop, they should be completely healed.

She doesn't need to know that I still visit the edge of Hickory to work myself over in order to feel *something*. This is where the best flowers grow on our territory, and I'll never visit her without one.

And maybe... maybe she might realize she has a choice to make after all.

AUTHOR'S NOTE

Thank you for reading *The Feral's Captive*!

This is the end for Quinn's part in their story. West will be the hero in the second book which is why he got the POV for the epilogue. However, if you want to get a peek inside of Chase's head? I wrote an extra steamy scene—*Chase and the Chains*—that is set about a month after this mating that is included in this edition!

Also, if you purchase a physical copy of this book—paperback, alternate paperback, or hardcover—send me your mailing address via email (SSpadeBooks@gmail.com) and I'll mail you a free bookmark and a signed bookplate!

Now, what's coming up next for the Sylvan Pack? West decides that maybe Chase had the right idea. If he can't convince Helene that he's the male for her, he might have to do something drastic—like maybe steal her?

Find out what happens in the second book in the **Stolen Mates** duet, *The Beta's Bride*. For now, keep clicking/scrolling/reading to get a sneak peek at the cover as well as its book description.

Also, if you want to read more about this universe? In *Never His Mate*, Gem is a female alpha wolf who is—initially—rejected by her fated mate. Unlike Quinn, she ends up with the male the Luna chose for her, but not until she disappears into the local Fang City for a year.

And if you're interested in reading the story about the Luna-touched female who is rumored to be able to break mate bonds? That's Elizabeth Howell, and she has her own story—featuring her vampire mate—to tell in *Hint of Her Blood*.

xoxo,
Sarah

A STOLEN MATES SHORT STORY
THE FERAL'S CAPTIVE
CHASE AND THE CHAINS
SARAH SPADE

THE FERAL'S CAPTIVE

CHASE AND THE CHAINS

SARAH SPADE

CHASE AND THE CHAINS

CHASE

You'd think that, after twelve years on my land, the wretched stench of hundreds of vampires living nearby wouldn't bother me as much as it does.

Probably because I need it as a reminder. With the meaty, rotten, *corpse* stink hitting me every time I walk out my door, I can never forget.

Even if I wanted to avoid it or get used to it, I *can't*.

Gotta give Henry credit. The only parcel of land available for me to claim back then is downwind from the Fang City. In Sacre Coeur, humans and vamps live together, with an impenetrable border surrounding the city; impenetrable, of course, unless you've got a vamp fang in your mouth or one hanging off a chain that you'd been gifted. Any supe with a nose and a brain would steer clear of any Fang City. It isn't worth the trouble.

And then there's me.

Even when the wind is still and the stink doesn't travel

all the way to my cabin, I can feel the vampire's cold, dark, dead magic on my skin. Alpha shifters are tuned to danger by design—and, though I lost my pack when I was sixteen so I've never been an actual Alpha to one, it works the same for any wolf born with an alpha's rank and dominance. Alphas are created to protect their packmates. I might've failed once, but even as I wear the fang that belonged to the bastard bloodsucker who killed my family, I live by one adage: keep your friends close, and your enemies closer.

Supernaturals are a ticking time bomb. I know that better than anyone. Though I came to Sacre Coeur an angry teen, looking to get revenge on the whole damn Fang City for the pain I was feeling inside, I finally realized that not every vamp was bad. Not every human was an annoyance.

Not every supe was damaged.

Lucius was. When he chanced upon the small pack I grew up in, he'd tripped so far into the hazy bloodlust that he went from vampire to rogue. He targeted the Wilder pack because we were shifters, and because he could.

I spent three years searching him down. At nineteen, I did. I wasn't feral then, but a lone wolf—and, undeniably, an alpha.

When I tracked Lucius to Sacre Coeur, claiming the territory as mine, Henry—the Cadre leader—couldn't ignore the shifter stubbornly prowling along the edge of his city. At the beginning, I challenge every bloodsucker insight, demanding they bring me Lucius so I could have my revenge.

As a peace offering, Henry did just that. He executed the rogue, bringing me his head and his fang.

Vamp justice. It's not for everyone, but I'm a supe. The fang hangs around my throat to this day, a sign I accepted his offer of peace.

Makes sense. In his own way, Henry's as much the Alpha of Sacre Coeur as I was to my patch of land and my empty cabin—and we both proved that again just his past month when another one of his vampires attacked my mate.

This time, I got to take his head, and Henry gifted Quinn a fang of her own so that she could feel safe walking around the woods that surround our home.

And if I purposely ignore the fact that she was running away from *me* when Nolan chanced upon her, it's because I have to. Remembering everything I put Quinn through while I was trying to kickstart the mating dance is a surefire way to bring that *thing* inside of me out again. It's been thirteen days, a new record, and I'd like to keep it like that.

Because not every supe is damaged—but I'm one of those who is.

Feral... When vampires give in to their bloodlust, they're rogues. When a shifter loses the balance between both of his halves, becoming more beast than man, we call it feral.

That happened to me. Only about a year ago, when the strain on my wolf being denied his vengeance became too much, something inside of me snapped. My wolf didn't care that Lucius was dead, only that *we* didn't kill him. He wanted to rip. To snarl. To tear flesh. To make beings *bleed*.

More than anything, though, he wanted to run.

Now that? That I could do.

Struggling against the desires of the thing I was when the beast came out—no logical thought, only urges and twisted emotions—I could run. I didn't think I would be able to outrun the ghosts of my family, the guilt of not being there to fight for them when the rogue appeared, or even the loneliness that had me nearly succumbing all the way to the *thing*. I wasn't try to outrun it.

I was trying to *distract* it.

Besides, when I lost control like that, I wasn't dwelling on what I lost, or what I couldn't have.

I'm an alpha. The Luna granted me all of this dominance so that I could take a mate, maybe lead a pack, but definitely create a family of my own. A new Wilder Pack. For more than a decade, it was a dream, but as though our goddess was punishing me for turning my back on her, on our people, she didn't help me find my fated mate.

She could have. During the ceremony that made an alpha wolf *the* Alpha, she rewarded her chosen leader with the names of their mate. Some even before that.

Not me.

I had no pack. No family. No *mate*—

—until the fateful day I ran hours and hours away from Sacre Coeur, living up to my name as I chased a sliver of happiness and peace, and I fucking *found* it.

When the feral wolf ruling me caught the scent of rainwater on the breeze during a sunny, summer day, the rage, the pain, the *ache* that tormented me became entirely focused on finding that female and, in whatever way I could, making her mine.

Fuck Fate. She wasn't the female the Luna might've meant for me, but I wanted her anyway.

So what if Quinn Malone, my gorgeous delta female, *did* have a fated mate of her own? Because she did. Damn it, she had *him*. The Beta of the Sylvan Pack. The bonehead who was handed Quinn on a golden platter by the Luna, only to reject her for another female.

I snort; I can do that now, since she chose *me*. He's an idiot. A she-wolf like Quinn... you fight for her. I would've. I *wanted* to. When I was working on trying to figure out how to get her to come home with me, to stay with me, just taking her wasn't my first idea. Though I had no idea how to approach a female, I thought I could at least introduce myself.

But then I realized that the feral would probably want to say *hi*, too—and his version would have me pulling her lush body beneath mine, rutting mindlessly because he was convinced she was his mate—and I couldn't let that happen. If Quinn met the feral before Chase, she'd never accept my pursuit of her.

Challenge the Beta, though? I liked that idea. Kill Reed and I'd prove I was the stronger male. That I could be the perfect protector for her.

Only... I watched her. I spent more time lurking around the wolf territory of the Sylvan Pack than I did in my own cabin during the nine months I stalked her, learning everything I could about the female who'd one day be mine.

All that time, she was waiting for her fated mate to

give in to their bond. She wanted him to. He was wavering. I could tell. I saw it happen with a fated couple in my old pack. No wolf can resist a half-bond. Either you finalize it or you break it, and since Reed kept her dangling on a hook for so long without outright rejecting her, I knew it was because he was going to take my female when he realized he had no other choice.

I couldn't let him finalize their fated mate bond. Not with the only female I'd found who actually soothed the savage beast inside of me. Whenever I was near Quinn, hiding just out of reach of her senses, breathing her scent into my lungs, hearing her voice as she playfully talked to herself even as her own heart carried as much ache as mine... the *thing* stayed settled. Always watching, always hungry, sure. If I let up for only a second, he'd break free, but I was strong enough to hold him back.

I felt... not whole. Not yet. But like I would be.

I am now.

My hand—not the furry, twisted paw that's there when the beast is loose—is resting on the door handle to the cabin. I give myself a full body shake, trying to get rid of the vampire stink clinging to me, then let myself inside.

Two steps into the living room of our cabin and my cock is already twitching the second her intoxicating scent reaches me.

My home smells of rainwater, and it's all because of Quinn.

Tonight, that's not the only scent I pick up on as I stalk toward the kitchen, though it's definitely the first one that hits me. My beloved mate had shooed me out of the cabin a couple of hours earlier, telling me that it was her turn to cook for me again, and that I could finally come back when the sun started to set for the evening.

Now... it's not that she was lying. Not exactly. My wolf knows instinctively whenever someone is lying to him; another perk of being an alpha, since dishonesty is one of those dangers and threats we pick up on. A month now since we've become forever mates, I can forgive Quinn a lot of her tiny lies; after how our relationship got its start, she's earned it. She rarely does it anymore, not since she learned that—despite being a feral—I never lost the ability.

I don't know why she was surprised. It's common knowledge in the shifter world that alpha wolves can do that. Being a feral? That part of me—the *thing*—is so much closer to pure instinct and emotion than even my wolf. Because of that, the feral's more sensitive to it. So, though I've been able to keep the *thing* back for the most part after our mating, I can still experience the world as he understands it.

Plus, I know Quinn. My mate wasn't quite lying to me earlier this afternoon, but she definitely was up to something.

I didn't care. My gorgeous mate was offering to feed me, and I needed to go out and do some territorial markings to reinforce the borders to our land anyway. If it made her happy to tell me to go, I'd kiss the hell out of her, then jog out the door until she wanted me back.

Pissing around our territory isn't a hardship. It's a *necessity*. I'm thorough, taking my time, because the safety of my mate is on the line.

I'll never forget how fucking scared I was that I would be too late to get to her after she ran away. With her fear rushing through the woods to slap at me, the tang of her blood driving the *thing* wild, I knew my worst fear had come true: a vampire had gotten its claws on my female.

My only regret is that I only got to kill Nolan just the one time...

Now, I might've made Quinn my captive once, but I refuse to do it again. If she wants to visit the garden I planted for her, or take the drive into Sacre Coeur, or go for a run on our territory to get away from me because, Luna knows, I can be too much sometimes... if I have to piss circles on every tree, bush, and stick to let other predators know to stay away, I will.

For Quinn, I'll do fucking *anything*.

Luna, she's so damn beautiful.

Her skin is pale enough that it shines like moonlight. Her eyes are a perfect shifter's gold, without a single hint of insanity lurking in their depths. She's got this soft, soft black hair that spills down her back. When I bury my nose in its length, it's like I'm standing out in the middle of a sunshower. It smells of rainwater and heat, and it does more to soothe my feral side than anything else.

Except, of course, when she opens that soft body of hers up to me, giving me pleasure that I only dreamed of.

Sometimes I think I *am* dreaming. Even now, watching her as she finishes eating her dinner, I still can't believe she's mine.

My plate is already empty. Quinn says her cooking is passable, and she isn't lying when she says that. She doesn't realize that the meaning behind her meals—that she's telling me that she loves me, and my little delta will provide for her alpha mate in her own way—makes it the most delicious food I've ever eaten.

But, as she reminded me when we sat down together to eat twenty minutes ago, she prefers it when I cook. She doesn't like to do dishes, either, and she tells me that she expects them all washed up before we turn in for the night.

If the order came from anyone else, I'd be snapping my teeth at them for daring to tell me what to do. But not my mate, and that's because she *is* my mate.

It's bad enough being a dominant wolf. Going feral is like walking on a taut string of barbed wire with a bunch of prowling, hungry lions below you. It hurts like hell with every step you take, but when you know that what's waiting if you fall is a million times worse, you suck it up. A little pain is better than being savaged, and I've learned how to navigate that fine line. I might not use the chains I installed in the basement when I decided I had no choice but to steal my mate away from her pack, but make no mistake. I'm never completely free—unless I've got Quinn to rely on to keep me sane.

Being around her? It's more than just how the beast reacts to her, or how my wolf accepted that hers was his mate the first time he ever saw her. Though her lovely brindle wolf is a delta, she is no submissive.

Thank the Luna. I'd eat a submissive she-wolf alive...

I always knew I needed a female who would stand

up to me, and once she realized that I was putty in her paws when it came to her, she never backed down again.

And, Luna, nothing in this world makes me go harder faster than when she jerks her chin up at me, golden eyes flashing, as she gives me a command that she absolutely expects me to follow.

Which I absolutely will.

She's my mate. I'll do anything she wants. Give her anything she desires. I'll buy her gifts, shower her with affection, plant her a thousand flowers so she knows that I love her more than anything.

If she wants to be the dominant wolf in our mating, I'll forever get on my knees for her.

And, since our mating, I've had that opportunity. It's the best.

Quinn tastes fucking *amazing* and, shit. I'm finished my meal and, already, I'm salivating.

My mate has the cutest little nick in her right eyebrow. She preened the first time I pointed it out so now I make sure to kiss it softly when we're cuddling after a mating, both my wolf and the feral too sated for me to worry about losing control during the afterglow.

Just then she's raising it in that habit of hers. "You've got that look again, you know," she says.

Busted.

Still, I try to act like I don't know what she means. "What look?"

"Your hungry look. Really, Chase? We just ate dinner. You even had seconds."

"Maybe I'm not hungry for food."

"Oh." Quinn's lips curve slightly, her eyes lighting up. "You in the mood for... dessert, baby?"

My nostril flare. Her rainwater scent is a soothing balm to my soul. But the rich musk of her arousal? It lights a fire inside of me. It's all I can do to keep from knocking the plates from the table, lifting Quinn up on top of it, and making her pussy my dessert.

I want that desperately. So much so that I wouldn't be surprised if I started drooling.

But this is Quinn's show. I knew she was up to something, and that mischievous expression on her face tells me that she's ready for me to discover what it is. The 'baby' seals it. My mate is full of pet names for me— something I've never experienced before—and 'baby' is my favorite.

I'm six feet tall, a hulking beast of a male even when Chase is in control, with enough baggage to fill a hotel, and she calls me 'baby' when she's feeling affectionate.

Affectionate, and *horny*.

"What have you got for me?" I ask.

I try to sound unaffected, to keep the game going.

I fail utterly, my voice dropping to a low rasp.

Though we never discussed it, I know that Quinn has a lot more experience when it comes to sex than I do; considering she was my first *everything*, it wasn't that hard to tell when she, at least, knew what she was doing. At sixteen, when most males were looking for a she-wolf to help them with their constant hard-ons and out-of-control hormones, I was busy burying the remains of my former pack. After that, my sole focus was on getting revenge. By the time I was a lone wolf, I was in my early twenties, I lived in a cabin bordering a Fang City, and I had no need for females.

Until, of course, I stumbled upon Quinn...

She darts out her tongue, playing at the corner of her mouth. Matching my rasp, letting me know that we're still playing the way that bonded mates do, she says, "A deal."

And... I'm lost. "What?"

Her golden eyes brighten. "I want to make a deal with you. There's something I've been wanting to do for a while now, and with the Luna almost full again, it's an itch I'm dying to have scratched. What do you think, Chase? You want to help your mate out?"

"You don't even have to ask," I tell her earnestly. "You know I'll do anything for you."

"Anything?" When I nod, she says something that would've had me on my guard if it was anyone else but Quinn: "Do you trust me?"

"Yes."

I don't even hesitate. With the bond stretching between us, I know that she's excited about what's to come next. And even if she wasn't? She's my mate.

I trust her with my life. I have to.

She *is* my life.

I trust Quinn with my life. I... I'm just not so sure I trust her with the silver chains in the basement.

I glance at the length of chain stretched out on the floor. The shackles are open, the key tossed in the far corner of the room.

She wants me to put them on. Willingly. Because she asked me to.

I will. For her, I *will*.

But first—

"Have I mentioned how much I love you?"

"Constantly, Chase, but if you want to again, I won't stop you."

Leaning over her, I press a quick kiss to the top of her head. Her scent wraps all the way around me, and though I'm a little uncertain when I straighten to see the chains winking up at me again, I'm ready to do whatever she wants me to.

"So. The chains…"

"Yup."

I place my hand on her shoulder, instinctively finding my mark near her throat. I stroke it with my thumb. "And this isn't just about you finally getting revenge on me for using them on you? Because I'm so fucking sorry, Quinn. I just… I wasn't thinking. The *thing* was."

"I've told you like a hundred times already," she says, patting me on my side. "It wasn't the chains that pissed me off. It was not getting a choice. The quicksilver, too, but remember: when I finally got to choose, I chose you, baby. There's no revenge between us. There will never be. So get that through your thick skull already, okay?"

Luna, I love it when she's forceful. "Yes, ma'am."

She rolls her eyes. "Don't be a dick."

"I thought you liked my dick," I tease.

"Oh. I do. A lot. In case you haven't figured it out, that's why we're down here."

Behind the zipper of my jeans, my cock jumps. It was

already as hard as it could get by the time I joined her in the kitchen. On our way down to the basement, I'd had to do a discreet adjustment, but now the poor thing is simply aching to get inside of Quinn again.

It's only been about five hours. An eternity to my poor libido.

"I'm ready when you are, Quinn."

She hold up her pointer finger. "Hang on. I said I wanted to make a deal first. You still up to it?"

Her voice has gone throaty. There's a promise of pleasure there I can't deny. "Of course."

"Here it us. We get naked, then you let me chain you up." Her fingers trail gently down my side, playing with the waist of my jeans before she steps away, reaching for the hem of her shirt. "I promise to make it worth your while."

Honestly? I'm a simple male. Even before my wolf splintered, turning into something more primal than he already was, I was never very complicated. I see things in black and white, what I want and what I'll take.

I want my mate. And Quinn? She had me at *naked*.

Flicking open the button on my jeans, I yank down the zipper, and quickly shuck them off. Since that's all I was wearing, I'm done before she's removed more than her shirt.

Quinn chuckles. "Eager, aren't you, baby?"

The truth is easy to admit.

"With you, yeah. Of course I am."

Smiling at my answer, she reaches behind her to unhook her bra. I bite back a moan when she removes it, showing me her gorgeous tits.

I swear, nothing feels better in my hands. My palms are already itching to feel their weight.

"Down, boy," she teases, and I'm not sure what she means more: the way I was already reaching out to caress her globes, or how my erection is bobbing toward her.

"You're still not naked yet," I tell her in a mock growl. I show her my claws. Regular shifter claws, not the monstrosities I have when the beast is free. They're still sharp enough. "This is your deal, but I can help you with that."

"Hey, we can't all walk around in a pair of jeans and that's all, you know." She casts an appreciative glance over my bare chest, then to my jutting cock as she bites down on her bottom lip. "Not that I'm complaining, Chase. Not one bit."

If it was up to me, I'd go naked all of the time if it weren't for things like pesky public indecency laws holding me back. My whole life, I've preferred to stick to a pair of jeans and nothing else, especially since I might have to shift to my wolf at a moment's notice; as a feral, I just have an excuse now. Hey. You can only replace so many shirts and boots and boxers before you realize that they're all a waste.

Then again, as Quinn shimmies out of her jeans, then tugs her silky panties down past her hips, I have to admit that there's definitely some allure when it comes to my female's underthings...

Once she's finally undressed, she points to the floor. "You ready?"

"My heart is yours," I tell her, dropping down to a crouch, then kicking my legs out in front of me so I'm resting on my ass. I move my back up against the cinder block wall, sitting next to the chains. "So is my body. You can do anything you want to me."

"Oh, I'm planning on it."

Quinn picks up her jeans. She roots around inside of one of the back pockets before pulling out two scraps of familiar grey fabric.

"One of your old shirts," she explains. "The one that tore when I grabbed you. I found it in the closet and figured you wouldn't need it as much as I do. I hope you don't mind."

"Not at all."

Most of my clothes are at least a decade old. Once I went through my last growth spurt, a lanky shifter turning into the alpha he was born to be, I bought enough jeans and t-shirts to fill a closet and left it at that.

Jeans are sturdy. Cotton? Not so much.

As if she's thinking along the same lines as I am, Quinn says, "We gotta get you new clothes, Chase."

I drop my gaze to my lap, looking at my cock. It already has a drop of pre-come on it. "Can shopping wait?"

My mate giggles. "Sure thing, baby."

Dropping to her knees, Quinn uses the piece of fabric to scoot the silver shackle closer to her. She kisses my ankle, running her fingers over the skin, before wrapping it with the fabric. Just like I did when I brought my precious captive to the basement, she's wrapping me with a protective layer so I don't burn.

She attaches the one shackle, doing it quickly so that the silver on the outside doesn't burn her. She does the same thing to my other ankle, complete with the kiss and the caress.

Sitting back on her heels, Quinn smiles at her handiwork. "Perfect," she says, and I think she's talking about how she has me shackled—until she firmly takes my erection in her soft hand.

Unh. I don't think I'll ever get used to the shock of her willingly touching me like that. It's so damn *good.*

She starts at the base, stroking me from root to tip. It's a leisurely stroke, no real force behind it, but her gentle touch is already enough to test my sanity—and she's just getting started.

"These chains," she murmurs, and I can't tell if she's talking to me or to herself. "You trapped me in them. I trapped you that one time. I was thinking... maybe it's time we use them for something good. Something like *this.*"

Tossing her hair over her shoulder, making sure my mark is on full display for me and my possessive wolf, she leans down, swirling her tongue over the head of my cock.

"Quinn." Oh, that feels even better, but I have to wonder: is she doing this because she wants to? Or because she's trying to prove something? This isn't the first time she's gone down on me, but the chains... I'm not so sure I understand what the deal with the chains is. "My mate. You don't have to—"

She cuts me off with a death grip on my cock. I strangle my groan as she squeezes the poor thing, pulling her lips away from my overheated, damp flesh.

"I know. I don't have to *do* anything. But... I love you, Chase. If this is one way I can show you, let me. Okay?"

I nod. "Of course."

"Good."

She lowers his head again, but not before I see her triumphant grin.

Mm. There really is nothing sexier than a confident female, except maybe *my* female as she takes my entire length between her lips again before slowly fucking me with her mouth and that wicked, wicked tongue of hers.

Consumed by her ministrations, I'm so turned on I can barely think straight.

I try anyway.

The chains are on my ankles. They don't stop me from patting her hair or caressing her cheeks as she sucks my cock. The silver—even with the grey t-shirt protecting my skin from its burn—is enough to dull the feral's razor-sharp edge of need, but that's all it does.

Unless she decides to bite me, then dart away out of my reach, I can't figure out why this was something she wanted to do so badly that she actually arranged for just this scenario.

And that's when, after hollowing her cheeks, making me throw my head back with how good her tongue feels on my cock, she lets my erection slip out from between her lips with an almost audible *pop*.

I fight back the urge to grab her head and guide it back to my dick.

I was so damn close!

Could she tell? Probably. Quinn seems to know my

body better than I do, and our mate bond would've told her that I was just about to erupt in her mouth.

"Quinn…" It's a plea. I don't even give a shit. I'll beg if I have to.

"I know, baby. But I want you to finish inside of me, okay?"

"Told you," I grit out, forcing my orgasm back. I was so close, and now that I know she's ready to mate, I have to hold on long enough to make it good for her. "I'm yours."

Tiptoeing over the chain, careful not to burn the bottoms of her feet, Quinn drops down over my lap.

Her eyes spark. "Got you right where I want you."

I hold out my arms, inviting her into my embrace. "I'm not going anywhere."

"I know. I've chained you to the wall to make sure of it," she teases.

Pressing up against my chest with one forearm while arching her back, she grabs my slick cock, then angles it so that our bodies meet. With a soft sigh, she pushes down on top of me.

The moment our groins touch, I exhale in pure contentment. Sure, my mate has me in chains, and my cock is primed to go off like a rocket, but there's nothing like that first connection when I know that the two of us are as close as two souls can be.

Well, except for when Quinn starts to ride.

Because that? That is fucking *magical*.

We've explored countless positions this past month. My wolf constantly grunts at me to take my mate from behind, but if I'm being honest? Nothing is as erotic as

Quinn riding me, her tits bouncing in front of me, her beautiful face twisted in an expression of power and pleasure as my little delta mate dominates her alpha male.

As Quinn sinks down on top of my cock, again and again and again, I wonder for the millionth time how I got so fucking lucky.

I don't know, and if anyone tries to take her from me, I'll rip their balls off and make them eat them, and I won't even have to be feral to do it. That's my possessive instincts racing to the fore. I'll do it as a human, and I'll be wearing a predator's grin as I do.

This is my female. My mate. If the Beta of the Sylvan Pack was too much of an idiot to realize that, oh well. No matter where she goes, I'll follow. I'll chase. Let her put me in chains if she wants. I broke out of them once before to get to her when I sensed the vampire terrorizing her.

Her fear slapped at me over the distance. Even then we had some kind of undeniable tie. Now we have a bond.

If something happened at this very moment while I was shackled and Quinn was suddenly gone, I'd gnaw off both feet, then run on bloody stumps to get to her. That's how devoted I am to my mate.

That thought in mind, suddenly, I understand what she meant before.

It's time to use them for something good...

Obviously, Quinn has bad feelings associated with this set of chains. I used them to trap her, taking away her choice. She used them to shackle my wrist after I betrayed her by biting her the first time she showed any interest in me.

I get it. Now that we're fully mated, she needs to dominate the chains just as much as she dominates me.

At that realization, I can't hold back anymore. I'm going to come whether I like it or not. So, reaching between our bodies, I rub frantically at her clit, hoping that I'll bring her with me when I go over.

Thank the Luna, I *do*.

Once I'm completely spent and she stops gasping the pleasurable pulses from her climax, Quinn eventually climbs up and off of me.

My cock slides out of her as she moves away, though the sight of her ass wiggling seductively as she crosses the corner before bending over to retrieve the key to the chains has it stirring again.

It's a shifter thing. Just like how we have advanced regenerative properties, super strength, and phenomenal speed, I can get it up again almost immediately.

And why wouldn't I? I'm insatiable for my mate.

My cock is willing. My chest is still heaving from the rush of my orgasm. Just… give me a second, I think. I'll be completely ready for another round then.

Maybe I can convince Quinn to take it up to the bedroom. She did her thing with the chains. Now it's my turn to lay her out beneath me while we leisurely mate. For that, I must prefer a mattress to the hard concrete floor I'm currently sprawled out on.

Luckily, my mate seems to have the same idea. At the very least, she's dropped to her knees, head bowed over one of the silver shackles on my ankles, key clutched between her fingers.

She starts to slip the key into the notch on the shackle, pausing before she can turn it.

Quinn always points out my 'hungry' look. I should really begin to do the same for his mischievous expression.

She taps her chin with her finger. "You know... I did have to sleep down here for like three nights when you had me chained up after we first me."

Telling her that we first met nine months before she knew I was stalking her isn't smart. I don't, but that doesn't stop her from what she's thinking.

With a slight smirk tugging on her lips, she pulls the key back out.

I blink. "You're not going to leave me naked down here after you just made me come like a fucking fountain, are you? I want to get my mouth on you," I tell her, my voice dropping to a growl. "It's my turn. I want the dessert you promised me."

Through our bond, I can tell just how much that turns her on. My mate... she's such a tease, and I *love* it. "You drive a hard bargain, Chase. What else will you give me to free you from the chains?"

"Fuck the chains. If you come over here and sit on my face, I'll give you any Luna-damned thing you want."

"Good answer. Just for that, I'll let you loose first."

I wasn't kidding. If she wants to keep me down here in chains, I'd do it. For a taste of her, and because I owe her. I'll probably spend the rest of ours lives making it up to her—no matter how many times she tells me she forgives me—and I'll look forward to every second of it.

For now? My mouth is watering for her.

True to her word, Quinn sticks the keyss back into the notch, releasing the first shackle. While I reach down to remove the fabric band she has around my ankle, she makes quick work of the second.

I rip off the second piece of fabric as Quinn gets back to her feet.

Now where does my mate think she's going? She said I could have my dessert.

I'm *starving* for it.

I swoop her up in my arms, squeezing her to me. My cock is back at half-mast and stiffening quick. It wouldn't take much to shift her so that I could get back inside of her where I belong.

But that's not what *I* want.

I'm a fucking alpha. A feral, too. What good is all of my dominance and strength if I can't use it to rip a delighted squeal out of my mate?

Bracing my bare feet against the concrete floor, I heft up my arms, lifting Quinn as high as I can. She's a smart female; she would know exactly what I was doing even if I hadn't already mentioned face-sitting to her. So, hooking her legs over my shoulders, she scoots until my pussy is hovering near my mouth, and my fingers are biting in her ass cheeks.

"You know," I murmur, the heat of my breath making her squirm, "I'd give you whatever you wanted no matter what. Not just because you unchained me."

She threads her fingers into my hair, jerking my head so that I'm perfectly positioned where she wants me.

Just now, this *is* what she wants.

"Yeah. I know," she tells me, her voice a purr that's

somehow fitting for a she-wolf. "It was still more fun this way."

As I use the flat of my tongue to give her my first lick, groaning when I taste my seed mingling with her wetness, I have to agree with Quinn.

The chains. The head. The mating… now me pleasuring my mate for dessert after a delicious meal that proves she loves me as much as I'm a slave for the female I once had as my captive?

Oh, yeah. This is *definitely* more fun…

AUTHOR'S NOTE

Thank you for reading *Chase and the Chains*!

I hope you enjoyed this little snippet into Chase and Quinn's mated life. After their book was over—and I gave West the chance for readers to get inside of his head during the epilogue—I thought it might be a little treat to see what Chase is like. And, of course, Quinn just had to get back at him for the chains ;) A she-wolf might forgive, but she *never* forgets.

And if you want a sneak peek at the second book in the duet—featuring Helen and West—keep reading. I've added the first chapter here for you :)

xoxo,
Sarah

CANARI

THREE YEARS BEFORE CHASE TAKES QUINN IN THE FERAL'S CAPTIVE...

HELENE

My brother might be the Alpha of the Sylvan Pack, but when he has something he has to say, Bishop usually comes to me.

He's not the only one, either. As the Omega, I have my own cabin in the heart of pack land, about a ten-minute jog from where the Alpha cabin is set. Unlike Bishop, I'm available for any packmate in need around the clock, and it's not hard to find me.

Of course, that's not why Bishop makes an exception to his rule of expecting his subordinates to go to him when he's available in the den.

In Hickory, I'm the exception to nearly *every* rule.

It's partly because—except for his beloved mate—I'm

the only other Dupuis in Hickory; our parents are long gone, and we were the only two pups they had. More than that, though, it's my status as our pack Omega. I exist outside of the hierarchy, coddled and prized for the type of wolf that I shift into.

Which is why, when one of the deltas who serves on Bishop's pack council comes to my cabin to tell me that my brother wants to see me in his den, I'm surprised. I haven't been summoned by Bishop since the morning after his Alpha Ceremony eleven years ago when he told me that his fated mate was a she-wolf named Sofia Russo, and that she was coming to Hickory to bond with him.

That should have been my first clue that something was wrong.

My second? The fact that Tucker is the wolf who came to retrieve me.

If it was so important that I had to go to Bishop, I would've expected that he'd send his Beta. His right-hand wolf, West is the male that Bishop relies on more than anyone in the Sylvan Pack.

Plus, he's my chosen mate. We're not officially bonded—at West's request, we haven't performed the Luna Ceremony that would make our union unbreakable—but we've been in a committed relationship since we were nineteen. Five years now he's been my male, and with his possessive shifter instincts, he'd insist on escorting me to meet with Bishop.

Not that he's jealous of me being alone with the Alpha. Ew. Of course not. He's my *brother*, for Luna's sake.

But Tucker Madden? One of the wolves from our age group who used to sniff around my tail until I made it clear that I only ever wanted West? It doesn't matter that Tucker's been with nearly every unmated she-wolf in Hickory *except* for me. West wouldn't like me being alone with Tucker, even if it's on Bishop's orders.

So... that means he doesn't know, right?

I'm intrigued.

I shouldn't have been.

I should have thrown the door closed when I saw Tucker's toothy smile.

I didn't—and now he's holding the door to Bishop's den open for me. Once I stride past him, the short skirt on my sundress swishing as I move purposely toward my brother, Tucker nods at Bishop before disappearing.

We're alone. Me standing in the middle of the space when I realize that no one else is here except for Bishop. My big, brawny brother sitting behind his sturdy desk. His beard hides his expression from me; reaching toward him with my wolf, I can't feel anything as he blocks me from reading his emotions.

Bishop is the only one in the pack who can do that. His excuse is that he had a lot of practice since he practically raised me himself after our parents' deaths. Spending so much time around me as an omega pup, he developed a bit of a shield against my abilities. He doesn't often use it against me, but when he's trying to protect me —like usual—he has a habit of locking down around me.

Something's up.

When the Alpha is in residence, the den is rarely empty. Connected to the cabin that belongs to Bishop and his mate, the cozy space is a safe place. It's where any packmate can go meet with the Alpha and know that he'll listen to their concerns. Pack councils and meets are held in this room. It's always open when the Alpha's home, and I can't remember a time when I've walked inside of it and found Bishop by himself.

At the very least, the chair next to him usually seats the other half of the Alpha couple. But Sofia is notably missing, and Bishop looks even more stern than normal.

He waits until Tucker closes the door behind us before he lifts his big paw, gesturing at the empty chair opposite his desk.

"Canari. Please. Sit."

I still, my stomach going tight with instant nerves. My wolf chuffs softly, her head cocked to the side as she responds to my reaction. I can't help it. I think I'd been a little oblivious that this wasn't just a routine discussion with my brother until now, and I'm suddenly apprehensive.

I don't know what's worse, either: that it's just me and Bishop in the den, or that he called me 'canari'.

Canari. For as far back as I can remember, Bishop has had this little pet name for me. As we grew older, as he took on the mantle of responsibility, becoming Alpha at the young age of twenty-one, he didn't use it as often.

He's using it now, and I'm beginning to realize that something serious is going on.

Our parents died when I was barely a pup. I was five, Bishop ten, and while the rest of the pack gathered around us, making sure we wanted for nothing, Bishop did everything he could to take care of me.

Always the alpha, I think, giving him a small smile as

I move forward and finally sink into the seat opposite of him.

Canari...

The tragedy of our parents' death turned Bishop hard, but I was too young to be affected by it. Oh, no. That came much later. But when I was still too naive to understand what losing my omega mother so young meant, I entertained myself by singing little songs I made up that—even then—I hoped would make my stone-faced older brother smile.

Back then, Bishop was still a pup himself, walking around with the weight of the world on his shoulders. A silly song from his younger sister was sometimes enough to remind him that the world wasn't such a dark place, and he developed the habit of calling me 'canari'.

Little songbird.

As fitting now as it was then, I still love to sing—and I live to keep my packmates content.

Even before I knew exactly what an omega wolf was, my instincts always led me to make someone feel better. Sometimes it was at my expense, but it didn't matter. I was born to make my packmates happy. To calm them, to soothe them, to keep them on the right side of going feral...

I was the official Omega by the time I was sixteen. Following Bishop's lead, I've devoted myself to the Sylvan Pack for years. It's what's expected of me, and I'm happy to do it.

Just like, if Bishop has a task for me, I'll do that, too.

When he doesn't say anything, just watches me with a

scrutinizing look in his dark gold eyes, I decide to ask, "Where's Sofia?"

I love his mate. She's a sweet delta she-wolf from the River Run Pack, across the country from where we are, and the closest thing I've ever had to a sister.

He clears his throat. "She'll be here if you need anyone to discuss this with. If you don't want to tell me, I mean."

What? There isn't anything I can't confide in to my brother. From my first period to when I began a relationship with his best friend, he's always been there for me.

I make a face. "What are you talking about?"

"I had a visitor this morning. He came all this way from Darkwoods to meet with Helene Dupuis."

Wait... that's me. "Darkwoods?" I've heard of it before. It's the name of a wolf shifter pack territory. "The Gravetail Pack from Texas?"

I don't know a lot about all of the shifter packs in the United States. I have no intentions of leaving the Sylvan Pack, so it's never interested me. I only know about Gravetail because they're our biggest threat. Only about a three-hour run away from Hickory in our fur, if they decide to challenge the nearest shifter pack for their territory, it would be us.

"That's right. Three wolves asked for permission to see you. I sent them away until you agree, but one of them... he won't be deterred. He's coming back tomorrow unless you refuse to see him."

"But... why?" They have to have their own Omega, and since that's my only worth as a wolf—and Bishop keeps me so protected, no one should know about me from off pack land otherwise—I don't understand. "Why would a Gravetail wolf want to meet with me?"

"You tell me, canari."

I open my mouth. Before I can repeat that I have no idea what he's talking about, a whisper of a soft, feminine voice flitters through my mind. It's as quick as the wind, almost as intangible, but I latch onto it before it vanishes as suddenly as it appeared.

I echo the sound out loud: *"Rafael Cruces."*

Bishop exhales roughly.

Me? I suddenly feel like I'm going to bend over and throw up on the hardwood floor of the Alpha's den.

When it comes to finding our Luna-given fated mates, our revered goddess doesn't usually whisper the name to any wolves except for an alpha. It's traditionally been her gift when a new Alpha takes over their pack. It happened to Bishop when the Luna whispered Sofia's name to him, and I heard stories about the same thing happening to our former Alpha, Xavier.

Other packmates—whether we're deltas, omegas, betas, or even the elder gammas—recognize their fated mates more subtly. Eyes meet and, suddenly, the beginning of a mate bond is born between them.

Not me. The Luna just whispered Rafael's name in my ear, and I instinctively know that I'm meant for him.

Wait—

Cruces? "The Alpha of the Gravetail Pack is Luis Cruces, not Rafael. Right?"

Bishop nods. "Luis is the Alpha. His son is the Alpha-heir. He'll take over for his father one day, and when he does, he's asking that you accept him as your mate."

Because he knows my name.

Because the Luna whispered it to *him*.

Because he's my fated mate.

My whole life, I wanted to find mine. The one male meant for me, who would love me and protect me and keep me safe when I couldn't do it myself… the male the Luna would pick out as my perfect match, and who I would build a life with.

And then, at nineteen, I found my heart's mate. It didn't matter that the Luna didn't tell me he was mine. He *was* mine—

—but I'm not his.

That's what Bishop is telling me. For years, West put off performing the Luna Ceremony that would make us bonded mates because he was convinced that, one day, the Luna would tell us that we were fated.

We're not. And all that means to me is that there's a female out there who's more perfect for West than I am.

I take a deep breath, then ask, "Does West know?"

"No. When the Gravetail wolves came to ask for entry into Hickory, he was on patrol on the south side of our territory. He knows that Rafael and his entourage were here, but not why."

"Because it's Alpha business," I murmur, my voice catching in my throat.

That's West for you. He knows his place is at Bishop's right hand, but he trusts Bishop implicitly.

Some of the gamma wolves who were part of Xavier's inner circle thought my brother was making a mistake when he handpicked West to be his Beta. He had the right type of wolf for the job, and could be coached to have the right temperament, but their close friendship isn't the reason why he ended up with the position.

His absolute belief that Bishop will always make the correct decision for the Sylvan Pack is what makes him the perfect Beta.

Bishop raps his palms on his desk. "It's not Alpha business, canari. It's *your* business. Rafael came to proposition you. You get the choice. You can reject him. Just because the Luna said he's yours, he only is if you agree."

That's right.

A mate gets to choose, and so stunned at this turn of events, I'm not sure what to do.

I don't ask my brother for his input. His own actions precede him. When the Luna told him Sofia was his mate, he didn't hesitate. He might not have crossed the country to meet her, but he did make a call out to the River Run Pack the day after he became Alpha. She accepted his proposal without knowing a single thing about him, and they were bonded the next full moon.

That was eleven years ago. Proving that the Luna knows what she's doing, they've been madly in love ever since.

But I'm already in love with another male...

Do I love him enough to let him go? Can I keep West, knowing that I'm depriving him of the chance to find his fated mate?

His true love?

And Rafael... I've never met him before, but if he's going to one day be the Alpha of the Gravetail Pack, a union with him would erase the threat to the Sylvan Pack. I'd have to leave Hickory, of course, but I'd be leaving my home knowing that my new pack would be allies with my old one.

Put that way, what else could I do?

"If I agree, would I have to leave with him today?"

"Of course not. Alphas only take their mate once they have control of their pack. With Luis still the Alpha, it could be years before Rafael is in a position to make you his mate. You'd stay here with me, under my protection."

I'd stay with Bishop and Sofia. But West...

"I'll meet with Rafael," I tell him. "But let me talk to West first, okay?"

My brother is careful not to give anything away with his expression. "You've made your choice then?"

I... I don't think I even have one.

"Yes."

Bishop reaches his palm out. Knowing what he wants, I place mine in his. "Don't worry about West. He'll understand. He'll do what's best for you."

I know he will. West loves me, but he's as equally devoted to Hickory as me and Bishop are.

"And I'll do what's best for the pack."

Bishop didn't tell West about Rafael. He told me he didn't, and I also trust him implicitly.

But my chosen mate knows. I'm one hundred percent convinced that he does. Why else is he standing outside of my cabin when I approach it, pacing nervously, his hands empty?

The pacing is unexpected, but not as much as the fact that he didn't bring a flower for me.

He always does.

It started when he became the Beta of the pack at twenty-one. Until then, we were inseparable. Friends since we were pups, our relationship turned serious when we were nineteen, the two of us always together. He had his own cabin, but since I was given the Omega cabin when I took the position in the pack, he spent all of his time at mine.

But then our last Beta retired, becoming a gamma, and Bishop offered the post to West. I was so proud of him, even if that meant pack duties and responsibilities kept us apart more than I liked.

That's when West started bringing me flowers. Whenever we were away from each other for more than a few hours at a time, he would pluck one of the wildflowers that grew on the outskirts of pack land and bring it back for me.

A reminder that he loved me, he would say, and that I was on his mind even when we were apart.

Not today, though. As if he was in such a frantic rush to reach me, he didn't stop for a flower.

When he sees me, he jogs right for me. Throwing open his arms, he's about to hug me when I dance out of his reach.

I've never done that before, but I have to. Touching West right now... I can't.

I just *can't.*

And he knows.

"Tell me it's not true, baby. Tucker said... he said

that… *Gravetail*. He's trying to claim you as his fated mate. But that can't be. You're not his. You're *mine*."

Next time I see Tucker, I'm going to encourage his wolf to lose his libido for a few days. When he can't get it up, maybe then he'll stop interfering in other packmates' matings.

A lump lodges in my throat. I almost invite West inside my cabin to break his heart in private, but I chicken out at the last moment. Having him near, surrounded by his sandalwood scent… this is already going to be so Luna damn hard.

Why make it even harder?

"I thought I was, West. But Tucker's right. I'm going to promise myself to Rafael of the Gravetail Pack."

"What? No! You can't do that. Didn't you just hear me say that you're mine? You always have been. You always will be."

Only I'm not. He might not see that now, but he will. One day, he will.

"We're both meant for others," I whisper, holding back my sob. "It's better if we leave it at that."

"Better? Better for fucking *who*?"

West's eyes are wild. Normally a steely, dark grey so unusual for shifters, they're the vivid gold of his wolf peeking through.

"For you. For me." For your future mate. "For the pack."

He hears something in my voice. I thought I did a good job holding back my ache, but he narrows his gaze on me.

West is looking right into my eyes, and though his

type of wolf can't sense emotions like mine can, he knows me. He can tell how much it's killing me to do this, how much I'm already regretting this... and that only firms his resolve to push back against me.

"You don't have to do this. Screw the pack. This is about us. You and me, baby."

That's where he's wrong. A Luna-given mate is a gift. To refuse it is to insult our goddess. I can't do that. Just like I can't reject an alliance with the Gravetail Pack. And screw the pack? That's traitor talk. If Bishop heard him, I don't want to know how he'd react to that.

For so many reasons, I have to nip this in the bud. Least of all because of the tears welling up in my eyes.

"I'm sorry, West. My mind's made up. Don't make this any harder, okay?"

"I have to. I can't... okay, your mind's made up, Lane? How do I change it?"

I knew it would be rough, ending things with West. I didn't know it would be *excruciating*.

"You can't."

His jaw clenches.

"Weston, please—"

"I love you, Helene."

And that's exactly why this is as difficult as it is.

"I know."

But he'll love his fated mate more. That's why us shifters prize the idea of being blessed by the Luna to find that one soul. They're perfect for us, and when West finds his, he'll understand why I have to do this. For the pack, yes, but for him, too.

I want him to be happy. I don't ever want him to look at me and wonder: *what if?*

I don't want to look at him and think the same thing...

"For the sake of what we had, if you love me, then do this one thing for me: don't ever tell me again."

West runs his hands through his thick, dark brown hair, leaving the strands to stand up on end when he drops his arms back to his side. He looks at me like I asked him to slit his throat for me, and while he'll do it, it's only because it's what I want.

But then he thins his lips. "I love you too much to let you go. You know that, too?"

Actually... I do. "But you're going to have to."

West opens his mouth. I see his fangs gleaming, much longer than their usual canine size. His wolf is riding him hard, and only his iron-tight control is keeping him from shifting on the spot.

I brace myself, waiting for him to argue.

He doesn't. With one more long look at me, he spins on his heel and stalks away. In between one footfall and the next, it becomes a run, then a sprint. Within seconds, West is gone.

And I'm free to dash inside and let out the sobs I struggled to keep in.

I'm all cried out, and more determined than ever to go through with my choice.

Maybe it's a good thing that West had to run away

from me. I know I broke his heart—just like mine is shattered—but it's for the best.

Right?

When I hear the gentle knock at my door, I think it's Sofia. She stopped by about an hour ago, offering to sit with me while I worked through my emotions, but I respectfully asked her to come back later.

After making sure my yellow eyes aren't rimmed with red, my hair mussed from burying my face in my pillow as I sobbed, I straighten out my wrinkled dress and reach for the doorknob.

It's not Sofia standing on my porch.

It's West, and he's holding three wildflowers out to me: a brown-eyed Susan, a Shasta daisy, and a dandelion.

With a defiant expression on his handsome face, creased with lines that weren't there earlier and spattered with something that looks suspiciously like blood—but that's, hopefully, mud—West says, "You said I couldn't tell you that I love you. You didn't say anything about showing you."

That's West for you: determined and logical, and unwilling to ever give up so easily when he wants something.

That's how he convinced me to take a chance on him even when I always suspected that I wasn't his fated mate —and it's why I do something that I'll come to regret for years to come.

I accept the flowers.

'Til death do they part...

Omegas are prized. I've always known that. Just like I grew up knowing that I would need a powerful mate to protect me.

I wasn't worried. I had Bishop—my overprotective alpha brother—to watch out for me, and then I fell in love with his best friend, Weston. A beta wolf, he was high enough in the pack that he would be a good match. And he loved me, too.

I couldn't choose anyone better.

Too bad it wasn't my choice.

Three years ago, I discovered that I was fated to be the mate of the future Gravetail Alpha. Because of his rank, he couldn't claim me as his until after he was installed as Alpha, but it didn't matter. From the moment the Luna whispered my name to him, I was as good as promised to Rafael. With our alliance on the line, I had no choice.

And that meant I had to say goodbye to West.

Only... he didn't take it too well. Even after the Luna blessed him with a fated mate of his own, he rejected Quinn Malone, even while I counted down the months until I'd finally have to leave Hickory.

It's my duty. As an Omega, I don't have the luxury of choosing my own mate like Quinn did, and as much as it hurts, it's for the best when West finally becomes as cold and distant with me as he is with others.

I should've known better. After a five-year love affair, I should've known that meant he was up to something.

And when I wake up one morning with a ring on my finger and a mark on my shoulder, I find out exactly what it is.

Weston Reed has stolen me from our pack, and he won't let me go until I accept what he swears he's always known: that, fate or no fate, we're meant to be.

This Omega will be the Beta's bride—or no male's.

The Beta's Bride is the second book in the **Stolen Mates** duet. After Quinn found her forever with Chase, West decides it's now or never. He'll either have Helene for his mate, or... well, there is no *or*. And Helene? She begins to realize that he might be right.

Get it now!

PRE-ORDER NOW

PREY

WOLVES AND WITCHES AND CURSES, OH MY...

I never believed in the paranormal mainly because I never had any reason to—at least, not until I received a telegram from a grandmother I didn't know existed, inviting me to a small town that was nearly impossible to find, full of shifters and witches that shouldn't be real.

Of course, I didn't know that until *after* I agreed to visit her in her secluded home.

When I pull into town, I almost regret my impulsive decision to take this trip. Bordered on all sides by rivers and mountains and dense forests, Winter Creek is a trap.

Once you get in, it's just as difficult to leave. No one has cars here or internet service, and my own phone is a glorified paperweight as soon as I step off the train.

Speaking of the train... I discover too late that it arrives on its rickety tracks once a week if you're lucky. And, of course, there's the small matter of the curse.

Turns out there's a reason why my grandmother finally got in touch with me for the first time in twenty-five years. In Winter's Creek, there's a curse involving a coven of witches, the feral wolf who haunts the dark forest, and a woman from seventy years ago who looks enough like me to convince my grandmother that I'm the only one who can break it at last.

When I refuse, I discover that my grandmother isn't just the head witch of Winter Creek—she's the one responsible for the curse that's kept the town in stasis for the last seventy years. To break it, she's willing to do whatever she has to, including sacrificing me to the big, black wolf that's been lurking in the shadows, watching me since my arrival.

Because the beast in the woods is hungry, and I'm the perfect prey...

Prey is the first in a new rejected mates/fated mates series featuring Fallon Witt, a human woman who doesn't know anything about the paranormal—until she's thrown headfirst into it. While partly inspired by Beauty and the Beast, it also has elements of Little Red

Riding Hood—though, in this series, the big bad wolf is the hero, and the grandmother is the true danger in the woods of Winter Creek...

Out May 23, 2023!

KEEP IN TOUCH

Stay tuned for what's coming up next! Follow me at any of these places—or sign up for my newsletter—for news, promotions, upcoming releases, and more!

Website
Newsletter

ALSO BY SARAH SPADE

Holiday Hunk

Halloween Boo

This Christmas

Auld Lang Mine

I'm With Cupid

Getting Lucky

When Sparks Fly

Holiday Hunk: the Complete Series

Claws and Fangs

Leave Janelle

Never His Mate

Always Her Mate

Forever Mates

Hint of Her Blood

Taste of His Skin

Stay With Me

Never Say Never: Gem & Ryker

Sombra Demons

Drawn to the Demon Duke*

Mated to the Monster

Stolen by the Shadows

Santa Claws

Bonded to the Beast

Fated to the Phantom

Stolen Mates

The Alpha's Heart*

The Feral's Captive

Chase and the Chains

The Beta's Bride

Wolves of Winter Creek

Prey

Pack

Predator

Claws Clause

(written as Jessica Lynch)

Mates *free*

Hungry Like a Wolf

Of Mistletoe and Mating

No Way

Season of the Witch

Rogue

Sunglasses at Night

Ain't No Angel

True Angel

Ghost of Jealousy

Night Angel

Broken Wings

Of Santa and Slaying

Lost Angel

Born to Run

Uptown Girl

A Pack of Lies

Here Kitty, Kitty

Ordinance 7304: the Bond Laws (Claws Clause Collection #1)

Living on a Prayer (Claws Clause Collection #2)